ONE FOOT IN THE GRAVE:

AN ALMOST ZOMBIE TALE

Shanti Krishnamurty

ONE FOOT IN THE GRAVE:

Copyright 2015 by Shanti Krishnamurty

All rights reserved.

This book is a work of fiction. Names, characters, places, and incidents either are the product of the author's imagination or are used fictitiously. Any resemblance to actual persons, living or dead, business establishments, events or locales is entirely incidental.

Formatting by
(http://WildSeasFormatting.com)
Cover Art Renee Barratt
(http://thecovercounts.com)

Acknowledgements

Nikki, when you told me this quirky, silly short story would make an awesome novel, I was absolutely skeptical. I'm very grateful you convinced me to take a chance on such a funky project.

Amy, your eye for detail has been profoundly needed...and I'm so thankful for it. You are amazing.

Rama, you are part of every novel I will ever write. Your support has gone far beyond words and actions. You are the truest definition of the word 'sister'.

Isis, thank you for letting me use your name. You're the perfect half-zombie.

And, as always, there are more people than I can possibly name who have kept me moving forward when those dark moments hit. Thank you for your belief in me. Thank you for 'spreading the word'. You are the reason I write.

Dedication

This book is in all ways dedicated to God, who created the platypus; my husband, whose presence in my life proves God's sense of both timing and humor, and my boys, who love me enough to let me write.

One:

And so it Begins.

Andrew and I stroll across the sand to where the thick wooden timbers creak above our heads and the only light I can see is through the cracks in the thick slats. I relax and take my boyfriend's hand in mine. We haven't been dating long, but he's everything I've always wanted: smart, funny and pretty much all around drop dead gorgeous. Truly dark gray eyes I could sink into forever, long black corkscrew curls and, to top it all off, he's thin but not skinny. I mean, there are abs. What's not to love?

"Where are you taking me?" I grip his hand as he leads me deeper into the shadows under the pier; the shadows that house the druggies and the homeless. This is starting to feel less romantic, and a little more than scary.

"I just want to be alone with you," he whispers.

I shiver at the velvet honey of his voice.

"I—I want to be alone with you, too," I reply, though it tastes like a lie on my tongue. What I really want is to go back to where light is, even if it's the artificial light of carnival rides and open stores. But my body has other ideas. It sways toward him as he tugs me closer.

"Relax, Isis. You'll enjoy it." He starts to nuzzle at my neck.

I do enjoy it. I enjoy it a lot. My limbs feel like a

marionette's and my eyes slide shut. Right until the moment his teeth actually pierce the delicate skin covering my jugular vein.

"What're you doing?" I shove him as far away from me as I can. He falls and just sits on the sand, staring at me.

I glare at the shadow of him. His eyes look like they're kind of glowing. I hide behind my words. "You're such a jerk!" Okay, the word I want to say is a lot stronger than 'jerk', but there's no way I can say it. My mom would *kill* me if she ever found out.

"Wait, you don't understand—I'm not done…"

"Done with what? You know what…never mind. I don't even want to know. Whatever it is, you can keep it to yourself!" I slap my palm over the spot he bit, and a warm wetness oozes over my fingers. "You drew blood? I'm so outta here!"

Andrew rises to his feet. "It's just a scrape…Isis, you need to let me finish." His voice deepens into honey again, but by then I'm done buying whatever he's trying to sell.

"It's not just a scrape! I'm *bleeding*!"

He holds out a hand; I think to stop me from leaving. It doesn't work. I run as fast as I can back to the light, and then continue all the way to my car. I scramble for my car keys, clamber into the VW Bug's front seat and peel out of there like my butt is on fire. I don't even care that I'm leaving him stranded in Savannah. Let him find his own way back to Atlanta. I'm done.

I get home and just collapse into bed, fully dressed. I don't even brush my teeth. By the time I wake up the next morning, I'm really hoping everything in Savannah was just a blurry nightmare, but my fingers creep up to my neck and I feel the scab. My boyfriend actually bit me. I can't even come up with a plausible reason why he'd do it. I *totally* misjudged him. What a freak.

I fumble my way out of bed and into the kitchen. The coffee maker burbles its version of 'good morning'. I'm beyond grateful it's one of those programmable ones, because I feel like there's sand in my eye sockets. I fill my cup to the brim and take a sip of the inky goodness. The coffee burns its way down my throat, tasting like liquid mud. I shove the cup away and it spills across the table. Perfect. Today just keeps getting better and better. I decide right then that I'm not going to try cooking anything. With my luck, I'd set the apartment on fire and how would I explain *that* to my mom when she gets home?

It takes around two seconds to stick my feet into a pair of flip-flops. I pull the front door open, and a folded paper drifts to the floor. I bend down, grab it, and cram it into my back pocket. It's most likely a flyer for a church event of some sort. Thankfully, the elevator's empty and it doesn't take long to get to the ground floor of the building. I walk through an unexpected summer rain shower to the little hole in the wall that almost always has lines around the block. Today I get lucky. At least something's going right.

I amble inside. The owner, Ms. Adwell, waves me over to a booth. "Hey, honey, how are you? Is your mama still in China?"

I nod. "She called me when she got there, but then decided that in order to experience the 'real' tour she'd better turn off her cell." My mom's been gone for two weeks, taking an in-depth tour of the Silk Road. Honestly, I have no idea when she's coming back, other than 'eventually'. I'm in charge of the apartment in her absence. Luckily, she's got a full bank account, thanks to figuring out how to grow watermelons vertically and some very curious farmers. Last I heard, she's trying to figure out how to grow square grapes, and I'm not really sure why. I think she just likes the challenge of it.

The old black woman hmphs her reply. I don't think she approves of teenagers being left home alone for weeks at a time. Never mind that my mom's been treating me like an adult for years and I've been a primary on her bank accounts pretty much since time began.

The scent that suddenly weaves its way through the restaurant makes my nostrils flare. It's eggs and…something else. Something unrecognizable, but utterly desirable. My stomach moans its disapproval of my neglect. "What's Carl cooking?"

She stares at me from across the nearly empty restaurant. "Umm… honey, I'm pretty sure you don't want that."

I'm pretty sure she's wrong. "No, it's exactly what I want." My stomach rumbles again, backing up my statement.

"White folk around here don't usually order pig brains and eggs."

That can't possibly be what I smell. Gross. What kind of person eats brains for breakfast? Not me, that's for sure. I order my usual, instead. "Can I get French toast with powdered sugar, orange juice, and a side of cheesy scrambled eggs?"

"Of course, darlin'. Give Carl a few minutes to finish up Lucky Rickard's plate, and I'll bring it right out."

"Thanks." I lean back against the worn plastic booth, glancing over at the other regular in the diner, Lucky Rickard. I have no idea why he'd order brains for breakfast, but anyone who's survived as many heart attacks as he has can eat any darn thing he wants, I guess. I shift in my seat and feel the folded paper in my pocket. I pull it out and look at it.

"Are you experiencing odd changes? Craving even odder foods? Visit 2089 Vista Round Terrace if you need guidance." It's written in beautiful, curvy letters. It reminds me of how I imagine the Victorian era people would write. Elegant. It's weird that some stranger's writing me, though. Maybe it's one of those help centers that dot the metro Atlanta area. I close my eyes and tilt my head back until it rests against the cool vinyl.

"You sure you're okay?"

I open my eyes as Ms. Adwell places my breakfast in front of me. It looks *amazing* and smells...*disgusting*. My nostrils flare. I very reluctantly pick up my fork. "Yeah, I'm just tired."

She shakes her head. "Honey, you look beyond tired. You look almost dead. Eat your breakfast, then go home and get some rest. You obviously need it."

I need some food, is what I need. "Thanks, I'll do that." I stick the fork into the cheesy eggs. The idea of eating them makes the utensil weigh about a bazillion pounds.

'Just let me know if you need anything else," Ms. Adwell says.

I can't bring myself to actually bring the fork up to my lips. The eggs just sit there, looking cheesy and yellow. I take a deep breath in and that incredible smell wafts over me. I know Ms. Adwell said it was eggs and brains, but maybe I'm just craving the eggs. I close my eyes, say a tiny prayer. Eat the forkful. And throw up. All over the plate. My face flares bright, tomato red.

"Oh my gosh! I'm so, so sorry!" My stomach is determined to expel every single bit of food in it. I stumble to the tiny bathroom in the back of the diner, Ms. Adwell hard on my heels.

"Honey, are you all right? Sit down; let me get you a glass of water." She fusses over me as I collapse into a ball, pressing my face against the cool tile.

I moan around my dry heaves. I'm so unbelievably hungry. When Ms. Adwell opens the bathroom door, my stomach rumbles at the smell wafting inside. I give in. It's obviously *not* the eggs. "Can—can I have a small plate of brains?" I talk to the floor, partially hoping she can't hear me.

"Wash your face and come back out to your booth." She obviously heard me. My hopes are dashed.

I push myself to a sitting position and just…stay, head hanging. I can't believe I just asked for brains on a plate. I have no idea what's wrong with me, but this seriously sucks. But my mom's always telling me to face the world that exists, not the one I wish I had, so I do. I get up, rinse out my mouth and splash lukewarm water on my face. I look haggard. My wavy black hair still frames my face, the ends tickling at my chin, but my black eyes look haunted. I shudder and look away. I don't need a reminder of how sick I feel. After wiping the excess water off with a handful of paper towels, I'm sort of ready to go back to my booth and face the music…errr…brains.

A rush of saliva soaks my mouth when I see the plate Ms. Adwell left for me. All those little curls of meat mixed through the eggs. The eggs don't do much for my appetite. I push them out of the way, take a miniscule forkful of the brains and start coughing almost immediately.

"What's a matter? You swallow wrong?" Carl ambles toward me, his white apron tied around his middle. I have no idea how he keeps it so clean while he cooks behind the counter. But then again, it's not like I'm an expert on the whole cooking thing. "Told Adina white folks have no business messin' with brains n' eggs, but she wouldn't listen."

I smile up at him wanly. "They taste like pork. I didn't know they'd taste like pork."

He crinkles up his forehead. "Course they taste like pork. They're pig brains. Were you expectin' something different?"

I shrug. "They smelled *amazing* when they were cooking…" My eyes widen as my brain processes what I just said. "Raw," I murmur. "Holy cow, I need 'em raw." My stomach heaves at the idea, but there's nothing left to throw up.

"What was that?" Carl asks.

"Nothing." I take one last gulp of water to wash the taste of cooked food away. "I'm sorry. It's not your cooking, I promise. I just – I gotta go." I pull a twenty out of my pocket. "Tell Ms. Adwell bye for me, all right?"

Carl nods. "Hope you feelin' better soon, girly."

"Thanks. Me, too." The string of chimes over the door does its thing when I leave.

Whatever is happening to me, I hope it passes soon. The morning's been horrible, and I want the afternoon to be better. Puffy gray clouds dot the sky. Barring the rain, it looks like a perfect day, but I'm too frustrated to enjoy it. All I want to do is get some breakfast I can eat and start the day sort of over.

I stare at the brains splayed out across my counter. The idea of eating them raw makes me sweat. I mean, they're *brains*. I can't *believe* I'm about to try this, but I've got to get *something* in my stomach, even if it's nasty, raw meat. I dig in, trying not to think about what I'm actually doing. Before I know it, I'm shoveling the brains into my mouth as fast as I can, eating straight off the oiled paper like an animal would. I've been hungry before, but nothing like this...my eyes narrow and I stop in mid-shovel, a handful of raw meat clenched in one fist. I might know where to go for some answers; 2089 Vista Round Terrace, whatever that is. My laptop's still in my book bag, where it's pretty much lived since the summer started. After all, why use a laptop when my mom has a screamin' gaming desktop in her bedroom? I drop the brains; wash my hands with blazing hot water and lots of soap before dragging out the laptop and firing it up. I type the address into the Google search bar. Huh. It's a church. I'm not sure if I want to go or not, honestly. I've been to enough churches during my lifetime—all seventeen years of it—to choke a horse and endured more lectures...I mean, sermons...than I care to think about. But I have no idea what else to do with my day, so why not? After all, a church is a church is a church, right?

Two:

Weirdness Abounds.

So apparently all churches were *not* created equal. The one I'm staring at is...well, run-down would be putting it nicely. I'm pretty sure if I blow on it, it'll collapse into a pile of rubble and dust. I bite my lip, but take the twenty or so steps forward to the huge double doors. The rusty handles look like they're about ready to fall off but they turn easily enough to reveal a deep darkness I dread stepping into.

"Can I help you with something?"

The woman's voice is friendly enough, but I can't see anything other than a long sweep of hair.

I reach into my pocket and pull out the note. "I found this on my door this morning. This *is* 2089, right?"

"It is," the woman says. "Why don't you come inside, where we can talk?"

"Why're all your lights off?" I counter.

"I'm sorry, but our church isn't normally open on Sundays."

What? That doesn't make any sense to my Bible Belt upbringing. Churches are *always* open on Sundays. I mean, Wednesdays at church are cool because of all the kid and teen friendly stuff going on, but Sundays are worship days. Period. I don't even *like* church and I know that.

A warm glow fills the interior of the building. It's

like a thousand candles have been lit all at once. Now that I can actually see what I'm walking into, I step inside. Light gray stone walls rise up to high cathedral ceilings and archways framed out in highly polished wood line the way up to the altar. Looking up, I see that soft lightbulbs sit nearly hidden in shallow crevices over every other archway, giving the impression of candlelight without the possibility of burning the church to the ground. It's ingenious. Wooden pews are actually on the *outside* of the archways. I've never seen anything like it before; it's pretty cool in an odd kind of way.

The woman steps forward out of a small room; I can only assume it's where the light switch is concealed. I expect long skirts and a bright shirt, but she's dressed in blue jeans and a plain brown tank top. A tattoo I can't quite identify decorates her left shoulder. The more I focus on it, the more it seems to move. Which isn't even close to possible. I blink to clear my vision.

The hair I noticed before sweeps at her ankles as she walks toward me. "My name is Lydia, and you are?"

…wondering why on earth I'm here. But I hold out my hand for her to shake. "I'm Isis."

"Why don't we have a seat?" She follows her own advice and sits down in the closest pew. I follow suit. "Can I get you something to drink?"

I shake my head. "That's a really cool tat. Where'd you get it?" I'd love to get one, but I'm pretty sure my mom would give birth to shoes if I did.

"Someone I knew a very long time ago gifted me with it." The tattoo stretches across her shoulder cap, and I catch a glimpse of one bright orange eye. It looks beyond real. Whoever gave it to her was seriously talented.

"I'd like to know about the note, if you don't mind. Did you write it?"

She nods and leans forward. "I did, because you needed to read it, Isis. Tell me what happened to you last night."

My breath catches in my throat. "How—how do you know about that?"

"My...calling, for lack of a better word, is to help people like you."

My eyes narrow. "What do you mean by 'people like me'?"

"Are you sure you're ready to hear what I have to say?"

I'm really not, but I don't think it matters much, so I just nod. I must look kind of wild around the eyes, though, because she tries to smile reassuringly at me.

"I haven't been stalking you. At least, not in the way you're probably thinking."

The only thing I'm thinking is that this was a mistake and it's time to leave. I put thought into action and stand up. "This really isn't my thing," I start, but she holds up one hand.

"I don't mean to be cryptic, Isis, but it's hard to know exactly what I should tell you."

I tap my foot. It echoes. "How about the unvarnished truth?"

She laughs. "Not many teenagers use the word 'unvarnished' nowadays."

"I read a lot of books." My voice is flat.

A breath whooshes out of her like she's been holding it in. "Oh, good. That will make everything a lot easier."

"Y'know, for not wanting to be cryptic, you're doing an excellent job at being exactly that."

"I'm sorry," Lydia says. "Please. Take a seat."

I sit down on the very edge of the pew, ready and willing to bolt if necessary.

"The note was sent in order to get you to come here," she starts.

"Yeah, I got that part loud and clear. What's so important that I had to come?"

"The fact that you came tells me you already know the answer," she says.

I'm kind of scared to tell her about my raw brain fiasco. I'm actually kind of hoping *that* was a fluke and I'll be able to eat normally tomorrow. I mean, Lydia seems nice enough, but she's a stranger, so I just shrug.

She stares at me for a long minute. "I know you've got no reason to trust me," she finally says, "but you can."

"Look," I reply, "I have no idea who you are. But the note—" my voice falters. I clear it and continue. "The note was right. I've been craving...ummm...stuff I really shouldn't be craving."

"Not blood?"

She sounds surprised, and that freaks me out more than anything else. "Why would I be craving...*no*...ewww." Of course, it's not like craving brains is better than craving blood. Quite frankly, they're both on my 'never, ever, *ever*' list.

"That's interesting," Lydia says. "I thought you were a vampire, but you're obviously not."

"You thought I was a *what*?" But even as I'm protesting the idea of it, it makes sense. Normal guys don't go after their girlfriend's jugular, or any other vein, for that matter. Neither does a normal guy have eyes that glow kind of golden. "Andrew's a vampire." It explains so much.

Lydia nods. "But somehow you're not and I'm not sure what you are."

ONE FOOT IN THE GRAVE

I slump. "I'm not sure what I am, either."

"Are you willing to find out?"

Do I have a choice? I nod, certainly not expecting what happens next.

The rustling of massive wings accompanies what looks like a huge boulder dropping from the ceiling. I scream until it...lands? I scramble to my feet and hit the ground running. Lydia grabs at my arm, but I manage to elude her and make it to the front doors, pulling at the handles in a desperate attempt to Get. Out.

"Isis, stop, it's all right, he won't hurt you," Lydia's soothing tone really isn't doing the job.

There's no way in the world I'm staying. I have no idea what just landed in the sanctuary, but I'm not waiting to find out. "No way," I practically growl at her. "Let me out of here!" My hands are sweating profusely and I can't grip the stupid handles well enough to yank them open. "I." *Yank* "Can't." *Yank* "Stay." *Yank*. The final pull does the trick and the double doors fly wide. I'm so freaked out, I don't even really think about the throb in my left wrist; I just assume it's a mild sprain, and rush out into the daylight, relishing the feel of the sun on my face.

"Isis," Lydia calls after me. I have no idea why, but I stop in mid-flight and turn back to face her.

"You need help," she says. "That's what we're here for. I promise you, nothing bad will happen here. Please...come back in."

"This—" I wave my arm around to encompass the church specifically and everything surrounding it. "This is way too weird for me. I can't. I just can't."

"*This* is where you belong." She's practically begging me. "Trust me; I've been doing this a long time."

"Doing what? Introducing people to that thing in

the church?" It takes a huge effort to keep my voice down to something resembling a normal level. "All this crazy talk about my being different, about you thinking I'm a vampire…it's really so you can feed me to that…that *thing*, isn't it?"

Lydia bursts into peals of laughter. "I—oh my goodness, what an imagination you have!"

I fold my arms across my chest. "What? I was being serious!"

"There's no way that would ever happen." She starts giggling again, but quickly sobers up. "When you change your mind and need us, we're open from sunrise to sunset. Every day except Sunday."

I can't bring myself to tell her she's wrong; that I'll never set foot in the church again. I nod instead, determined not to ever come back here. There's not a chance in…heck.

Three:

So, What Now?

In a vain attempt to get my mind off the winged thing at the church, I decide to go home and sort laundry. I've been neglecting it since Mom's been gone and it's starting to crawl up the walls. If I don't get it done, I might find myself smothered in my sleep by jeans and t-shirts. Oh, and I've got to wrap my wrist in an Ace bandage; the sucker is really starting to ache and it's already begun turning colors, which is fairly alarming. I try to pull open the door to my apartment building, but my palms are still covered in sweat. I wipe my hands down the front of my jeans.

"Hey, Isis, how're things going?"

I smile. The voice belongs to Sam Allen, my lab partner in high school who just happens to be *the* hottest guy around. If you're into Vikings, and probably even if you're not. Seriously, the guy looks like he could bench press a semi. Oh, and he lives in my building. Lucky me. "Hi yourself, Sam. What's going on?"

He shrugs awkwardly. "Just delivering for Bruno's...he told me you came in and bought raw brains. What's up with that?"

Crap. "I...uhhh...just an experiment," I lie. "You know how my mom is."

"Your mom's awesome. Kind of weird, but awesome."

That pretty much sums up how I feel about her, too. I fidget from one foot to the next, not sure how to continue the conversation. "So, got any cool plans for the summer?" Gah, that sounds so cheesy, but I can't exactly take it back.

"Just working," he says. "My car insurance is killin' me. What about you? Still dating that Andrew guy?"

I shake my head. "Not anymore. We just had different...goals." Like he wants me dead and I want me alive.

He nods like he totally understands. Maybe he does. I don't doubt he's had more girlfriends than anyone else in our graduating class. He's just one of those guys: not a 'player', but not a monk, either. Popular.

"Did he do that to you?" Sam points at my wrist.

"Indirectly, yeah. But it's okay," I say. "It's just a sprain."

"What a jerk. Good thing you dumped him."

"I think so, too." Even though my heart aches a bit at the loss.

"I'd better get to delivering these." He juggles the small box of meats with one hand, and reaches for the door handle with the other. "Here, let me get that for you."

"Thanks," I say, and walk inside ahead of him.

"Hey, some of us are getting together tomorrow at The Coffee Jar. Want to come?"

I'd be crazy to say no. I've wanted him to ask me out, in any regard, since I was a freshman. "Absolutely. Just call me and let me know what time."

He nods. "Will do. See ya later."

I actually hum my way to the elevator. The day is definitely looking up and even the prospect of mountains of dirty clothes doesn't bother me.

ONE FOOT IN THE GRAVE

***

The next morning doesn't start out so badly. I check my wrist by wiggling it slightly, having wrapped it the night before. It feels wonky, but a visit to the doctor after I get control of the laundry should fix that. But first, I crack two eggs into a bowl; scramble them with two tablespoons of milk, then pour the concoction into a frying pan. It's not until I put a forkful of the delicious, perfectly scrambled eggs into my mouth that my stomach goes 'Nope!' and clenches itself into a knot. I don't even get a chance to truly enjoy the fluffy goodness before I'm racing for the bathroom.

It sucks, but I'm determined to eat *something* that's not raw meat. I've never liked steak tartar, and I'm not about to make it part of my regular diet. Not if I can help it. The pig brains were bad enough. I manage to keep three minuscule bites of a banana down by sheer strength of will. It's stupid, but it totally makes me feel like a winner. I grab the full laundry basket and head to the elevator. There are definitely days I wish my mom had paid for an apartment with washer/dryer hookups. Today is one of them. I don't want to deal with people, and my building is full of nosy little old ladies. I push the down button, and wait a few minutes. It doesn't take long for the doors to *woosh* open.

A tiny old woman smiles at me, showing off a set of beautiful pink gums. "Why hello, Isis. What a nice surprise! Doing your laundry?"

What else would I be doing with a basket of dirty clothes? "Hi, Mrs. Castemar. How are you?"

"I'm peachy, dear, just peachy." She peers at me over her bifocals. Yeah, she's pretty much a stereotypical little old lady. "You look peaky. Have you been sleeping all right?"

"I've been restless lately," I admit. "I've got a lot on my mind."

"But school is over." She reaches out to pat my arm, but stops midway. "Oh, dear, what happened to your wrist? Did you break it? Shouldn't it be in a cast?"

I shake my head, even though I really have no idea. "It's just bruised really badly."

"Oh, dear." She fumbles around in her purse. "I have some ointment my daughter sent me. It's miraculous, actually. Makes bruises disappear almost instantly."

I seriously doubt that, but it can't hurt, right? I start to unwind the bandage. I haven't looked at my wrist since yesterday, so I'm expecting that kind of weird 'dead' skin. What I don't expect is for my hand to fall off. I instantly go numb.

Mrs. Castemar blinks for a moment. I wait for her to scream; heck, I wait for *me* to scream, but neither of us does. She just bends over, picks it up, and turns it over in her palm. "It looks so real."

That's when I notice no blood is pooling onto the floor. I open my mouth and the lie just rolls off my tongue. "It's a prosthetic wrist. I had an accident when I was young. I'm so sorry!" I hold out my other hand for my errant limb. She hands it back to me. I put it on top of the laundry, not entirely convinced what's happening is actually happening.

"Well, you need to be careful with it, dear. Whatever you're using to hold it on, it's not working well."

It's called muscles and veins. And yeah, they're not doing their job well. Or at all. I don't have a clue what's happening, but I suspect it has to do with Andrew and the weirdness under the pier and my newfound appetite. Or lack thereof.

ONE FOOT IN THE GRAVE

The elevator dings and the door slides open at the ground floor. Mrs. Castemar smiles as she steps out of the elevator. "It was wonderful seeing you, dear. Don't lose your hand."

If weirder parting words were ever said, I sure don't know them. "Thanks," I say as the doors slide shut again. I'd like to say the idea of continuing on to the basement is out, but the amounts of laundry I have to do are truly staggering. I stare at my wrist, shrug, and toss the hand onto the pile of dirty clothes and wait while the elevator continues its journey down. Laundry'll be so fun to do one-handed. I can't wait. The door slides open and I'm there; the machines staring at me through the doorway; lined up in two neat rows with the dryers pushed back against the far wall.

Luckily for me, the basement is completely empty, so I don't have to explain the hand. I reach into the basket and put it on the edge of the washing machine for safe keeping. It's not until after I start the load of laundry, though, that I hear the telltale *thump thump thump*. My eyes flick up to the top of the machine and yup. The hand's gone. I close my eyes and sigh. Well, that's one way of washing myself, though not the one I would have picked. Call me super lazy, but I'm not going to fish around searching for it. I'll call it a tennis shoe if anyone comes in and wait until they do their laundry before I transfer mine to the dryer.

The washer stops its spin cycle. I hope my hand's in one piece. I mean, regardless of what I said to Mrs. Castemar, it's kind of irreplaceable. I reach in and start pulling the laundry out and back into the basket. My left hand is sitting at the bottom of the washer, intact. I fish it out and put it on top of the wet clothing, then transfer the whole mess into the dryer.

I figure as long as the dryer's on the lowest setting, my hand should be fine.

The *thump* of the hand kind of lulls me to sleep. I wake with a start when the dryer buzzes. Hoisting everything back into the basket, I haul it back to the elevator, ride it upstairs and, finally, close the apartment door behind me. Then I slide to the floor and cry. Or rather, I try to. My shoulders heave, my throat tightens up, I start to sob, but that's it. I have no tears. My eyes are bone dry. I wasn't a biology geek in school, but I'm beginning to suspect that Andrew has a *lot* more to answer for than I originally thought. And yeah, while the idea of a doctor flits across my mind, I discard it almost as quickly. I'm pretty sure whatever is going on, a doctor isn't going to be able to fix it. I'd rather not be turned into a research paper for some medical journal. And telling Mom is pretty much out of the question. I love her and she's awesome, but I don't think even her open mind is open enough for a daughter who eats brains. As much as I don't really want to, I think it's time to go to church and talk to Lydia and the flying rock.

Four:

Is This Really a Church?

I don't want to go back to the church but here I am, debating whether or not to go inside. Of course, I will. I have to. My blood is congealing and my freakin' *hand* fell off. Rewrapping it was an exercise in patience, and something I never, ever want to have to do again. So that means I need answers. Badly. I hope Lydia is inside. No sooner does the thought cross my mind when the doors open and the red-haired woman pokes her head out.

"Isis! It's so good to see you. Come in. Please. I have a quick errand to run, but I'll be back in a few minutes."

I bite my lip, not particularly interested in going in without her, but really. What else am I going to do? I edge my way inside, peering up at the ceiling just in case the 'priest' decides to drop on my head.

"What are you doing?" The voice reminds me of rocks tumbling down a mountain; something I experienced first-hand once when I visited the Southern California coastline. It's unnerving, to say the least.

A sound like two large pieces of granite moving shivers its way up my spine. *Something* is in here with me and it sure as heck doesn't qualify as human. I look around, but don't see anything, which makes the hair on the back of my neck stand to full attention.

"Ad—admiring the ceiling," I stutter. Stupidly, because honestly, who'd admire a ceiling, unless it was the Sistine Chapel.

"I've always liked our ceilings, but then again, I'm a bit partial to them."

There's no nice way to ask, so I blurt it out. "Are you the thing that flew down from the ceiling yesterday?"

"I'm the priest here, yes."

It's only kind of an answer. I'm not sure what to do with it. "What are you? I mean, besides the priest."

Rumbling laughter fills the sanctuary. When it finally dies down, a scraping sound like I'd imagine tectonic plates rubbing together takes its place. "Is it all right if I come closer?"

I'm not super happy with the idea and wish Lydia'd hurry up with her 'errand' and come back already. "I guess…"

What I'm expecting is an old man, hunched over, face wrinkled and careworn. I don't know why, I hear the grinding as he approaches, but it still scares me when I finally get a good look at him. True, he's old. He's also pockmarked, made of stone and three quarters covered in moss.

Holy crap, the priest's a gargoyle. I fumble my way to the nearest pew, which, as it turns out, is farthest from the doors. "But…you don't exist!" Granted, it's not the brightest thing I've ever said, but there it is.

The thing grins at me. At least, it shows me two rows of super long, super sharp teeth. I'm hoping it's a grin and not a prelude to dinner. "When is the last time you looked closely at the architecture on a church?"

I blink. "Ummm…" is my oh, so intelligent reply.

My mom would be so proud.

"Gargoyles have existed for a millennium, and we're not the only ones. I created this working church around that fact, after all."

Whatever *that* means.

It continues as though my shock is nothing new. Maybe it's not. Who knows. "Is there a specific reason you came here?"

"Lydia invited me back. See, I've got this problem." I kind of waggle my left hand in his direction. "Can you do anything about this?"

In return, the creature holds up its claws. "I can't unwrap the bandage. Would you mind doing it?"

I do as it asks, and, as I knew it would, my hand drops to the stone floor.

"Ah, I see your dilemma," he says.

It's kind of hard not to. "I don't know what's happening to me," I confess. "All I did was go on a date with my boy—*ex*-boyfriend, and when I woke up, everything started going pear-shaped." I'm still not entirely convinced this isn't some kind of hallucination brought on by Andrew and his neck chewing fetish, but it can't hurt to explore the options. "Do you know what's happening to me?"

I didn't know creatures made of stone could shrug until that moment. Somehow that fact makes the whole conversation more normal.

"Let's backtrack a minute," the creature says. "You're already acquainted with Lydia, but I'm Father Moss."

I giggle at his name. I can't help it. "Seriously?"

"It was given to me before I collected lichen," the priest replies. "It's a family name."

Wait. "Does that mean there're more of you? I mean, were you actually born?"

Father Moss flexes his shoulders. Rocks groan.

"I was created, as were my parents and my grandparents. We were all carved by the same man, you see."

I nod, even though I really don't. I always thought *creation* implied a soul. Can you even carve something with a soul?

"But we aren't here to talk about me," he continues. "Have you experienced any other symptoms lately?"

Ummm...yeah. I fill him in: raw brains, eating like an animal, everything.

"You need to use our computers," Father Moss says.

"Oh, I have a laptop," I say. "Just give me the name of the website and I can look it up at home."

"Our computers are a bit more specialized than that," the gargoyle says.

I frown, but before I can ask him what he means, the doors pull open and people start spilling into the sanctuary. I guess he wasn't kidding when he said this was a working church. It's not like hundreds of people or anything, but it's enough to make me flinch backwards and clutch at my unattached hand. I don't really get a good look at any of them; they just file in and start to fill up the pews in front of me.

"Excuse me," the priest stands up and his clawed feet dig into the pitted marble flooring. Little chunks fly up around him. A grinding sound accompanies the sight of wings unfolding from his back, and my breath catches. The wings are beautiful quartz, the light from the stained glass windows catching and reflecting the purple of the stone. "It's time to start services."

Having grown up in churches across Georgia, I fully expect a relatively normal service, though in retrospect, I have no idea why. I mean, the priest *is* made of stone. I turn to face the altar and bow my head.

Father Moss clears his throat. It sounds like a monsoon storm of boulders, but it doesn't slow the low rumble of chatter from everyone. Cleary, no-one's new except me. He clatters those gorgeous wings, and the sound dies down. "We've got a new visitor tonight."

At that, most of the heads swivel in my direction and suddenly I'm the center of attention. I also get an up-close view of the people sitting around me. The word 'bizarre' doesn't do them justice. "What the...frick."

"What's your problem?" The girl directly in front, probably the only one in the room *not* staring at me, turns in the pew. I gasp. Her eyes are huge, green, and slit vertically, like a cat.

As usual, my mouth gets in the way of my brain. "What the heck are *you*?"

Those eyes narrow. "Rude much?"

"Let it go, Noelle," Father Moss says.

She subsides, but not without glaring daggers at me first. Great. My first enemy.

Five:

In Which I Learn What I am.

"Everyone, this is Isis," Father Moss says.

"Hi, Isis," everyone except the chick in front of me, Noelle, says. I feel like I'm at an A. A. meeting in the Twilight Zone. Everyone is deformed: there's a kid around my age whose hands are massive paws. That can't be real, can it? And what about the guy who grins at me, his canines needle sharp? My gut tells me those have *nothing* to do with body mods, but the alternative – that they're real – is even weirder.

I'm pretty sure the gargoyle sees the whites of my eyes, because he motions to me with one clawed hand. "While everyone mingles, let's go to my office."

I nod. I don't think I'm ready to learn the truth of why all these people look so freaky. Computers feel safer. They only do what they're told, after all. Nothing more and nothing less.

"When I said our computers are specialized, I meant that the search engines go deeper than normal ones," Father Moss says. "They were designed by an old friend."

I shrug. Okay, so he doesn't use Google. No biggie.

It doesn't take long to reach the office. It's not like the church is massive or anything. I actually expect a closed and locked door, but there's only an archway. That makes sense, I guess, since the priest doesn't have fingers to grip a doorknob. The gargoyle gestures me before him. I walk in and sit in one of the comfy looking computer chairs, facing away from the arch. Behind me is a row of high tech desktop computers. Nice.

"What did Lydia tell you about our church?" The priest squats down on his haunches, wings folded across his back.

I think back. "Not a thing."

"Let me guess...you started finding strange notes lying around?"

"I found a note, yeah. Is that some kind of conspiracy to get people to come here?"

The gargoyle laughs. "Not really. Lydia specializes in finding and helping certain groups of people." He shrugs and small pieces of stone fall from his shoulders in a gritty cascade. "Your kind of people."

"What do you mean, 'my kind of people'?" I lean forward in the chair.

"Isis, what do you think you are?"

The question kind of throws me. "Well, for starters, a high school graduate...but that's not what you mean, is it?"

He shakes his head.

"Do *you* know what I am?" I feel a bit like the little bird in that kids' book *Are you My Mother?*

"I have my suspicions," Father Moss says. "But I think it's something you need to find out for yourself. I *will* tell you this, however. This church, these people...they're all here for the same reason you are; because none of you fit completely into either reality."

I blink. "There's only one reality. Isn't there?"

Someone knocks at the archway and I turn to see Lydia. "Hey, can I come in?"

"Please," Father Moss replies. "We were just getting to the sticky part of the conversation, anyway. It might be easier coming from you than from me. Besides, I need to tend to my flock."

"The freaks." Sometimes I really just need duct tape for my mouth. I'm sure of it.

"They're not freaks, Isis," Lydia corrects me. "They're halves."

I feel about as smart as the closest telephone pole. "Halves of what?"

The gargoyle answers me right before he steps through the archway. "Supernaturals, Isis. Just like you."

"You're crazy. He's crazy." I'm not really sure who I'm talking to at this point, because Father Moss is gone and Lydia is just standing there, staring at me. "This isn't Narnia. It's Atlanta."

Lydia takes the chair I'm sitting in and spins me around so I'm facing the computers. "Type H.V.V. into the search bar."

I put my hand down on the mouse pad. "Don't you mean H.I.V?"

"No," she says. "I mean H.V.V."

I guess I don't do it fast enough, because she leans over me and types it into the Google search bar. My heart begins to stutter when I read what appears on the screen.

'Human Vampiric Virus: A condition found in 0.000000001% of the population in which a human begins to take on the traits and mannerisms of a zombie (including the consumption of raw flesh, decomposition, madness and eventual death). Attributed to the swamps of Louisiana, it is spread via blood to flesh contact. There is speculation whether the virus exists or is, in fact, a rare mental disorder with no known cure.'

I lean back in the chair, pretty much as far away from the screen as I can get without tipping over backwards. "Zombies don't exist."

"Tell that to any practitioner of voodoo."

"I can't be half a zombie."

She looks pointedly at my still unwrapped stump. "Your hand tells me a different story."

I glance down. "You mean because of the lack of blood?" I'm pretty sure I should be freaking out more, but it's all so unreal.

Lydia peers into my eyes. "I think you're in shock."

"I can't cry," I blurt, apropos of nothing.

She pats my arm and I shake her off. "No, you don't understand. It's not that I don't *want* to cry. It's that I can't. There's something wrong with my tear ducts."

"That's interesting," Lydia murmurs.

"No. No, it's not 'interesting'. It's freaky and it's bizarre and it's weird. But it's *not* interesting!" My voice rises on the last word.

"You're not the only one who's gone through this, I promise." Her voice calms me down. A bit.

"I'm not? There are others like me? Other half-zombies?"

Her eyes are sympathetic. "We're all like you, Isis. Well, not Father Moss or me, but everyone else here is a half-something or other."

"Then what are you?" Maybe that chick in the sanctuary is right. I *am* rude, but it's too late to take it back now.

"I'm a witch."

I'm distracted from my own plight, which may have been her intent. "Like in the Salem Witch Trials?" I remember vaguely reading *The Witch of Blackbird Pond* when I was around ten years old.

Didn't that have to do with Salem, or the Puritans, or something?

"Those women *weren't* witches. The Witch Trials were nothing more than maligned women being drowned and hung for man's ignorance."

I swivel the computer chair back around so I can look at her without straining my neck. "Were you— were you one?" I inch the chair back toward the computers. If she's one of *those* witches, she's really old…and probably really dangerous.

"I wasn't one of those women, no."

Lydia answers the exact question I asked, but I'm not stupid. I rephrase the question. "Were you alive back then?"

"Oh honey, I've been alive for *years.*" She laughs and sits down in the chair next to me. "But yes, to answer your question, I was. However, I will not tell you about my past, so please don't ask. What happened back then wasn't pretty and I have no desire to relive it. Besides, you're getting distracted. As I said, everyone in the sanctuary is a half. They've all struggled with finding themselves. You're not alone. Not anymore."

"How'm I supposed to 'find myself' when I don't even understand what I am?"

"Come back into the sanctuary with me," Lydia says. "Meet some of the others. Who knows, you might wind up with some friends."

I think of the girl with the cat-slit eyes. "Doubt it." But I follow her out of the office, because I'm already here and why not?

It figures. The first person to come up to us is the fang guy. I try to smile, but I'm pretty sure it looks more like a grimace than anything else.

"It's okay, Isis," Lydia says.

I'm not reassured. Especially now that I know

those weird canines he has are the result of being a monster. Excuse me. *Half* a monster. Like that makes it so much better.

He grins at me. All the rest of his teeth are normal looking. He'd even be kind of cute if it wasn't for the fact that when his mouth closes, his fangs rest on his lower lip. "You look kind of freaked out," he holds out his right hand. "I'm Daniel."

Oh. Crap. I've left my hand sitting on the left side of the keyboard in the priest's office. "Ummm...Hi," I mumble. "Sorry about my hand."

He glances down at my stump. "Oh, wow. So...what are you?"

I frown. "Excuse me?"

"You know...we're all halves here. I'm a half-vampire. What're you?"

"Z—z—zombie," I stutter, wondering if I'm really having this conversation.

"Cool, so you're an undead, too."

Wait. "I'm a *what*?"

Daniel grins again. "You know. Undead. Like...not alive."

I blink. Weirdest. Conversation. *Ever.* But he's been nice so far and I like him. "So what's the deal with the cat-eyed chick? Is she undead, too?"

He flushes. "You mean the half-fae? Nah, she's not undead. That's Noelle."

"Yeah, she's—interesting."

"Like a fungus? Plan on putting me in a petri dish, maybe?"

Crap. Of *course* she's behind me. I breathe deeply; in through the nose, out through the mouth, just like Mom taught me. I turn. "That's not what I meant," I start, but she doesn't let me finish. Not by a long shot.

"What's your malfunction? Why are you here,

anyway? Slumming?"

"Noelle, she's new," Daniel says. "Give her a break, why don't you?"

"Why should I?" Boy, she's got enough anger to keep an entire city lit.

"Look," I say. "I don't know what I did to set you off, but I'm really sorry, okay? Whatever it is, I didn't mean it."

She stares at me for a long minute. "That's just about the worst apology I've never heard."

Before I can say anything else, the green haired half-fae storms out of the church, slamming the doors shut behind her.

"Wow. Is she always so volatile?" I'd rather use another word, but my mom's always telling me that ladies don't swear.

Daniel shrugs. "It's Noelle. You get used to her."

Yeah. I don't see that happening any time soon. Or ever. My cell phone rings and Elvis' Jailhouse Rock fills the sanctuary. I blush and fish the phone out of my pocket, quickly pressing the down volume button before answering. "Hello?"

"Hey, Isis."

Six:

It's a Date!

I'd recognize that slow southern drawl anywhere. It's Sam. My eyes widen. It's *Sam*. What the heck am I going to say? I can't believe he actually called.

I turn my back to everyone and lower my voice. "Hey, Sam. What's up?" There. That sounds natural and not like I'm standing in the sanctuary of the weirdest church ever.

"You still up for a Coffee Jar run? Farrie, Rhett and I are going to run by there before heading to Savannah."

"I'd love to come," I say.

"I can swing by your apartment and get you in, like, ten minutes."

"I'm not home, but I can meet you at the Jar," I counter. "I'm not too far from there."

There's a pause and a flurry of conversation I can't hear, then Sam's voice comes back loud and clear. "Okay, yeah, that'll work." The phone beeps.

I turn back to Daniel. "Sorry, I've got a —"

"A date. Yeah, I heard," the half-vamp says. "Having a life when you don't really, y'know, *have* a life is harder than you think." He smiles and it looks a bit sad. "But good luck. I hope it works out for you, I really do."

"Thanks, Daniel." This time, when I smile at him, it's real. He seems like a nice guy. Fangs and all. I head for the front doors.

"Uhhh...Isis?" Daniel calls me back. "You forgot something."

I frown.

"Were you planning on leaving your hand here?"

Startled, I glance down. I somehow completely spaced that my hand is sitting on Father Moss's desk. I guess because I'm right-handed. But that leads me to another issue. "Would you do me a huge favor?"

He looks cautious, but nods. "Sure."

"Wrap my hand back onto my wrist?"

His sigh is relieved. I wonder what favors he's had to do before, but it's really none of my business. I barely know him. "I'll be right back."

I wade through the other people, glancing briefly at the paw handed guy. He catches my eye, raises one eyebrow, then turns back to the girl standing next to him. *She* looks totally normal. I wonder what her super power is. She's gotta have something, or she wouldn't be here. Then again, with the way she's clinging to paw guy's hand, she might just be a visitor. I don't even know if that's allowed. Maybe I could bring Sam... if this is going to be my life, it might be nice to have a bit of normal in it.

Father Moss isn't in the office when I get there, so it's a quick in and out to grab my hand and get back to where Daniel's now standing with paw guy and the chick.

"And this is Isis," Daniel says, as if he totally knows me.

The girl, a cute multi-color haired pixie, smiles. "I'm Bekah and this is Albin. It's great to meet you. Is this your first time here?"

I don't really have time to chat, but her question gives me the opening I want to ask a question of my own. "I'm new to all this. What about you?"

She laughs. "Oh, it's not like that. The most unusual thing about me is my hair."

"And all...this," I wave the hand in my, uhhh, hand to encompass the whole church, "doesn't mess with your head?"

"It did at first, yeah. But Albin's paws aren't ever going away...so neither am I."

It must be nice to have a love like that. My thoughts flit back to Andrew. He really *was* perfect...except for the biting part. But if Andrew was so perfect, why am I going to coffee with Sam? My life's obviously not going to be anything close to normal ever again. Maybe trying to be something I'm not just isn't worth it.

"Aren't you supposed to be going on a date? If you give me your hand, I'll re-bandage you." Daniel holds out his hand for my loose one.

"I—don't know if I should go." I give him my hand and hold out my stump. He carefully wraps the ace bandage around my wrist and the errant hand.

"There. Good as new." He smiles at my raised eyebrow. "Well, okay, not quite, but it's the best I can do."

"See," I say, "that's what I'm talking about."

"I don't know you well enough to give you advice, Isis, but if it was me, I'd go." He kind of one shoulder shrugs at me. "If someone asked me out, I'd go even if they *were* completely human."

"You're right," I decide. "I'll go. Thanks, Daniel."

"Hey, it's what I'm here for."

I doubt that, but it's nice of him to say.

"Have fun," Bekah says.

I hope I see her again. She sounds like she has her...stuff....together and I could talk to someone like that. Someone who might just understand what I'm going through, but who's not half a monster, that is. I hear Daniel saying, 'zombie,' as I pull the doors shut behind me. I'm waiting for it to bother me, but, surprisingly enough, it doesn't. Weird how things change so quickly.

It takes me around fifteen minutes to reach The Coffee Jar. I pull the Bug into a parking space right in front and clamber out. It'd be just my luck if they weren't even there anymore, but they are, seated at the counter, hands wrapped around their cups.

Sam glances at the door and breaks into a wide grin when he sees me. "Hey, Isis, you made it!" I wonder if he's been watching the door. I'm suddenly really, hugely, glad I decided to come.

"Grab a cup and join us. Move over, Farrie." He nudges the short, heavyset guy whom I recognize as one of the football players from my sophomore year.

"Sure thing. Cop a squat, Isis. I don't bite. Much." Farrie laughs and Sam glares at him until he moves over a stool.

"Don't mind him," Sam says. "He doesn't mean anything."

I slide onto the stool. "Hi, Rhett."

"S'up?" The smaller boy on the other side of me nods. "You comin' with?"

Uhhh...I frown. "Coming where, exactly?" He can't mean what I think he means, can he?

"Shut it." Sam swivels on his stool so he's facing me. "It's summer, Isis. I thought..." he flushes. "I thought you might want to come with us. You know, a road trip."

Oh, *heck* no. I can't even imagine what my mom'd say to that one. Me and three guys? Yeah. *So* not going to happen. "There's no way," I start, but Sam holds up one hand to stop me.

"No, that's not...I mean..."

I didn't even know Vikings *could* blush, but his face is flushing again. "Sara and Rose are meeting us there."

"I can't. My mom's in China and I have to stay close to home." And there's no circumstance, *none*, under which I'm ever going back to Savannah. But they don't need to know that part.

Sam gulps down the last of his coffee. "That sucks."

Kind of yes, kind of no. All I can do is hope he'll ask me out again sometime. Like, on a real date, not something that includes his tribe.

"Ready to bounce?" Farrie slides off his stool, leaving his empty cup on the counter.

"Dude, were you born in a barn?" Rhett follows suit, but tosses his cup into the trash can. It's an impressive shot, considering the trash can is at the other end of the long counter. But then again, Rhett's the youngest player in school to be offered a full ride basketball scholarship to the college of his choice. He's the pick of the litter.

"I'll call you later, Isis." Sam winks at me before he follows Farrie and Rhett out.

All I can do is hope. This does suck.

Seven:

Me, Popular? Nah.

I'm seated at the row of computers in Father Moss's office. It's been a week since the whole Coffee Jar incident and Sam *still* hasn't called, but my mom has, which got me thinking. If H.V.V. is a virus, then there's bound to be a cure, right? After all, viruses don't exist in a vacuum. So now my end-goal is to figure out not *if* I can be cured, but *how* I can be cured. Thus far, I've learned exactly nothing.

"Service is about to start."

The voice startles me and I swing around. Dear Lord, why is it always Noelle? I sigh. "I'm about done here."

Instead of leaving, she saunters into the office. "What're you holed up in here for, anyway?"

I have no idea why she's so invested in starting up a conversation. Noelle hates me and the feeling is definitely mutual.

"You've been in here every day last week, and now here you are again. Sitting in that chair; in front of that computer. For hours on end."

She's obviously not going away any time soon without an answer. "I'm looking for a cure." I wait for her to laugh.

"Is that all?" She plops down in the chair next to me.

"It's kind of a big deal to me," I snap.

"It's easy to be cured, Isis." Noelle reaches into her pocket, pulls out a butterscotch candy, unwraps it and pops it into her mouth. "All you have to do is find, and kill, your maker."

"*Excuse* me?" *Kill* someone? Kill *Andrew*? Is she serious?

She nods. "Werewolves do it all the time."

"Why're you telling me this?"

She gets up and brushes off her pants, as though there were crumbs on them. "The sooner you get your cure, the sooner you leave us all alone." With that lovely parting shot, she walks out.

Typical Noelle. What a...pain. I'm not sure whether to believe her or not, but what she says sounds perfectly reasonable. Which should worry me, but it doesn't. I type 'werewolf cure' into the search engine and *bam!* There it is; a whole list of cures ranging from medieval to modern times. I have a lot to read through, but it's not like I don't have the time. Frankly, I'm surprised Noelle told me the truth. I wonder what her 'end game' is, because there's no way she's helping me out of the kindness of her heart. I'm not even sure she's got one. The question now is...can I actually hunt down my ex and kill him? My stomach rumbles and suddenly all doubts are gone. I can't go through life eating brains. I just can't. And Andrew *is* a monster. So it's not like I'll be killing an actual person. Maybe it'll be as easy as luring him into the sun. Then it won't be my fault. Technically.

"How's it going?" Daniel's voice startles me, but then again, he always startles me. He's stealthy. I think it's because of his vampire blood. At least now I know how Andrew moved around without making any noise.

"It's going." I tilt my head back and up to look at him. Yup, he's wearing his canine caps, which is only a little less creepy than when he *doesn't* wear them, because the white plastic tips of the caps rest on his lower lip. I wonder if he can get the caps in different colors…

"You know you're not going to find out anything about the undead by sitting in front of a keyboard, right?"

"Wanna bet?" I point to the screen. "I just learned that werewolves can be cured."

"Weres aren't undead," Daniel points out.

"But they're still monsters." As soon as the words leave my mouth, I want to take them back. I don't see Daniel as a monster. He's too nice.

"Not all monsters are monsters," the half-vampire's voice is full of hurt.

"I know," I mutter. "Sorry, I'm just frustrated."

"Do you ever go anywhere? I mean, other than here?"

I shake my head. "Not really, no."

"Go out with me," he mumbles into his wisp of a beard.

I swivel around in the chair to face him. "*Excuse me?*"

"I mean…not *out* out. Just, y'know, out."

I raise one eyebrow, waiting for the explanation.

"I don't mean on a *date*," he rushes on. "More like…an outing. Tomorrow night."

I haven't been out since Andrew. I wonder where we can go. Daniel and his fangs aren't exactly low profile.

"I see *you're* making yourself right at home."

Why's she back? It's like she's incapable of leaving me alone. If Daniel hadn't said Noelle was a half-fae, I would swear she was part cat. The woman *always* hears what I'm saying. *Always.* I don't know why she has it out for me, but holy cow, I'm tired of it.

"Oh, look," I'm pretty sure my smile would melt concrete. "It's a wingless fairy."

She stalks toward me, but Daniel steps between us.

The half-fae glares at him before marching away, her back stiff.

"I am getting sick to death of her," I growl. "I really wish she'd just leave me alone."

"Noelle's sensitive," Daniel says. "What'd you do to chap her hide?"

I lean back in the chair. "Nothing, as far as I know. She's just being ugly for no reason." Even as I say it, I know it's not *exactly* true, so I amend my answer. "When I first got here, I asked what she was. I didn't mean anything by it, but c'mon. Those eyes aren't what I'd call normal."

He laughs. It's nice. "Boy, you really know how to make friends, don't you?"

If anyone else said that to me, I'd be pissed off. But Daniel's already proven himself to be one of those nice guys you pretty much find only in books, so I just shrug. I'm not particularly interested in making friends with Noelle. A shared avoidance would be great, but that doesn't seem to be on her radar.

"Okay, so what about this outing?" I change the subject away from the half-fae.

"It's an underground club," Daniel says. "Just a place for us to hang out, get to know each other. You know, the normal stuff."

I'm pretty sure what Daniel thinks is normal, isn't. And I have one more rather pressing concern about the whole thing. "How do I know you won't try to bite me?" Call me paranoid, but the possibility *does* exist.

A frown wrinkles his brow. "Why would I bite you?"

"I assumed...I mean...well, you *do* drink blood, don't you?"

He tilts his head to one side. "Do you really want me to answer that?"

He takes my silence for assent.

"I have to drink blood, but I don't drink people."

My opinion of him goes up even further. "Then what do you do? Drink animals?"

Daniel shakes his head. "I just go visit the local blood bank."

"That's people," I state.

"Yeah, but it's not directly out of their necks or anything, so you're not in any danger."

He's trying so hard to be reassuring. It's cute. "All right, I'll go out with you."

"Great," he says. "So I'll pick you up around seven?"

I'm not thrilled with the idea of any halves knowing where I live. "I'll meet you here."

"I'll have Lydia call you and set something up. Unless you own a modern Gothic gown, that is."

"Wait, you didn't say anything about dressing up..."

He grins at me. "It's a club, Isis. Don't you want to fit in?"

Before I can think of what to say, he leaves.

I stare at the screen for a moment before hitting the 'print' button. My eyes are blurring. The printer buzzes to life, then spits out a single piece of printed paper. I grab it and start scanning. It's full of weirdness, but all I really want to do is go home, climb into some comfy pajamas and go to sleep.

Eight:

The Wrath of Mom.

I'm not paying much attention to anything when I walk up the steps to my apartment building; after all, I've lived here for close to six months. It's home. My inattention is my downfall, as it turns out. The apartment door is ajar. Not a lot, but enough to be worrisome because I'm 99.999% sure I locked it earlier. I fumble in my pocket for my pepper spray until I hear a very familiar voice.

"Isis, is that you?"

"Mom?" Seriously, she's home? She didn't say anything about coming home when I talked to her last week. What's going on? "Are you okay?"

"Quit yelling at me from the hall," she chides. Never mind that I'm not yelling at all. I'm practically at the door by now. "You sounded weird on the phone, so I cut my trip a little short."

I dread what she's going to say once she gets a good look at me. It's not like I resemble anything close to healthy. In the span of one week, I've gone from pasty white to, well, undead; a kind of yellowing ivory. I'm definitely not anything remotely attractive anymore. I push the door all the way open and walk inside.

"Great good gosh, what's happened to you?" My mom totters forward on her 3" heels, still one of the shortest women I've ever seen.

I fold my arms across my chest. "I...uhhh..." My mom is a force of nature when she wants to be; she's like a tiny tornado wrapped in 4'8" of long skirts and hippy-esque tops. I'm not sure how to handle it.

Her eyes narrow. "What are you hiding, Isis? What's that marking on your wrist?" She grabs at me, but I move away.

"It's nothing, Mom. Honest."

I've been finding little tubes of crazy glue in Ziploc baggies on my doormat, along with the same handwritten note: 'Dearest Isis, I hope the glue helps with your prosthetic wrist. Let me know if you need any screws. My grandson works in hardware supply. Yours truly, Rohanda Castemar.' It's hilariously creepy. But it's better than walking around with an Ace bandage all the time.

"Sit down. I'll make you..." I pause. Double crap. I don't have anything in the blasted 'fridge except raw brains. I mean, why stock food I'll never eat?

"I looked in the refrigerator already. Isis, what on earth is going on?" She stares at me, her arms crossed and a familiar, determined look plastered on her face. There's no way I'm going to be able to lie my way out of this.

"You'll think I'm crazy," I hedge. "I mean 'lock me up, throw away the key' crazy."

Mom nods, though I'm not sure if it's in agreement with my statement, or a gesture for me to continue.

I pull my wrist out of her grasp. Gently, because I don't want to risk the glue coming loose. "Remember Andrew?"

"Sure, the nice boy you were dating before I left for China. Did something happen between the two of you?"

I try to stifle a snort of laughter. 'Nice boy',

indeed. "He got me sick."

Mom's eyes widen. "Did he give you A.I.D.S, Isis? I swear to the Father, if he gave you A.I.D.S. I'll kill him."

If only she could. "No, Mom, I don't have A.I.D.S." I blurt out the truth. "He gave me H.V.V."

'He gave you...what? I've never heard of that." She taps her foot on the carpet. "Whatever you're trying to say, just spill it."

"I'm a half-zombie, Mom." There. I say it and wait for her response.

It looks like Mom's eyebrows are going to crawl into her hairline and hide. "A half-zombie,' she says. "How'd it happen? Is it reversible?" She's taking the whole thing a lot calmer than I did.

I really don't want to go into any details. "It was a hickey gone wrong."

"Andrew." Her voice is completely flat. She is beyond pissed. "Are you sure you're a zombie?"

"Half. And yeah. I'm pretty sure."

She stares at me.

I wait. Mom isn't stupid and she reads a *lot* of fantasy, so I know she knows what a zombie is. After a minute that I'm sure lasts much, much longer, she sighs.

"Well, that explains the raw brains."

And, just like that, she accepts my situation.

"Please don't tell anyone." My voice shakes a bit.

"No, dear, of course not. Where would I even begin to explain this?" Mom's preoccupied, and I wonder what she's planning. It doesn't take long to find out. "Now, what are you going to do about it?"

I'm not sure if telling her my plans is such a good idea. I doubt she'd condone her daughter killing anyone. Then again...I sigh. "I have a piece of paper that talks about cures."

She presses her lips together. "Cures, huh? Can I see it?"

I pull it out of my pocket and hand it over. She unfolds the paper and starts to scan it. "Isis, this is about werewolves. I see nothing that applies to you."

"Someone at...at church...told me it would work."

Her eyes light up. "You're going to church? Oh, Isis, I'm so glad!"

Welcome to Georgia, where even hippies have religion. "Yeah, well." I'm not ready to tell her about Father Moss or Lydia, and definitely not about Noelle. I steer the conversation back to the original topic. "If this person is right, then I can be human again."

"So you're planning on what? Trying everything on this list and hoping it works?"

"Why shouldn't I?"

"Because there are some rather inappropriate things on this list. There's no reason to be that desperate." She peers at me. "Unless...you haven't...those aren't *human* brains in the 'fridge, are they?"

"Oh, *ewww*... no, Mom, they aren't. I'm not eating people!"

"Then we'll figure something out."

I narrow my eyes. "Why is this so easy for you to believe?"

"The only other option is that you've somehow contracted leprosy. No leper I've ever heard of eats raw brains, though." She peers at me. "Unless you're a new strain...are you, Isis? Are you a brain eating leper?"

I frown, not quite sure she's joking. "No. Definitely not."

"I believe it was Sherlock Holmes who said, 'When you have eliminated the possible, whatever remains, however improbable, must be the truth.'"

"You're quoting an opium addict, Mom. You know that, right?" And a completely made-up character, but I'm not going to argue *that* point with her.

"That doesn't make him wrong," she snaps.

I close my eyes. "Okay, you win."

She immediately backs off. This is how our conversations go, though. She quotes an obscure source to cement her point of view and I give in to her 'greater wisdom.' Never mind that, in this case, she's absolutely right. "Have you tried calling Andrew yet?"

"Why would I call him? He's the one who caused this."

"How does a human turn another human into a half-zombie?"

I was wondering when she'd get around to asking *that* question. I take a deep breath and let it out slowly. "Andrew isn't human, Mom."

"But he's such a *nice* boy. I mean...except for the zombie turning part."

"Mom. He's a vampire. I have no idea what happened, but he bit me and I woke up like this." I kind of wave my arms around.

"Then we definitely need to find him. What's his address?"

"I...no, Mom. This isn't your problem, it's mine."

"Don't be ridiculous, Isis. If it's your problem, it's my problem." She yawns. "Darn jet lag. I need to get some sleep. Are you up for coffee later?"

Oh, how I wish. I start to answer her, but the corner of my mouth tears open.

"Damnit," I swear, and then cringe.

"Isis Blue! Don't you dare swear in front of me!" Mom points her index finger at me while she chews me out.

"Yes, ma'am." I fall back on old habits even though I can feel the hairline tear in my cheek widening. "Ummm...Mom?" I interrupt her. "I need some crazy glue."

"...swearing is the Devil's...What?" She breaks off to stare at me.

"Yeah. It's in the top drawer in the china hutch, left side. Crazy glue. Please."

"Oh my...word, Isis, your cheek!" She rushes to the hutch and does as I ask. Good to know that even under the weirdest circumstances imaginable, Mom's great in a crisis.

I reach out to take the glue from her, but she doesn't let it go. "No, I'll do it." Her hand shakes. I find myself wondering whether I'll have a half-smile like Heath Ledger's Joker when she's done, but I don't complain. All things considered, her attitude's been great.

"There, all done." She hands me the glue. "I'm sorry it's messy, but I'm not used to this sort of thing."

"It's okay, Mom," I say. "I'm just glad you stayed."

"When I should have run screaming, you mean?" Mom smiles at me. "You're my daughter. What else am I supposed to do?"

It's a good question and one I'm pretty sure I don't have the answer to. Not yet, anyway.

Nine:

The Hunt Begins.

I wake up, stretching my arms high above my head. Is it tomorrow? I turn my bleary eyes to the clock and double check. Yup. It's tomorrow. Ugh. That means the date with Daniel is tonight. As if last night's fun with Mom wasn't enough, now I have what I never imagined I'd have again. A date with a vampire. It's the title of the worst campy movie ever. I sigh and roll to the edge of the bed, where I sit up and feel the glued cut on my cheek. Thankfully, it's holding, because I'm not up for having Frankenstein screws in my face. I already feel freakish enough.

I stumble to the bathroom and splash cold water on my face. I grab my bathrobe off the back of the door, put it on, and slide my arms into the soft, fuzzy sleeves before belting it closed. The part of me that's human longs for bacon and eggs for breakfast, or even sausage gravy with biscuits. But the zombie part demands raw piggy brains. Again. So I shuffle my way into the kitchen, awake but not functioning at 100%. Kind of zombie-like, if I do say so myself. I'm so tired of brains. I wonder if there are such things as zombie doctors...like voodoo doctors, but for the undead, and if they can help me eat 'real' food. After all, I'm still half human.

"Morning, Isis!"

My mom is just a bit too chipper for my taste. "Hi,

Mom, what're you doing up?"

"*Trying* to get back on a normal sleep schedule." She pours herself a cup of amazing smelling coffee and a tsunami wave of jealousy washes over me. I want coffee. "Besides," she continues, "you've got nothing in the 'fridge except brains, and I'm simply not up for eating those. Ever."

I sigh and tie my hair into a swift knot before reaching into the 'fridge and grabbing one of the many covered Tupperwares. I don't blame her one bit. Sitting down at the table, I open my brains and stare into the bowl, trying to summon the energy to eat.

"Do you want to go grocery shopping with me?"

Ugh. I so *don't*. "Ummm...not really, Mom. The smell of food kind of makes me queasy."

My mom makes lightning fast decisions, I'll give her that. "Then I need to buy you your own 'fridge; one of those dorm sized ones should work great for your bedroom."

"Seriously? You'll do that?"

"On one condition," she says.

I stab my fork into the plastic container and get around three squiggles of brains onto the tines. "Which is?"

"Get off your rear and call Andrew. Get his address so we can go pay him a visit later today...tonight. I don't want him to explode before I get a chance to kill him."

I love my mom. I really do. "I can't tonight, Mom. I've got...a date."

She frowns. "All this is happening and you're going out on a *date*? Isis, what's wrong with you?"

"I'm half alive, but I can't eat. I'm half dead and I'm starting to decompose. What could possibly be wrong?"

ONE FOOT IN THE GRAVE

"A lot less snip would be appreciated, young lady. Now tell me about this date. Who's it with, where'd you meet, and when will I get to meet him?"

"His name is Daniel, I met him at church, and I'm not sure. He's...shy."

The ringing phone cuts our conversation short, for which I'm extremely grateful. Mom reaches it before I do.

"Monroe residence, Marilinn speaking." There's a pause. "Yes, may I tell her who's calling?" She holds one hand over the mouthpiece. "It's someone named Lydia."

I replace my fork with the phone, wondering how she got our number. Then again, I firmly believe she's a Salem Witch, so it was probably easy-peasy.

"I'm heading out to the store." Mom mouths at me. "Is there anything you need?"

"Extra volume shampoo and conditioner." I say. "Lots and lots of conditioner." My hair's becoming drier and drier. Maybe my body's stopped producing the oils it needs to stay healthy? I blame zombiedom.

As soon as my mom leaves the apartment, I speak into the mouthpiece. "Hello?"

"Isis, it's Lydia. Daniel told me you'd need a gown for tonight, and I might have just the thing in your size."

"I wear a small," I say, positive she has nothing in my size.

"It used to belong to my daughter, but she's since outgrown it. Why don't you come by my house around six tonight and we'll make sure it fits. I'm at 4263 Hagwood Circle. Do you know where that is?"

It's not too far from me, actually. I nod, then remember I'm on the phone. "I'll be there tonight. Ummm...thanks."

"Sure thing. See you then."

I put the phone down. I'm not going to call Andrew. One: I already know his address and two: all that'll do is give him the chance to deflect my questions. The best course of action is to confront him face to face. I glance at the microwave. The light green numbers blink 12:30 p.m. He's probably at home. Maybe he's even still asleep in his coffin, if vampire legend holds true. If I hurry, I can get to his house before he wakes up. I push away from the table and head for my bedroom. I'm not horribly worried about what to wear, so I just throw on a pair of holey jeans and a shirt that unfortunately says 'Brainzzzzz...it's what's for breakfast, lunch *and* dinner!' with a picture of a cartoon zombie chowing down on a defenseless teddy bear. I grab my keys and pepper spray off my nightstand and head down to the apartment garage.

I love my car. It's not anything special, but it runs. It's a bright blue '74 Volkswagen Beetle, which is a tribute to my oh-so-wonderful hippie upbringing. It even has a huge flower painted on the driver's side door; an orange carnation. I climb inside and crank the engine. It turns over immediately, thanks to my mom's utter paranoia about car maintenance. I stick it in first, pull out of the garage and into traffic. Andrew's house isn't far from me, which was great when we were dating. Now...I'm not so sure. At least I can get over talking to him quick. It'll be like ripping off a Band-Aid; it'll hurt for a second, and then be over.

I make a left-hand turn into Andrew's neighborhood and navigate the small streets until I reach his house, where I park the Bug and idle. I'm not ready to get out and confront him. I have no idea what to say. 'Hey, Andrew, guess what? You turned me into a monster and, oh by the way, you *suck*?'

ONE FOOT IN THE GRAVE

Hmmm...probably not. I don't even know *how* he did it; just that it happened. Maybe it was just a freaky accident and he has no idea. It's possible. Maybe I don't have to kill him, after all. I open the door and get out. A curtain flickers open, then shuts again, so I know someone's home. My heart's beating like a triphammer. I straighten my shoulders. It's time.

The guy who answers the door definitely isn't who I'm looking for. He looks exactly like a transplant from a California surfer movie and not a bit like Andrew. Which makes sense, considering he's not my ex.

"Yeah, can I help you?"

"I'm looking for Andrew," I say. "Is he home?"

"Wow, he hasn't been here in, like, forever." He yawns.

"He didn't leave a forwarding address or anything? I find that pretty hard to believe."

"Dude, seriously, I don't know where Andrew is. He left, like, a week ago." He scratches at his ear. "He might be at Jennette's. Maybe."

I glare at him. "I don't know Jennette." She must be the next girlfriend and, as angry as I am at Andrew, I'm kind of pissed he replaced me so fast, too.

"Well, I don't know what else to tell you. He's not here."

I stifle my frustration. "Do you know if he's coming back anytime soon?"

"I doubt it," the guy says. "He was pretty freaked out, actually. Paid up his portion of the rent, grabbed some of his stuff and bolted."

Great. Terrific. Now what am I supposed to do? I turn to leave.

"Wait; is your name Queen, or something? You're his girl, right?"

I turn back. "I *was* his girl, yeah. Why?"

"He left something for you. Hold on a sec." He shuts the door in my face. Nice. It doesn't take long before the door opens again and surfer dude shoves an envelope at me.

I take it out of reflex more than out of any real desire to see what's in it. "Did he say anything?"

The guy shrugs. "Just something like 'if she comes by, give her this'."

He's so full of information, I can hardly stand it. I wait for him to say something else, but he just stares at me. I guess I have to walk away first. "Thanks."

"See ya." The door slams shut and that, as they say, is that. I walk back to the Bug, climb inside, and stare at the envelope. I have no idea why Andrew would write me, or what he could possibly have to say. But it feels like more than one sheet of paper, so whatever it is, it'll probably be worth reading. Maybe. I flip it over, open it, and take the two sheets of stationary out.

'Isis,' it begins, 'I wish I could take back what I did to you. Not because I'm ashamed of trying it, but because it didn't succeed.' I almost crumple up the letter right then and there, but my curiosity gets the better of me and I keep reading. 'I wanted us to be together, and that was the only way I could think of to make it happen. Any harm I may have caused you wasn't at all my intent.' I'm not quite sure how he might have thought turning me into a vampire wouldn't be harming me, but I can feel my anger at him seeping away 'I'm sure by now you've figured out what I am. Normal boyfriends don't bite their girlfriends. At least, not like,' I flip the page over. It's blank, so I turn to the last page in the envelope. 'I did. I know telling you now I didn't want to be alone anymore won't help you forgive me, but I hope you do anyway. ~Andrew.'

Crap. How am I supposed to kill him now that he's asked for my forgiveness? Won't doing that make *me* into the monster?

Ten:

Breakdown, it's all Right.

I turn the ignition over and head home. The entire venture only took around an hour, so that leaves me with five and a half hours to burn, and nothing on my agenda. Or so I believe until I walk into the apartment and hear the low hum of voices coming from the kitchen.

"I met one of your new friends at the grocery store. Come in and say hello." My mom says.

My brain starts whirling around. Who could she possibly have met? "I'm kind of tired. I was just going to head to my room and take a nap." I'm not particularly tired, but I don't much feel like socializing, either.

"Don't be rude. Come in here."

I sigh. So much for that deflection working. "All right."

Our kitchen is tiny. Like, there's room for a table and a couple of chairs, but that's pretty much it. I guess it's a typical apartment kitchen, but I don't know. The last place we lived was a commune, which has its own concept of space. My mom is sitting at one of the chairs, and Lydia's planted in the other.

"I thought I was going to meet you at your house," I say.

"Fate had a different idea," she says matter-of-factly. "Unfortunately, I don't have your gown with me, so you can come get it early."

"How did you know that's my mom?" I'm not going anywhere with her until I know how she found my mom in a grocery store.

"I scryed for her."

"You used *magic* on me?" My mom, on the other hand, doesn't sound creeped out at all. It's obvious she's fascinated by the idea, which is pretty disturbing.

Lydia nods. "Only a tiny bit. Magic is practice and discipline and study and using it takes almost more energy than it's worth."

My mom nods as though that's the most natural answer in the world. I just kind of twitch one shoulder upward. "So why do I have to go with you, again?"

"Is she always so stubborn?" Lydia asks my mom.

"I raised her to be an independent thinker," my mom replies. "You can go with her, Isis. It's all right. She's told me all about the church and your...date."

"Oh my gosh, Mom, it's *not* a date." I protest. "Daniel just said he'd help me, that's all. I didn't tell you because it's not that big of a deal."

"It *could* be a date, Isis, and you need to get out. You look positively unhealthy."

"Really, Mom? 'Unhealthy'?"

Even Lydia stifles a snicker.

My mom glares at both of us. "I'm doing the best I can under the circumstances. My child, my *daughter*, is undead...this isn't exactly something that was ever in the parenting manual!"

Her voice starts to fray and I see tears forming in her eyes. The last time I saw her cry, I'd accidentally dropped a gallon of apple juice on her big toe right after she lost the nail. She just...wept. I was only five, but I still remember swearing I'd never make her cry again. It's a promise I've kept until today.

"Mom, I'm sorry, I wish I could..." What do I wish? I can't go back to being completely human without killing Andrew...can I? It's not a question I want to ask in front of my mom, so I just trail off.

She smiles at me, but now I see the cracks in her façade. She's really having a harder time dealing with this than I am. Lydia seems to understand that, too, because she gets up from the table.

"I really appreciate you letting me come over, Marilinn, but you look a bit frazzled. We really shouldn't take up any more of your time. I'll keep Isis overnight to give you a chance to rest."

Wait...I'm spending the night at the witch's house? When was *that* decided? "Spend the night? Mom!"

Before I can move, my mom grabs me by the elbow. "Excuse us, Lydia. Isis and I need to have a chat." She hustles me into her bedroom and shuts the door.

I normally love my mom's room. It's bright and bold and filled with greenery. She's got plants all over the place except on the bed itself. It's like a greenhouse, but without the humidity and windows. We can't exactly paint the walls, so she enlisted me and we hung curtain rods everywhere, then draped long silk scarves along every surface. It's eye bending, to say the least.

"What happened to your manners, Isis? I *know* I raised you better than that!"

"Mom, she's a witch," I start, but she's having none of what I'm saying.

"And you're a half-zombie. And Andrew is a vampire. What's your point, Isis?"

I try again. "You don't even *know* her. How do you know she's not a serial killer in disguise or something?"

She laughs. "*You* know her and she works at a church. I think you're safe."

And just like that, I know I'm going to be shipped off to the witch's house.

Eleven:

It's a Witchy-Witch.

Lydia lives in a cottage. It's a true, hand to God cottage complete with rosebushes and an immaculate lawn. As a matter-of-fact, it looks sort of like some of the houses straight out of Lord of the Rings – the hobbit holes, or whatever they're called; but without the round doorways or being covered in dirt.

"Go on in." She opens the door wide and gestures me inside first. I step over the threshold. I'm not sure what I expect, candy furniture and gingerbread walls, maybe? Whatever it is, it's not anything close to what I see. The interior is cozy; a fire even crackles in the fireplace. I frown. Wait a second, it's summer-time, and she's got a *fire* going? It's weird. Not to mention, how many people keep a fire burning when they're not home?

"I made some tea," the red-haired woman says. "Do you take yours with cream and sugar, or plain?"

Tea with cream and sugar sounds interesting...too bad I can't have any. "I can't drink anything except water." This whole half-zombie thing is sucking.

"I'm sorry, I forgot. Have a seat," Lydia waves at the couch; a big, comfy monstrosity taking up a full three quarters of her living room. "I have the perfect dress for your date. Just hang on one second..." She trots down the hallway, leaving me totally alone in her living room. Maybe she's got some specialized security or something. Either that or she's super trusting. But if she's as old as I think she is, she wouldn't have survived the Trials by trusting...my thoughts are just squirreling around everywhere. I slide my shoes off, sit cross-legged on the couch and glance around the room. Sandstone colored walls hold pictures of cacti and pottery shards. In fact, the whole theme is really Southwestern.

"Try this on, it should fit you." Lydia holds out what looks like yards and yards of red velvet. I'm no seamstress, I can't even sew buttons on, but it looks well made.

"Why are you giving me this?"

"I'm familiar with the club Daniel is taking you to," she says. "You need to be dressed appropriately. This should cover it."

"Are you sure a dress is necessary?" I take the gown from her.

"You'll be gorgeous." She physically turns me around. "The bathroom's through there."

"Thanks." I hold the dress close.

"Well, hurry up and try it on!" Lydia admonishes me. "I can't wait to see you in it!"

I open the bathroom door and step inside, closing it behind me. I start to pull the dress over my head, then realize the stupid thing isn't unzipped. Ugh. Wriggling back out of it, I reach for the zipper, but it's not where normal zippers are. I search and finally find it, starting under the armpit and continuing almost to the waist. Whoever made this thing needs to die. I mean, why would anyone make a dress like this on purpose? I finally get it undone and slip the gown over my head, fastening it shut and tightening the corset. Opening the door, I step out into the empty hall.

"Uhhh...Lydia? I'm..." I don't know what I am. Dressed? Definitely. Ready? Maybe.

"I'm in the bedroom. Come on back! I have a full length mirror in here." Her cheerful voice guides me to the furthest room in the house. I walk back, holding the gown up with one hand so it doesn't drag across the wood flooring.

The witch is insane. It's the only explanation I can come up with as I stare at myself in the mirror. The gown itself is stunning. It's floor length blood red velvet and has this super cool hood thing on the back which covers my neck. There are also extra-long sleeves and a square neckline. Oh, and did I mention the corset?? Yeah, the thing has a corset! It's crazy, but she's adamant.

"It's incredible on you," she bubbles. "Your white skin in that gown is sheer perfection!"

I run my hands down the beautiful red fabric. It really is a gorgeous gown. "Ummm...is there an age limit at this club?"

She laughs. "No. There's only one entry requirement and you definitely have it."

Before I can ask her what she means, she changes the subject. "Daniel will be here to pick you up about six thirty. That gives us four hours. Is there anything specific you'd like to do?"

I bite my bottom lip, then blurt out the one thing I wish I could do well. "Garden."

She arches one red eyebrow high. "Excuse me?"

"I'd like to garden," I repeat. "My mom is excellent at it; nothing she grows ever dies. Like, ever. I always wanted to learn how to grow like that, but I never really could. There's something in the dirt that makes me all red and spotty, so gardening and I never mixed well. But maybe being part zombie, I can do it now."

"All right," she says. "I have a small plot of land out back, and some herbs I've been meaning to plant...you can help me with that. But first, we need to take care of your wrist. Going into the club with a bandage just highlights the fact that you've been injured. I have some tiny screws in the junk drawer. I'll get them while you get changed, then we'll fix your wrist and continue with our day. Also, I have some gloves in the shed. We'll set you up with those, since some people have an adverse reaction to our lovely Georgia red clay. You might be one of them."

I can't wait.

***

Daniel picks me up at six thirty. Not six thirty one, but six thirty on the dot. He's quite...punctual.

"You look fantastic, Isis." Lydia leans in to hug me. I hug her back. The gardening was awesome and I feel more relaxed now than I have in weeks.

"Thanks for the loan," I say. "I'll bring the gown back to church tomorrow."

She waves a hand. "Oh, no, don't bother. My daughter doesn't wear it anymore. You can keep it."

I can...what? "Ummm...thanks." I have no idea where I'll ever wear it, but I'll try to find a place.

"I hate to break this up," Daniel says, "but the taxi's waiting."

I wave goodbye to the witch, who watches us from the porch until I get into the cab.

"Don't you drive?" I ask.

The taxi surges forward into traffic, our driver honking wildly at an unsuspecting car in front of him.

"Of course I do," Daniel leans back on the vinyl seat, and lowers his voice to a whisper. "But blood makes me drunk."

"Huh?" I'm lost.

"Drinking blood is like drinking alcohol to me. I can't drink and drive."

Huh. That's interesting. "What club are we going to?"

"The Blood Bank."

I snicker. "Seriously? You're taking me to a club called *The Blood Bank*?"

He flushes. I thought vampires could only do that once they'd fed...ewww...I decide not to pursue that line of thought.

"What's the address?" The cab driver asks.

"1532 Peachtree Street." Daniel rattles off the address as though he's been there a lot. Maybe he has.

The cabbie turns his head and glances at me. "Well, at least you're dressed for it."

"You look awesome," Daniel agrees. "Did Lydia loan you that?"

"She kind of insisted." I shift around on the seat. "So how does this club work, anyway?"

"What'd you mean? It's a club."

I lean close to him. I definitely do *not* want the cabbie to hear my next words. "Lydia mentioned something about an entry requirement."

He shakes his head. "I'm not sure what she was talking about. There's a cover charge, but that's so the band gets paid."

The cabbie turns his signal on and spins the wheel at the same time. As a result, I find myself practically sitting in Daniel's lap. His face flushes beet red even as I lever myself off.

"Sorry 'bout that," the cabbie mutters. He doesn't need to apologize. I'm not leaving him a tip for planting me in a guy's lap. I'm pretty sure I can do that all by myself, if I want to.

ONE FOOT IN THE GRAVE

"1532 Peachtree," the cabbie says, putting the car in park.

I glance at the meter. $45.03. Holy crap, getting here is expensive! I reach into a hidden pocket in the voluminous sleeves of the Gown de Goth Lydia encased me in, but Daniel shakes his head.

"I got this, don't worry about it."

All right, I won't. It's his party. Sort of. I eye the front of the club. What I'm seeing is very different from what I think I should be seeing. The lights proclaiming 'The Blood Bank' are neon yellow and bright blue, not black and blood red. I thought the club would be a lot more 'in your face' than it is. A bouncer stands at the door, arms folded across his chest. He eyes me up and down when I climb somewhat ungracefully out of the cab.

"You lost?" He asks with a glimmer of a smile.

I don't expect that and it kind of throws me. "Ummm... I don't think so. I'm looking for a club..." I trail off. Daniel is still in the cab and I wonder what he's doing that's taking so long.

His smile widens into a full blown grin and his arms unfold. "The Blood Bank *you're* looking for is downstairs."

Daniel strolls up to me and the bouncer grins at him. "Long time no see, man."

The half-vampire shrugs. "I've been kind of busy."

"It's cool," the man says. "You 'n your date can go on in."

Daniel nods. "Thanks. Tucker still manning the front?"

"Uh-huh."

"Wait here while I pay for us," Daniel tells me.

It's easy enough to do. There's a lot to look at. From the outside, I'd thought there would be those weird glitter balls hanging everywhere, but it's not like that at all. Instead, there are round wooden tables every four feet or so, with two and three chairs at each and a stage on one side. But instead of a beautiful woman crooning 1940's music from the elevated stage there's a ginormous drum set. It's a bit out of place, but who am I to judge?

"Are you ready?" Daniel's approach startles me and I swing around to face him.

I paste a smile across my face. "Let's do this." I drag a bit of my hair forward and feel some piece of flesh come off in my hand. Crap. I close my hand around it and pray it's not my ear. I don't want to have to glue on more body parts. I sigh and follow Daniel across the floor and behind the stage to a plain wooden wall.

"What's up with the wall? I thought we were going downstairs."

Daniel passes his hand across the wall and a panel slides open. A wrought iron spiral staircase, its railing a dragon's tail spiraling down into a black that's blacker than black, greets me.

I halt at the top, apprehensive. I'm not entirely sure I want to go down there.

Daniel stops, his foot already on the first step. "What's the matter, Isis?"

My chest feels tight. "I'm—why're there two clubs?"

"The upstairs one is for full humans. The other one's for people like us." Daniel lowers his voice. "It's a club for supernaturals."

Twelve:

What Fresh Hell is This?

"**A** club for supernaturals," I repeat. "Why'd you lie to me?"

He blinks at me with innocent hazel eyes. "I never lied. I said I'd take you to a night club. This is a night club."

I sigh and follow him down the staircase. It really irritates me that he's right. "What kind of creatures are going to be down there?"

"Oh, the usual crowd: vampires, ghosts, a few weres, maybe even a revenant or two."

"Don't ghosts just haunt people?" I ask. I'm not even sure what a revenant is, but it doesn't sound pleasant, either.

Daniel shrugs. "I've heard that."

"Then what're they doing down there?"

"They don't *just* haunt people, Isis. Ghosts have lives too, y'know."

Actually...that never even occurred to me; that ghosts would do anything besides wave chains around and scare people. I'm distracted from that thought by another one. "You said there are vampires?"

"They're undead, so yeah."

I point out the not so obvious. "Daniel, Andrew tried to turn me...what if the vamps down there decide to make me into a happy meal?"

"They won't." He sounds awfully sure of himself.

My eyes narrow. "How do you know that?"

Daniel's nostrils flare. I take a few steps down and away from him.

"What're you doing?" My free hand clutches at the iron railing. If he lunges at me, I'm a goner. I just know it. This stupid dress wasn't made for running.

"Relax," Daniel's voice is soft. As a matter of fact, it sounds a lot like Andrew's did right before he tried to eat me. I swallow hard.

"Daniel, what're you *doing*?"

The half-vampire shakes his head. "Sorry, I...nothing. It happens sometimes." His voice sounds normal again and I try to relax.

"Well...stop," I instruct him.

He shrugs. "It just..."

"Happens," I finish. "I know, I know."

"The point," Daniel says, "is that you don't smell normal, so you'll be safe downstairs."

I'm skeptical, but what choice do I have? I've trusted him this far. I nod and continue down the stairs. The door that greets me at the bottom is huge. I mean it's castle massive with two metal beams on either side that I'm sure sit across the door when it's not in use.

My eyes widen and I turn back to Daniel, who's on the step above me. "Are you sure it's open?" I whisper, not because anyone can hear me, but because it feels like I should.

"Of course." He pushes past me and knocks three times.

I can't help myself. I giggle. Daniel throws me a glare. "What's so funny?"

I gesture. "This is. I mean, there's the staircase, you knocking three times. The whole thing is hilarious."

It's obvious he doesn't have a clue what I'm talking about, so I elaborate. "Don't you ever read? Good grief, this place is like every cliché in a horror novel, Daniel!"

"It's stairs and a door, Isis. What's your problem?"

I start to answer, but my attention is caught by the creaking door. I turn away from Daniel and my jaw drops. Not onto the floor, thank goodness, but actually open.

The...I'm not sure what to call it...creature...standing in the open door looks at us and takes a deep breath in. I watch its chest rise and fall, because that's easier than looking at its face.

"Hey, Tucker. How's tricks?" Daniel addresses the thing and, much to my shock, it replies. Its voice is the chill of the grave. I shiver.

"Daniel," my date's name hisses out from between molding lips. "Did you bring me a bite?" It grins and I see an up-close mouth full of broken and stained teeth.

"Ummm...not this time," Daniel flicks a quick glance at me. "This is my...uhhh...she's not food," he finishes.

The thing extends its hand, expecting me to shake it, I guess. Its skin is as pasty white and gross as mine. As usual, my mouth runs away with my common sense.

"Are you a zombie?" I extend my hand in response, but forget about the small piece of flesh. It falls to the floor.

It doesn't answer my question, just stares at the tiny chunk, its mouth drooping open. "You going to eat that?" It finally asks.

I bend over and pick it up. "It's part of my ear," I blurt out.

"Oh, well then...can I have it?" A line of drool snakes its way down its chin.

"Tucker, she's not alive," Daniel steps into the conversation.

The corpse tilts its head to one side as it observes me. "There's blood," it states after a brief silence.

This is getting creepier by the minute. Luckily, Daniel rescues me.

"Tucker, trust me, she's a guest, not dinner. No eating." He takes me by the hand and leads me past the creature. I can feel it watching me as I walk away.

"What the heck *is* that thing?"

"That's Tucker. He's pretty cool for a revenant."

I stare at him. I have no idea what that is.

"He's a reanimated corpse."

Oh. Ewww, that's kind of revolting.

Now that I'm past the...Tucker, I glance around the huge rectangular room. It's pretty dimly lit and I can't see much past the small circle of luminance Daniel and I are currently standing in. Leather couches take form as my eyes adjust. I can see shapes moving around the place, but they're not walking in the traditional sense. They almost glide across the floor, flickering in and out of existence, depending on the half- light to keep them solid.

Daniel pushes at my shoulder. "Go on. Mingle."

"Mingle with what?" I ask. "I don't see anything."

He points to the shapes. "Those. There." He lowers his voice. "They're the vampires."

Oh. My mouth dries. I'm not super eager to approach them and strike up a conversation. The gown I'm wearing feels tighter than it did at Lydia's house and my heart starts to race.

One of the forms pauses in mid-glide, half in and half out of a circle of light, and turns to face me. I still can't see what it is beyond a dim shape, but I can sense its interest.

"Uh, Daniel? That doesn't look friendly." I inch closer to him. So I'm a zombie chicken. I mean, chicken zombie. Darn it. Either way, I don't want to talk to the vampire staring at me from across the room.

"No-one'll hurt you here. I already told you that. I'm going to get a drink." He grins at me before striding toward a corner of the room I assume has a refreshment table. Or a bar. Or a freezer full of bodies.

The shadow/thing/vampire glides closer.

"Uh, hi," I say as it draws near to me. I clear my throat and try again. "Can I help you with something?"

The vampire moves into my light circle. It's a long-legged female dressed in a business suit.

"You smell...intriguing," she says. "What are you?"

Well, that's more abrupt and to the point than I expect. I decide to return the favor since it looks like Daniel was right and I'm not on the menu.

"I'm a zombie."

The woman's almond shaped eyes narrow. "You don't smell like a zombie."

"I'm a half-zombie. Maybe that's it."

She shakes her head. "No...you smell of decomposing flesh and blood. A zombie-vampire hybrid, maybe?"

Oh, disgusting. I wonder if they make industrial strength perfume. I just might need a gallon. Or eight. "No, I am...I was...human."

"But you have been consorting with vampires...I smell it, though it is an old scent and not recent."

Then it couldn't be Daniel. Besides, she'd smell

human on me if that was the case...wouldn't she? The answer hits me hard, even though I kind of already knew it. I *have* been consorting with a vampire...and not recently, either.

She smells my ex. There aren't enough showers in the world...

Thirteen:

Inka, Binka, Bottle of Ink.

"You interest me, zombie."

"I don't mean to." I cross my arms.

"Nevertheless." The vampire holds out one hand. "I'm Ink."

"I'm Isis," I say, taking her hand in mine. It's cool to the touch.

Her hand closes around mine. Firmly. She clearly has no intention of letting me go. "What brings you here?"

She's an anonymous vampire; there's no reason in the world not to tell her all about Andrew and Father Moss's church. Except for the sheer embarrassment of it. So I tell her about discovering the church, but not about my ex, ending with 'And so Daniel asked me out."

"I am familiar with the gargoyle's church and the reasons behind it." She tilts her head to one side. "Are you?"

"Not really." I shrug. "Do I need to be?"

"Have you met the witch and her daughter yet?"

I blink. "I've met Lydia, but who's her daughter?"

Ink shrugs. "It's not my concern," she says. "Merely an idle curiosity."

I file it away for future reference. "Why isn't there music playing down here? I saw the drum set upstairs."

She nods toward the center of the room. "We don't need music to dance."

I look. My heart clenches. A woman with long red hair and skin whiter than mine is whirling gracefully through the filmy beings littering both the shadows and the circles of light. She is tall and long legged; there's not an ounce of fat anywhere on her, and when she smiles at me my palms remember how to sweat.

"What's that?" My voice cracks on the last word. Holy Mother, whatever that thing is, I want no part of it. Ever.

"That's Lorii Martin, our local banshee."

"Don't banshees kill people?"

The banshee stops whirling and walks toward us, hips swaying. When she speaks, her voice is liquid smoke. "I'm not a murderer. I only let people know when their time is over."

Oh. "How do you do that?" I have to ask. Of course I do.

"My screams are knives from Heaven. I shred souls and give those fortunate enough to hear my true voice time to put their petty human affairs to rest."

"Lorii!" Ink snaps, and the banshee's eyes refocus on me.

The woman blinks incredible green eyes and smiles again. "But I'll never visit you," she says. "You don't have enough soul to shred." She stamps her feet in a one-two pattern, and whirls back to the center of the floor.

I spin to face Ink. "Is she saying I have no soul?"

"Would it make a difference?"

I stare at the vampire. "Of *course* it would! How can I be alive without a soul?"

"If you cannot tell, how can it matter?"

ONE FOOT IN THE GRAVE

My mouth snaps shut. I think this is a conversation better suited to someone with experience in spiritual matters. Someone like Father Moss. Speaking of...this seems as good a time as any to get some fantasy clichés answered, and Ink seems really nice. For a bloodsucker. "Can vampires set foot on holy ground?"

"With special dispensation from the priest, yes. Otherwise we burst into flames. Much like what happens to us in direct sunlight."

"Why do undead eat humans?"

"That has an easy answer. We need blood to survive, and they have it."

"Does that mean *I'm* going to eat people eventually?" My hands start to shake at the very idea.

"It has been many years since a half-zombie has existed. I am not sure anyone knows what you will, or won't, crave over the centuries."

"*Centuries*? I'm going to live for *centuries*?" My voice rises, attracting the attention of other shadowy figures. They begin to move closer, almost like a pack. I think I might have just gotten myself into trouble. I ease closer to Ink, whose narrowed eyes tell me she's not thrilled at the extra company.

"Who's the new toy?" The first creature to reach us grins, showing a mouthful of razor sharp teeth. I have no idea what it is, other than scary. Whatever it is, however, it's sharply dressed in a gray suit with a red silk tie.

"She is not for you, and she is not a toy." Ink snarls. "Move along."

"She has flesh."

That's enough. I step forward. "Okay, for one: Yes, I have flesh, but I'm fairly attached to it. For two: I'm not...uhhh...I'm not human, so I'm off the menu."

A cold, dry sound escapes its lips, like a million

dead autumn leaves caught in a dust devil. It takes me a minute to realize it's laughing. Drool snakes its way down its chin and begins to drip onto the floor. I back up until I'm pressed against Ink's side.

"I don't care if you're human or not. You are not protected *here*. That makes you food."

"She's under *my* protection, ghoul." Ink smiles and, as I watch, her canines elongate to points sharp enough to rival the ghoul's teeth. "Back off."

The creature bares its teeth. "You are tolerated, *vampire*, not protected."

"I can protect myself." Ink states. "I have no need for his protections."

The ghoul backs away, and the shadowy figures that never quite materialized follow it.

I let out the breath I've been holding. "What was that about?"

"Not everything here is friendly," Ink says. "This is not a place to let your guard down. Ever." She half smiles. "Unless you're Lorii, of course. No-one in their right mind takes on a banshee."

I was under the impression banshees did nothing but scream; other than being freaky loud, was that really a big deal? I might have to do some research on the subject so I don't mistakenly get on her bad side. It'd suck to die now that I might have a cure for my issues.

"Your date has been gone for quite some time. Have you been abandoned?"

"He's not really my date," I say. "He's just a friend."

"Your friend, then," she corrects herself.

I shift my stance slightly. "He wanted a drink and told me I should mingle."

"As you can see, some things here are decidedly *un*friendly, even toward other monsters. Until you are protected, it would be wise if you didn't mingle."

I frown. "What kind of protection are you talking about?" I have visions of mobsters and, what are they called? Shakedown men? Wise guys? Something like that.

"The ghouls belong to the owner of this club," Ink says. "They aren't terribly happy at the idea, so they tend to flex their muscles whenever someone interesting shows up unexpectedly."

"Does that mean I need to meet the owner?"

The vampire shrugs. "That's up to you. Do you plan on coming back?"

I look around. As strange as it sounds, I feel comfortable here. I mean, barring the incident with the ghoul. No-one is looking at me weirdly. Heck, no-one's paying any attention to me at all. It's more than I can say for anywhere else I go. Not that I've gone a lot of places in the last week. I finally nod. "Yeah, I'll be coming back."

"Then you really do need to meet the owner. We can go now, if you like."

"I need to let Daniel know where I am first." Why I feel loyalty to the half-vampire, I'm not sure, but it'd be mean to leave.

Ink raises her face to the ceiling and closes her eyes. She speaks without opening them. "He's at the bar, drinking." Opening her eyes, she stares at me. "I'll wait here for you."

The idea of watching Daniel drinking blood, even if it's from a glass, quite frankly turns my stomach. I change my mind about finding him. "No, that's okay. I'll talk to him later."

"Follow me," the vampire says.

I follow Ink across the floor. "Where're you taking me?" And why am I not worried about going somewhere with a vampire I never met? It's not like my track record is great, but then again, neither are most of my ideas, honestly. So this is nothing new.

"I told you, the owner. He frightens Tucker, so he tends to stay out of sight when the club is open. It makes things easier on everyone."

I really don't want to meet the creature that can frighten the revenant at the door, but I've already committed myself to whatever Ink has in mind.

"Come on," Ink says. "It's just on the other side of those lights."

Apparitions appear in front of us, drifting in and out of the lit circles we walk through.

"Are those ghosts?" I ask, though I'm sure I know the answer. At least they're not more ghouls.

"Yes. They like it down here. It makes them feel…alive." One brushes against Ink's face and she brushes it away. We continue across the floor to a blank wall that's clear of everything. It's like a space in time that everyone, and everything, avoids. Ink places her hand on the wall and it slides open.

Fourteen:

Cap'n, There be Monsters Here.

"**C**ool!"

The vampire smiles at my enthusiasm. "You're quite young." She raises her voice. "Nacelles, I've brought you a visitor."

A deep voice climbs above a host of moans and growls. "Did you bring my ghouls a treat?"

What *is* it with the undead and their obsession with eating people? Oh yeah. They need blood.

Ink gestures at me.

"I—Ummm...Hi." Great. I sound like a blithering idiot. Not for the first time. "I'm Isis, and Ink told me I should meet you?" That's sort of better.

"And why would she do that?"

I still can't see what's speaking to me, but it sounds like a Mack truck drove over its throat once, then backed up and did it again. Multiple times.

My eyes flick to the expressionless vampire standing next to me. "A ghoul tried to eat me in the club."

"My ghouls get peckish from time to time. It's the nature of ghouls to eat."

"It's the nature of me to live," I snap. "I'd really like to keep it that way."

"Isis," Ink hisses. "Watch your tone."

"You're bold to come into my club, tempt my pets' appetites, then take umbrage when I point out the obvious," the faceless voice says. "Come closer."

"I'd rather not. No offense, but how do I know *you're* not going to try and eat me?"

"I don't eat."

"Everyone eats," I scoff. "Ink told me even the undead eat."

"Ah, but I am so undead that I no longer require food."

How is that even possible? I take a step forward, curious to see the creature. "Are you sure the ghouls won't eat me?"

The creature laughs. "Don't worry. My ghouls are under my control. They won't eat anything I don't allow. Ink, bring her closer." The vampire gestures at me.

The growls grow louder as I trail Ink through the open doorway. The door slides shut behind me. I bite the inside of my cheek. And immediately spit out a gob of flesh. Gross.

"Did you just spit on my floor?" The creature asks.

"I…uhhh…yeah, sorry." I bend over and pick up the soggy mass. Blech. Now what? I stuff the bit into one of my pockets.

"I'm looking forward to meeting you face to face."

Well, gee, doesn't that just make me feel all warm and tingly. I continue walking down the hall, which is beginning to feel like it goes on forever. Just as that thought crosses my mind, a shape forms a few feet in front of me. I squeak and take a step backward.

The figure laughs and stretches out a hand. It's skin, stretching taut over bone. Like in the movie 'The Mummy'. I reach out and take it. It's cool to the touch, but I guess that makes sense since the guy's practically a skeleton.

"What are you?" I know I'm asking that a lot, but it doesn't make sense to stop.

"Why, Ink, did you not tell our young guest what to expect? Nacelles Caldmer, lich, at your service." His voice is more gravelly than Father Moss'. I wish the old gargoyle was with me. I don't know what good he'd be in this situation, but then again, I don't know what good I am, either. His fingers scrape over the screws in my wrist. The lich hisses.

"Interesting. Why do you have screws in your wrist, Isis?"

"I'm half a zombie. My hand fell off."

"How inconvenient for you," Nacelles says. He steps closer. I force myself to stand still. His eyes are almost nothing more than hollow sockets in a long since rotted skull, but I can feel them boring into me. "Is that why you've come to my club?"

"No disrespect meant, but I don't know what a lich is."

"Is that all? Why, that's a simple answer." He bows in my direction and I find myself staring at actual holes in his skull. I'm pretty sure those didn't appear overnight. "I'm a magician," he straightens up. "When I was quite young...well, much younger than I am now, I recreated myself in this form."

"But why would you do that?" I stare at him, at the almost mummy-like leathery skin. What possesses someone to do that to themselves?

"I craved more power than being a simple magician gave me," he says.

I'm pretty sure 'magician' signifies something completely different than David Copperfield, but I state the obvious anyway. "So you're an undead magician."

"I am an undead researcher," the lich corrects. "I do not perform children's parlor tricks. Now, back to my original question; what brings you into my club?"

"Actually, I'm looking for someone."

Nacelles cocks his head to one side. "Does this mysterious someone have a name?"

"His name is Andrew."

"I'm not familiar with him. Ink, could he be one of your kind?"

The vampire shrugs gracefully. "He could be. There are always more vampires being created. But he could also be one of the were-breed. They are even less discriminating than we are."

I shake my head. "Oh, no. He's a vampire. He's *definitely* a vampire. He even tried to bite me. So now it's my turn."

Ink's eyebrows raise and I can feel Nacelles' intense interest. "You plan on biting the vampire back?"

"No. I plan on killing him."

"To what end?" Ink asks. "Nacelles, can I *please* have a chair?"

The lich waves his hand and an honest-to-gosh office chair appears. The vampire sits down, crossing her legs at the ankles, like I've seen pictures of supermodels do. "Now, as I was saying, why on earth would you want to kill Andrew?"

"You mean other than the fact that he tried to chew on me? Because I want to be human again, and killing him will accomplish that."

"Whoever told you that lied," Ink says flatly.

I've never believed in the term 'boiling blood' until now. She lied to me. The half-fae actually *lied*. For a split second, everything around me gains a reddish tint. "I've got to go. How do I get out of here?" I have to go back to the church. I don't particularly want to, but I don't know where else to find Noelle. And finding her is my top priority.

"The same way you came in, I'd imagine," Ink replies.

"What about the ghouls. Will they attack?"

The lich shakes his skull. "They know not to touch you. You'll be safe."

That's a relief. "Ummm...thanks for..." I'm not sure what to say to either of them, quite frankly. Thanks for not letting flesh eating monsters devour me? Thanks for introducing me to the oddest club in the history of clubs? "Everything," I finally finish.

"Come back anytime," Nacelles says. "You're an interesting mix and I'd love to chat more in depth."

"I'll think about it," I promise, more out of polite habit than any real commitment to any reoccurring conversations with the lich.

"I'll find your...friend...and give him your best," Ink promises.

Daniel hasn't even crossed my radar, so I'm glad she remembers him.

"It has been millennia since I have seen a half-zombie," I hear Nacelles say to Ink as I walk away. Her reply is muffled by a sudden influx of growls.

Terrific. I have a gauntlet of ghouls to run. And run I do. Past rows upon rows of human-like monsters with rows upon rows of bared, razor sharp teeth, dressed in identical gray suits with identical red silk ties. The growls increase as I race by. I catch flickers of red eyes glaring at me and one pair of golden eyes that wink out of existence almost as soon as my brain can register it.

Fifteen:

Tuesday Night's Alright for Fightin'.

It doesn't take me long to reach the church. I gun the Bug all the way there, praying I'm not stopped by some overeager officer of the law. The doors are shut, but it's Tuesday. I know for a fact that the church is open for business. I pull the Bug over to the curb and hop out. Closed doors aren't going to stop me. Not today. Not when Noelle lied.

My fists slam into the doors. "Open up! Noelle, if you're in there, open the doors! Right freakin' now!"

The doors fly open. "What on God's green earth..." Noelle stands there and it's all I can do not to punch her in the mouth.

"You *wanted* me to kill him," I snarl. "Why? What was the point?"

"Oh, that."

"That," I stalk toward her, "was a crappy thing to do."

"Don't pretend you never considered it," she replies, her arms folded.

"Of *course* I considered it!" I snap. "That's not the point!" By this time, I'm in the sanctuary.

"That's *entirely* the point! You *want* to kill him. I gave you the perfect excuse. It's not my fault that you don't have the guts to see it through!"

"You've been after me since I walked in the doors of this church, Noelle. What, exactly, is your problem?"

The half-fae steps into my personal bubble and it takes just about all I have not to step back. I know where this is heading. I was a kid once. "I want you to stay away from Daniel, but that's not happening."

I guess that means she heard about our date. I don't want to deal with her and her obsession with the half-vampire, but it looks like I'm not going to have much choice in the matter. "Look," I say," I don't want to fight with you. I'm really not interested in Daniel. This is about Andrew."

"Screw Andrew. Every time I turn around, you're right there, next to Daniel."

This isn't going to end well. I just know it. "He's helping me out with something, Noelle. That's it."

"Yeah, yeah. We all know about your little quest for your boy toy, or healing or whatever." She smirks. "Didn't anyone bother telling you that we're unfixable? What makes you so special?"

Wow. "We're all special, Noelle." Even to my own ears, I sound pretentious and stuck-up. And what Noelle says next just confirms it.

"Where'd you get that little gem of wisdom? Out of a Cracker Jack box?" She snorts a laugh. "Do you actually *believe* the tripe you're spewing?"

She's being ugly. I'm over it. I take two steps toward her. She doesn't back down. "I don't know what bug crawled up your...backside...and died, but get over yourself, Noelle. I'm not here to steal Daniel. He's so not my type."

"Actions speak louder than words," she growls. Her eyes start to glow and I swallow. Hard. I think I just made a colossal error in judgment. I raise my hand in a 'stop' kind of gesture. And I'm pretty sure my heart doesn't just skip some beats, like normal, but stops altogether, because my fingers aren't fingers anymore. They're freakin' *copperheads*. As in the snakes just about every Georgian is familiar with. As in venomous snakes that are doing their best to gnaw on me. I do what any self-respecting person would do. I scream. And shriek. And shake my hand hard enough that my wrist pops, hoping my fingers will fly off and slither far, far away.

Noelle laughs. I look down. My fingers are fingers again. They're flesh colored, with no forked tongues where my nails should be. Just five fingers, like God intended. I narrow my eyes and shove the half-fae backward. She flies through the air and slams into the far wall before sliding down to sit, stunned, on the floor. Guess I'm stronger than I thought. When did *that* happen?

"Children, that's enough!" Father Moss's voice is loud enough to wake the dead.

I'm rooted to the ground. I've never been strong before. Like, ever. I'm so busy wondering about it, I don't even realize Lydia is standing in front of me until she says "Blessed be." I sag immediately, wanting nothing more than sleep. What did she do to me?

"Lydia?" Father Moss calls. "Is everything all right?"

"We're fine here." Lydia gazes into my eyes. "Aren't we, Isis?"

I nod. "What happened? Is Noelle okay?"

"She's fine. Want to tell me what started the fight?" The witch's voice is soothing and close to hypnotic. I wonder why she cares.

"She thinks I'm dating Daniel." Lydia's eyes are an astonishing shade of green. They remind me of these plants I saw once at the Botanical Gardens in Atlanta: a green so vibrant it almost doesn't look real. Bottle green; that's the color.

"Did you try telling her you're not?"

I frown. Wait. Why am I so fixated on her eyes? I shake my head, but the feeling doesn't go away. I rub at my eyes, but answer her anyway. "All she wants to do is argue." Then I remember the snakes. "And turn my hands into snakes." My head clears. "She turned my hands into *snakes!*"

"Isis, calm down," Lydia says, but I'm having none of it. Now that I'm not staring straight at her, I recognize the feeling.

"You mesmerized me!" I accuse.

She shakes her head. "That's a vampire's ability, not mine."

"Then what'd you do?" I cross my arms.

"It's a simple spell," the witch answers. "But not one you should have been able to break."

Out of the corner of my eye I see Noelle get to her feet. "Is she going to attack me again?" And speaking of which... "What's up with the snakes?"

"Noelle can bend reality," Lydia replies. At my blank look, she elaborates. "Your fingers weren't actual snakes. My daughter is a mistress of illusions."

Noelle is Lydia's daughter? That explains the illusions. Or, who knows, that particular parlor trick could come from her father. I have no idea what kind of power a witch/fae hybrid might have. And, lucky me, she hates me. I'm so screwed.

Noelle eyes me from behind Father Moss's wings. A huge bruise is forming on what I can see of her shoulder. "Coming back for another round?" She rolls her head from side to side. "I can do that."

Father Moss hisses and clatters his wings. Noelle glares at me, but subsides.

So I'm the one who has to be the big girl. Fine. I hold out my hand. "I'm not trying to steal Daniel," I grit out. "He offered to take me to a club. That's it.

And that still doesn't explain Andrew."

Noelle stares at me for a long moment before answering. "Daniel told me it wasn't a date," she admits, which just pisses me off even more.

"You already *knew* about it?"

"Back off, minionette, he's mine."

And, like a dog, she wants to pee on her territory. Then I blink. "Did you just call me a minionette?"

"You're not tall enough to be a whole minion…"

"Come at me," I growl. Forget Father Moss. I'm so finishing this.

"Isis, Noelle, enough! We're all adults here. Try acting like it!"

There's nothing like having a creature you always thought was imaginary yell at you to make you feel around an inch tall.

I sigh. "Noelle, Daniel is all yours. I promise. I don't want him." The only person on my mind any more is Andrew, and not for the reason she thinks. But I'm not going to tell her that. Ever.

"You know Isis is telling the truth," Father Moss says. "Noelle, end this childish behavior at once."

The half-fae sighs. "Fine." Her next words sound like they're pulled from the depths of her, slow and reluctant. "I apologize for turning your fingers into snakes."

"And?" Lydia prompts.

"Mo-ther!"

I've never heard Noelle sound so childlike before.

"Noelle Mykayla Louren A'Damier, complete that apology at once!"

"I'm sorry I lied about Andrew."

It's the most half-hearted apology I've ever heard, but it's probably the best she can do.

ONE FOOT IN THE GRAVE

"We can't have fighting in this church," Father Moss says. "If you can't abide by the rules of the sanctuary, then you can't stay. Noelle, that applies to you just as much as it does to Isis."

"What?" Noelle protests. "That's not fair. This is my *home*. She has a life. Let her live it elsewhere!"

"She needs this church just as much as you do," Lydia says sharply.

"So what? We're all supposed to cater to her and her whims because she's a half-zombie? That doesn't make her any more special than the rest of us! Ask Albin, or Terra, or anyone else who comes here!"

"That's *enough*," Father Moss says. "Noelle, go to your rooms. Isis, is there a reason you're here, other than to antagonize Noelle?"

That is *so* unfair. "I didn't mean—"

He gives new meaning to the term 'flinty eyed'. "What you meant and what you caused are two very different things."

"I would suggest you go home, to your own apartment, and think about what happened here tonight. Come back Thursday and we can discuss it," Lydia says. I guess staying at her house tonight is off the menu.

My heart sinks. Noelle smirks at me before flouncing away.

"I'm sorry," I mumble. "I'm really, really sorry." I slouch out the front doors, down the sidewalk, and back to the Bug. It's time to go home and explain to my mom why plans changed.

Sixteen:

I Suck.

My mom drums her fingers on the kitchen table. Her eyes are red and swollen. I can only presume that I'm the cause. "So this gargoyle said you couldn't come back?"

"No, Mom. Lydia said I couldn't come back. Not until Thursday."

"Because of the fight with her daughter."

"Right." I sit, slumped, across from her, dressed in a pair of green Grinch footie pajamas. "I was just so angry. I pushed her and she *flew* across the sanctuary. Now I'm afraid to touch anything."

"You don't have super strength, Isis. That's a myth."

"Mom, you weren't there. You didn't see it. I cracked one of the stone pillars." I'm trying really hard to stay calm, but my voice has other ideas. It keeps spiraling upward.

"Sweetie," she reaches across the table and takes my hands in hers. "It'll be okay, I promise."

I pull one hand free in order to tuck my hair behind my ear, forgetting completely that part of it's missing. My mom, on the other hand, notices immediately and reacts accordingly.

"Isis Blue, what happened to your ear, and where is the rest of it?"

Crap. "It's, ummm, in the dress Lydia gave me."

"*What*?" Her eyebrows crawl up to her forehead and take residence there while she waits for my reply.

"Part of it came off in my hand at the club Daniel took me to," I reply. "Honestly, I forgot all about it."

"So you shoved it into your pocket? Isis, what's *wrong* with you?"

"Seriously, Mom? What's right? Apparently I'm starting to decompose. I don't *know* what to do about it. I certainly don't want to wear screws in my wrist for the rest of my life. Death. Whatever!" I fling my hands into the air. The left one goes sailing across the kitchen and lands, with a thunk, on the stovetop. Of course it does. The apartment falls silent.

"I thought you had screws in your wrist." My mom's voice is hoarse.

"I do. They must have come loose during my fight with Noelle. I'll get it."

"While you're up, get the bit of your ear, too. I'll put it in a baggie of ice to preserve it and first thing tomorrow, we'll head to the hospital. Maybe they can reattach it, like they do with fingers."

"And pretty soon I'll look like Frankenstein. Thanks, but no thanks."

"You're acting like this is an option, Isis." She leans forward. "Let me assure you, it's not."

"Mom," I protest, "it's not just going to stop. I'm not suddenly going to turn normal again."

"Do you actually think I don't know that? Do you actually believe I have my head buried so far in the sand that I don't understand what's really happening? I'm doing the absolute best I can, Isis, but believe me when I tell you that I know the truth. I promise you, I *know* it." By the time she finishes speaking, the tears are dripping down her cheeks.

"It's decomposition, Mom," I say quietly. "A

doctor won't help."

She nods. "I know, but I don't know what else to do." Defeat weaves its way through every word she utters.

It takes me two steps to reach her, wrap my arms around her, and give her the biggest, hugest hug I can before I continue to the stovetop and pick up my hand.

"Do you—do you want me to help you with that?"

I shake my head. "I'm just going to go to bed. But thanks." I smile to take some of the sting out of the rejection.

"I love you."

"Love you, too, Mom." I walk into the single bathroom, swinging my hand in my...errr...hand. Placing the hand on the edge of the sink, I awkwardly squeeze the toothpaste onto my toothbrush. With everything starting to decompose, I'm just grateful I still have teeth. But I brush carefully, making sure I barely massage each individual tooth with the electric brush before spitting and rinsing. I leave my hand in the bathroom. There's really no point in keeping it by my bed. I'll get my mom to help me with it tomorrow. I pause at the entrance of my room; pleased, as I always am, at the homemade chain mail canopy draped on the four posters of my bed. I hated making it *while* I was doing it, but now I think it's pretty darn cool. I crawl into bed and close my eyes. Sleep would be a blessing.

The dreams start almost immediately. Crazy, twisted dreams of eyes with little arms and legs; eyes following me down dark, twisted hallways, and six foot tall talking skeletons covered in rawhide. I open my mouth to say something, but my lips fall off. It's only once I bend over to pick them up that I realize I have no hands, either.

ONE FOOT IN THE GRAVE

I scream myself awake.

"Isis, it's all right."

I don't recognize the voice and lash out when a hand begins to smooth my hair back from my forehead.

"Isis, stop, it's Mom. It's all right. You're awake now."

I start dry sobbing. "It—it was horrible, Mom. I was running down a hall and all these red eyes were following me and growling."

"It's that club," she says. "It's giving you nightmares. I really don't think going back there is a good idea, honey."

And that's when it hits me. "Actually, Mom, it's the perfect idea. I *have* to go back."

"What are you talking about? How's going back the perfect idea?"

"Nacelles is a magician." My words come slowly as I noodle out exactly what I'm trying to say. "So theoretically, he could stop me from decomposing. Right?"

My mom rubs her eyes with the palms of her hands. "I suppose it's theoretically possible. But is it wise?"

Probably not, but that isn't going to stop me.

Seventeen:

The Blair Lich Project.

Nacelles drums his finger bones on his table. "Ink, you know my services don't come cheaply. Why would you bring her to me?"

The vampire leans back in her chair. "She came to the club to find you, Nacelles. I found her pressing random panels on the wall. Did you really want me to let her continue doing that?"

He doesn't answer her, but turns to me. I swallow.

"What brought you here, Isis?"

I reach into my pocket and pull out my bits of ear and cheek, carefully preserved in a quart sized baggie with two ice packs. My mom is nothing if not super-efficient.

"I see," the lich says. "And you wish me to what? Reattach them?"

"Can you do that?"

"Isis, be careful what you ask for. Magic has a price," Ink cautions me.

"I don't need him to reattach them," I hurriedly reassure Ink. "I'd just prefer it if nothing else fell off, y'know?"

"I will need a payment of some kind from you," Nacelles says. "It's the only way the magic will work."

"Is that why you're willing to help me?" I ask. "What's in it for you?"

"I'm a lich by nature and a researcher by trade." He leans toward me across the table. It takes everything I've got not to send the chair I'm sitting in flying backward. "You are a fascinating conundrum, Isis. Quite frankly, I wish to study you, but in order to do that, you need to stay whole."

If that's the price I have to pay...and speaking of prices..."You said I had to pay you?"

The tall creature nods.

I catch a glimpse of something hound shaped at his side, but even as I blink, it vanishes and I'm not sure I really saw it in the first place.

"What kind of payment are you talking about?" I ask.

Nacelles' shrug is oddly graceful. "It's nothing we need to discuss yet."

"Ummm...I disagree," I say.

"Come with me," Nacelles commands. "I find this room damp and uncomfortable for extended conversation." He waves one hand and the room we're currently in lights up, which means I get to see the hound shape clearly. Except that it's more than one shape. And they're large. I mean, they're *huge*; like brahma bulls huge. And they're all drooling.

Ink notices my wide eyed stare. "They're hell hounds," she responds to my unanswered question. She holds out her hand and one of the monsters flickers in and out of reality until it reaches her. Then, much to my surprise, it swipes her hand with its tongue. Okay, so hell hounds aren't always evil, either. Boy, this night is turning into some sort of an education.

"Isis, this is Maxx." Ink introduces me.

The gigantic beast opens its jaws. "Isisss," it repeats.

Oh. My. Gawd.

"Maxx is my companion of many years," Nacelles says. "I watch over him and he returns the favor."

Maxx opens his mouth in a wide, doggy-like grin. It would be cute if it wasn't for the strings of steaming saliva dripping from fangs as long as my pinky.

"That's...nice," I say.

"She is nervous," Maxx states the obvious. His body isn't pure black, like I originally assumed. Undertones the colors of magma coat the animal's fur. I stretch out my hand, but before I can touch him, he pins me with a golden eyed stare. My hand drops back to its side.

"It's not you," I can't believe I'm attempting to placate a dog, but it seems to be the wisest course of action. "I just – this is all so new to me." I eye the hell hounds still standing at silent attention behind the lich. Regardless of what Nacelles might think, none of them look particularly friendly.

"Maxx, would you please take your pack and return home? It appears I won't need your services, after all."

The massive animal bows his huge head and barks once. The hounds behind him begin to flicker out of existence until the room is empty.

I breathe a sigh of relief. The hell hounds freak me out. "What kind of services do they perform?"

The lich stares at me for a long moment before answering. "Maxx is in charge of pest extermination, among other things."

I don't even know what to say to that, so I keep my mouth shut.

"Ink, I would greatly appreciate it if you would go up and bring Blair downstairs. We will need her assistance."

The vampire nods her assent and leaves.

ONE FOOT IN THE GRAVE

"Who's Blair?" I'm determined not to show my nervousness, but my voice shakes and declares me a liar.

"She's a ghost. She's going to help me stop your decomposition."

I frown. "Really? They can do that?"

He nods, but I can tell he's not really paying attention to anything I'm saying.

"So what exactly is going to happen next?"

"Once Ink gets back, I will cast a spell that will transfer some of Blair's energy to you. The supernatural blending of your forces will allow your body to stop your decomposition."

I'm sorry I asked. I sigh and rest my head on the table in front of me. My undeath just keeps getting more and more complicated.

"Are you all right, Isis?"

I open my eyes. The first thing I see is the ghost Nacelles had mentioned hovering *in* the table.

"Uhhh...yeah," I reply.

"Blair, I could use your help over here, please."

The ghost nods and drifts away.

"Isis, have a seat over there."

I look where the lich is pointing but don't see anything to sit on. "Ummm..." I trail off.

"Oh, I do apologize." The lich waves one hand and a comfortable looking couch appears.

"Neat trick," I say before realizing how trite that sounds. The creature in front of me pretty much sold his soul for magic and here I am, making light of it. "I mean, that's kind of cool." Yeah, that sounds so much better. Sheesh.

"This won't hurt," Nacelles promises. "As long as you stay still, everything will be fine."

Crap.

Eighteen:

One of These Spells is Not Like the Other.

The couch is super comfy and I slouch down, my back against the deep purple cushions. Ink sits cross legged next to me while Blair hovers in the background.

Nacelles rubs his hands together. "All right, then, let's get started. Blair, I need you to put your hands on Isis' shoulders. I'll be using your energy to fuel the spell."

"What if Blair dematerializes and can't come back?"

"Hmmm?" The lich is pulling books out of thin air and flipping through the pages before allowing them to float to the ground at his feet. I'm pretty sure he's not listening to me at all.

"Nacelles?" I raise my voice.

"Huh? Oh." The lich focuses his non-eyes on me and I kind of wish I hadn't said anything. "Blair will be fine," he replies. "I won't take much from her."

"And you're okay with that?" I turn my head and ask Blair, but the ghost just shrugs her reply. It does make me wonder if she can speak at all. It's obvious she's sentient, since she obeyed Ink's command to come here.

"She's done it before," the lich snaps.

"You've stopped decomposition before?" I ask. "What? How? Why?"

"You forgot to ask who's on first," Nacelles says.

Even under the circumstances, I laugh. Who knew the undead could be so alive? Blair rests her hands on my shoulders. Pins and needles race down my arms and into my fingertips. I flinch. Ink reaches over, taking my hands in hers.

"Nacelles knows what he's doing," the vampire says. "Just close your eyes and empty your mind. It'll be over soon."

I try to do what she wants, but I keep hearing Nacelles fidgeting around and at one point some sort of liquid is sprinkled over me. It's not congealing, so I assume it's not blood, but I crack open my eyes a sliver just to make sure.

The lich stands in front of me, his skeletal hands stretching out like he's attempting to bless me, Pope style. He's muttering to himself, and from the snatches I hear, it ain't pretty.

"It's not working... it should be. I don't understand why..." His voice is quiet, but audible.

Ink whispers. "What's wrong, Nacelles?"

"I'm pouring Blair's energy into her, but it keeps seeping out again."

Awesome. I'm a sieve. Lucky me.

"Ink, I want to try something," Nacelles says. "Blair, you can go."

The tingling in my arms vanishes. I open my eyes and pull my hands away from Ink's. "What's going on? Did the spell work?"

The lich shakes his head. "Not exactly." I must look confused, because he continues without my asking. "The spell itself worked; exactly the way it's supposed to. It just didn't work on you."

I want to cry, but I have no tears. "So I'm unfixable."

"You're more of a challenge than I first thought,"

he says. "But I wouldn't say you're unfixable. I want to try the spell again, but this time using Ink's energy."

"Do I have to close my eyes again, or can I watch what you're doing?"

Nacelles shrugs. "I don't suppose it matters. If the spell will work, it'll work regardless."

"What was the point in shutting my eyes anyway?" I roll my neck and hear joints pop in release. Or protest.

"Not everyone I've come in contact with is comfortable with magic, and humans less so than others. I thought you'd appreciate not knowing what was happening."

"Look," I say, "I didn't even know magic was real until recently, but I've read about it my whole life. I definitely want to know what's going on."

"All right, I'll be sure to keep you informed." He raises one stiff eyebrow. I almost expect the dry skin to crack, but it doesn't. "Would you like a play-by-play, or just a summary of what I'm doing?"

Ink laughs. "Leave her alone, Nacelles. Let's get this over with. I'm getting hungry."

Ewww.

"Ink, take her hands again, and be sure to relax, please." His voice is particularly insistent. I wonder if that's because she's a vampire. Aren't they supposed to be super-fast as well as strong?

"What do I have to do?" My voice squeaks.

"Not a thing," the lich reassures me. "Just be still and try to keep your mind empty. It'll make my job easier if I don't have to sift through your thoughts while casting."

"Wait, you're going to probe my brain?" This isn't sounding like such a hot idea, after all. I know nothing like that happened when Blair was helping, but maybe things work differently with Ink, since she's not a ghost.

It's Nacelles' turn to laugh. "Nothing so melodramatic," he says. "Now, let's begin."

Ink nods and I take her hands in mine, watching the lich in front of us.

Nacelles bows his almost skeletal head and holds his hands out as before. A deep green mist, almost forest in color, begins to appear. From where, I have no idea. It's like it's just seeping up from the flooring. It takes all my will power not to curl my feet underneath me, away from the tendrils reaching out for my ankles.

"Stay calm, Isis," Nacelles whispers. "It won't hurt you."

"What is it?" My voice is low, even to me.

"Shhh," Ink reminds me I'm not supposed to move at all and I subside. I don't know what the lich is doing, or why I trust him, but I hope he can stop me from decomposing. I'm tired of losing body parts.

"Thrice curl, thrice entwine, thrice be still and once be mine," he says. I watch as the mist does what he directs. It curls three times around my ankles and then tightens. Finally, it lies still against my flesh, releasing me to twine around him.

"Gather life and bring it forth," the lich continues, "from a distant, darkened source. Creaking, groaning, howling moans, deliver up the secrets of thy bones."

Ink screams. And screams again when the mist begins to wrap itself around her.

I try to pull my hands away from the vampire, but she refuses to let me go. Her face twists in agony and I realize she can't cry any more than I can, though I'm sure she wants to.

When the mist finally releases her, she slumps further down into the couch. I stare at the green cloud-like stuff. I'm pretty positive I don't want it touching me again.

"It's okay, Isis," Ink gasps. "It won't hurt."

"Y'know, I keep hearing that, but your screams told me a whole different story."

Her smile does nothing to reassure me. Still, Nacelles gestures and the weird mist oozes itself toward me. I close my eyes and brace myself, but nothing happens except I feel like I'm being enveloped in a damp cloud.

"There," Nacelles says. "Go ahead and open your eyes, Isis. It's over."

"How do I know if it works?" I ask. I don't feel different, but then again, would I?

"If you keep losing bits and pieces, you can assume it didn't work." The lich replies. "But it did."

Ink nods. "You have some of my physical energy. I felt it leave my body and watched it enter yours. It worked."

Nineteen:

Paying the Piper.

"I owe you something, don't I?" I say.

"My services don't usually come so cheap, but I have something specific in mind for you," Nacelles says. "But first I must attend to Ink."

The vampire on the couch shakes her head. "I'm fine."

I glance at her. She looks pretty much like she did before, so I guess that means she's not lying. High school never covered 'Vampire physiology', go figure.

"So...what do you want from me?" I ask Nacelles.

"I need you to walk Maxx outdoors for eight weeks, rain or shine. Teach him about the world upstairs. He's spent his entire existence working, so navigating the world isn't something he's used to." The lich peers at Ink. "Does that seem a fair price for some of your un-life?"

I'm not sure what shocks me more; the idea of walking a hell hound through the streets of downtown Atlanta, or the knowledge that I carry some of Ink's actual life in me. I thought it was just energy. "Does that mean you're less immortal than you were?"

The vampire shakes her head. "No, it doesn't work that way. I transferred some of my life to you, but it didn't affect my existence. It's hard to explain, and now's not the time. And Nacelles? Don't involve me in your payments." She stands up. "I didn't do it for you, nor do I need Isis to pay me. This is your game, not mine."

"You are the one diminished by what I did."

"And it's your hell hound you're telling her to walk. Down Main Street, U.S.A., no less."

The two of them seem to have forgotten about me, which suits me down to my toes.

"Maxx wants to roam," the lich replies. "I can't walk him. And neither can you. Not without bursting into flames."

"What about your ghouls?"

Watching them is like watching a game of tennis.

"My ghouls have better things to do than walk my companion. Besides, even I'm not callous enough to release them where their appetites can be fulfilled."

Nasty. "You mean eating people, don't you?"

"Not just people, Isis," Nacelles says. "Flesh of all kinds; living *and* dead."

In that case... "You *do* mean just Maxx, right? I don't have to walk the whole...the whole herd, do I?"

"A group of canines is a 'pack', not a herd, but yes. It'll be just Maxx. The others have shown no interest in the surface, though that may change after Maxx tells them about his ventures."

So...I guess I can add that to my non-existent resume... "Hell Hound Walker." That sounds totally legit. I sigh. "Okay, when do I start?"

"Tomorrow," he replies. "I will inform Maxx tonight and he'll meet you at your apartment."

"Ummm...I'm pretty sure people will notice him walking down the street," I say.

"All I need is your address. I will ensure his discreet arrival."

"1465 Peachtree Street, Apt. # 218, Marietta. Do

I need to buy dog food or something?"

He shakes his head. "I'll make sure he eats before he arrives. I doubt he'll be staying the night, so food isn't necessary."

Well, that's a relief. I'm not sure how I could fit a dog the size of a bull into my apartment. Might be problematic. Plus, the little old ladies would notice. And that's not even considering my *mom's* reaction to the whole thing.

"I believe that takes care of our business," Nacelles says. "Ink, it's always a pleasure seeing you." It's a clear dismissal and I take it as such, rising from the couch, which vanishes as soon as my feet hit the floor.

"Thanks for stopping the decomposition," I say. That can definitely go on my list of never before spoken sentences. My mom would be so proud that I remember to say thank you. "Will I see you again?"

"I doubt it," he says. "Unless you need another spell, of course."

I hope that's never the case. Magic is weird and not my favorite thing to experience at all.

"What do you think of us?" Ink asks as we walk back the way we came. I'm just grateful there aren't any hell hounds hanging around in the hall.

"What us are you talking about?"

"The undead, of course."

"It's interesting," I say. "The only thing that really freaks me out, other than the ghouls, is the banshee."

Ink laughs. "Lorii's fascinating. You should talk to her sometime." She throws me a glance. "Y'know, after you find the answers you're looking for."

"You don't think I'll get healed, do you?"

The vampire shrugs. "It's never happened before. Once turned, you tend to stay turned. It's the way of the world."

"But I'm not 'turned,'" I protest. "Not really."

"You aren't human and you've decomposed enough that you can't ever *be* human again." She stops walking at the hidden door and turns to face me. "What are you hoping for, Isis? Some cure you can pass on to the rest of the half creatures? I hate to tell you, but there isn't one."

My human pride rises up at that idea. "Just because you don't know about it, that doesn't mean it's not out there, waiting."

"How old do you think I am?" She straightens and her voice begins to slide into that liquid velvet I last heard coming from Andrew and Daniel, though I'm not sure he counts, since it was weak and didn't really affect me.

I just shrug. It's really none of my business.

Her eyes widen.

"What?" I don't like the way she's staring at me. Not like I'm lunch, but like I'm something she's never seen before.

"You should have answered that," she says.

"I don't care how old you are." I don't understand what the big deal is.

She shakes her head. "That's not the point. You shouldn't have had a choice."

I still don't get it. "So?"

Ink puts hands on her hips. "Do you know nothing about vampires, Isis?" She sounds exasperated.

"Just what I've read."

"What abilities do vampires have?"

I think back to the last book I read that had vampires in it. "Unnatural speed, turning into a bat, mesmerizing…" I trail off as my brain catches up to the rest of the conversation.

Well, hot damn, I'm immune to mesmerizing.

That could come in handy... and I wonder if that's why when Andrew tried it, it didn't work out. Maybe I have a natural immunity...

Twenty:

Hot Dogs and Chicken.

Still thinking about what Ink told me, I walk in the door of my apartment, peel myself out my jeans and tank top, pull on my comfy zombie P.J.'s and bless the idea of nice cool sheets. Can I bring a hell hound to church or does that violate some obscure churchy rule I don't know about? I should've asked Nacelles, but it didn't occur to me at the time. As a result, the question keeps niggling at me until I fall asleep.

I'd love to say my sleep is totally dreamless, but it's not. It starts out normally enough, I guess. Andrew and I are on the pier, holding hands and laughing. He asks me to walk in the sand with him, down by the water. I nod and the next second we're so close to the waves they're lapping over my toes.

"Isis, come here." His voice is buttery soft. I step close enough that his arms go around me.

"I love you," the words he never said in reality roll over me, but my heart stays cold.

"I want to tell you something," I reply, cupping his cheeks and pulling his head down to mine.

"What?" He whispers, but I don't answer. Instead, I open my mouth so wide my jaw unhinges and drive my now pointy teeth into his skull to get at his brains.

I wake up shaking and covered in sweat. What the frick was *that* all about? I eat pork brains, not human ones. Gross. There's no way I'll be able to sleep now, even though my eyes feel like sand's been poured into them. I roll out of bed. The sun is peeking through my blinds and dust motes dance in the filtered light. My stomach rumbles and I realize it's time for my usual morning routine, even though I'm fairly sure it's not morning anymore. I plod to the kitchen to grab my usual, eyes blurry and brain only half-functioning.

"Rise and shine, Isisss."

I shriek, one hand held up to my sort of racing heart. "What. The..." I glare at the hell hound parked in my kitchen. I didn't even know he'd fit. "Maxx, what are you *doing* here?"

The big dog's tail starts to thump. It sounds like a bass drum. "Nacelles gave me your address. I walked."

Okay, Maxx is huge. I mean, he's smaller than a brahma bull now but not by much, to my untrained eye. I don't hang around bulls much. Or at all. People must have crossed the street, and themselves, when he walked by.

"I didn't realize you were going to be here first thing."

"I was bored, so I came early. Is that all right?"

Now how am I supposed to say 'No, go home'? He's obviously happy to be here and I'm not that mean. "You're unexpected, that's all. I didn't expect you to show up in my apartment. And quit wagging your tail! It's..." I glance at the microwave clock. "It's 2 in the afternoon? Well, be quiet anyway. Please. You'll wake my mom up."

Somehow the massive dog manages to look ashamed. "Your mother is not here, but I am sorry for getting so excited. It has been a long time since I have been able to explore and Georgia is a new experience." His tail slows down until only the tip is whacking against the low lying pine cabinets.

I'm intrigued in spite of my pique. "Where are you from, then?" What I want to know is if he's from the Biblical Hell, but I have no idea how to ask that without sounding rude. Then again, he's a dog. Would rudeness really make a difference? My mom would say 'yes', but she's never faced this kind of situation, either.

Maxx cocks his shovel like head at me. "I am a hell hound." His voice is half words, half growls.

Forget it. I ask. "Are you from Hell? I mean, the actual, physical Hell?"

He sits. "I did not realize your agreement with Nacelles would include a history lesson." His diction is perfect. Not a contraction in sight. I wonder where he learned to speak.

I lean against the counter, furthest away from him. Not out of any real fear...one on one in a lighted room he's not as terrifying as he was last night...but because he's taking up all the space.

"All your owner told me is that I need to walk you for eight weeks."

Maxx sighs and a warm, moist breeze wafts over me. "He is my companion, not my owner. I choose to be with Nacelles." He bares his teeth at me. I hope he's grinning. "It was more fun than Hell."

"I'm not sure how to say this, but you're kind of huge-ish to be walking around in broad daylight. Plus your drool steams."

"Consider, if you will, where I am from," Maxx says. "I cannot control the temperature of my saliva."

"Maxx, do you know what you are?" I begin to giggle. "You're a hot dog!"

He snorts. "I cannot believe you are the one Nacelles chose to help me see the world."

I hold up one hand. "I'm sorry, I am." I snicker again. I'm sure I don't sound sorry. "But how am I supposed to walk you? I don't think walking you around my apartment is exactly what Nacelles had in mind. Besides, I have no idea how I'd explain you to my mom. She'd have kittens if she saw you in here."

The dog's brow crinkles. "How can your mother have kittens?"

"It's just an expression, Maxx. She can't actually give birth to them."

He cocks his head to one side. "Ah. Well, I have certain abilities so I can walk in the world. I can shift the sense of others' reality around me, as well as bend time."

Say what? "I have no idea what you just said."

"I can disguise myself, and move through the realities of this world and Hell," he breaks it down for me.

"That's a pretty neat trick. How'd you learn to do that?"

"I worked for a demon," Maxx says. "You do know what hell hounds are for, correct?"

I shake my head.

The dog sighs again. "We are created to bring escaped souls back to Hell. Most times, that involves moving around during the daylight hours and transferring souls from this reality to that one." He shakes and the magma tones shift places with the top coat of fur for an instant before reverting back to a shiny black.

What an awesome job. No wonder he chooses to hang out with the lich instead.

"Did you escape Hell? How'd you get away?" I lean forward, my still rumbling stomach forgotten in my fascination.

"I left," Maxx replies. "Hell is a choice for those of

us created there."

While that's interesting, I don't want to get involved in anything resembling a religious debate. "Can you go into a church?"

"Is there a reason I would want to?" He blinks those huge golden eyes at me and I resist the urge to run my hands through his fur. It just looks so soft.

I shrug at first and then realize I do need to tell him. After all, I don't want to miss my Thursday night meeting. "I go to church on Thursday nights."

"Oh," the hell hound replies. "Well, yes, I can enter holy buildings. I am not restricted to unconsecrated ground." He yawns and a long string of drool hits the floor, steaming. "But church sermons bore me. I may leave instead."

"Oh, *this* church is interesting. I promise you'll want to stay." I like the idea of his company. He's growing on me.

"I will keep that in mind." Maxx rises to his feet. "When can we go for a walk?"

"I thought we'd go out after dark," I say.

"I saw a huge metal animal on my way over here," he counters. "We could walk around that a few times." He blinks at me with his huge doggy eyes and yes, I melt. I'm such a sucker.

"Okay, the Big Chicken it is. Transform yourself, or whatever you do, so the cops don't get called."

Maxx shakes and his body folds in on itself until he's the size of a Rottweiler. "Whose idea was it to build a chicken?"

The smarty pants in me wants to say 'God's', but I know that's not what he's asking. "The Big Chicken's attached to a KFC – Kentucky Fried Chicken – restaurant. I have no idea who built it. But it's pretty neat. The eyes and beak move." It sounds stupid when I say it aloud, but that chicken is a

Georgia landmark. "Ummm...you know what a chicken is, right?"

"I do," he answers. "I lived for a time on a farm. It was an interesting experience."

"I don't have a leash, but I might be able to borrow one. And I need to eat breakfast before anything else." My stomach rumbles a counterpoint to my words. "Can you please move so I can reach the 'fridge?"

Without any warning, Maxx isn't there anymore. I hear my bed groan. My eyes widen. He could have phased himself anywhere in the apartment, and the stupid dog chooses my bed?

"Maxx, did you just break my bed?"

"Would you rather I lay on your mother's?"

"No, I'd rather you don't lie on a bed at all!"

"Very well." Maxx's voice now comes from my living room. "Since it bothers you, I moved."

"Thanks." I open the 'fridge, grab my normal Tupperware and a spoon. "Will my eating in there disturb you?" I don't wait for an answer and when I enter the living room, I see him first thing. Sprawled across my couch; taking up every single inch of space.

"Do you mind?" I make flapping motions with my hands. "I'd like to sit."

He slides off and curls into a ball on the floor. "I apologize. I should have asked."

Now I feel ugly. "It's okay." I squish over to the left. "Is there enough room for you now?"

Maxx nods and retakes his place. "Thank you. You are quite kind."

I pop the lid off the plastic bowl and dig out a spoonful. I'm so tired of eating raw meat, I could scream, but I'm pretty sure it wouldn't help.

The hell hound's nostrils flare. "Are you

eating...brains?"

"Of course I am!" I snap. "I'm a zombie, aren't I? It's what I'm supposed to eat, isn't it?"

Maxx's upper lips curl and I'm pretty sure he's not smiling at me. The throaty growl confirms my belief. I swallow as I stare at him and remember his true size. He could do some serious damage and while I'm not thrilled at what I am, neither am I ready to explore the afterlife. "I'm sorry, I'm just frustrated."

His lips lower. "Then reduce your frustration by getting dressed and taking me for my promised walk. I'd like to see the iron chicken up close."

"Steel," I correct. "The Big Chicken's made of steel."

The Rott glares at me and I continue eating. Who knew hell hounds could be so bossy.

Twenty-One:

Who Let the Dog Out?

I borrow a leash from one of the little old ladies down the hall. She frowns at me when I ask, but all the ladies in the building have stopped asking questions. I think Mrs. Castemar has been chatting about my weirdness.

Maxx is as excited as a normal dog, prancing around and acting all goofy. It'd be cute except for the fact that it's a pain to get the choker over his head.

"You. Need. Obedience. Classes." I gasp. "Sit. Still!"

He settles down at once, thrusting his head through the metal chain and cocking his head sideways. "I was only practicing my part."

I glare at him. "You can do that once we're outside. In here, it's just you and me." I adjust the sweatshirt I'm wearing. "Maxx, can you change my shape, too?"

The dog shakes his head. "My abilities only apply to me. Why?"

I shrug and open the apartment door. "Nothing, it's just...I'm pale."

"Not any more than others I have seen," he reassures me. "If you were that concerned about it, maybe you should not have worn a color that emphasizes it."

"It's Emo," I explain. "A fashion that's, uhhh, in fashion right now." It's also one that I pretty much hate, but that's an irrelevant fact. Being dressed in black lets me walk around pretty much unnoticed by the masses.

"It does not look like any fashion I am familiar with." Maxx pokes his head out of the apartment and surveys the hall. "We can exit."

The elevator bell dings and I hush Maxx with the universal sign of my index finger pressed to my lips. I turn and close the door to my apartment, being sure to lock it. I'm scared that, if someone found my supply of brains, the police would arrest me or something. And my mom would *definitely* be more than miffed about having to bail me out.

"Why, Isis, I didn't know you owned a dog!"

I turn with a sigh. Of all people, it's Mrs. Dixon, the nosiest of all my nosy neighbors.

"Hi, Mrs. D."

Maxx wags his tail.

"What a beautiful boy. Is he friendly?"

"He's not mine. I'm just watching him for a couple of months."

She trots up to Maxx, who presses against my legs, but without putting any weight against me. I appreciate the gesture, because otherwise he would knock me over.

"Oh, look at that fur! What a sweet baby you are!" She buries her hand in the ruff at his neck. "What a good boy," she blathers on. "But, dear, his skin is quite warm. Have you taken him to the vet?"

Maxx rumbles low in his throat. If he was a cat, I'd swear he's purring. I tug on his leash and begin to walk away. "I'll take him in first thing tomorrow."

"Be sure you do, dear!" She calls after me.

I wave in response, eager to get outside, since

I'm sort of camouflaged in plain sight. The elevator doors slide shut behind us. "Maxx, is there a reason you won't let me touch your fur?"

"You could have been badly burned."

"But Mrs. Dixon touched you, no problem."

"I am not currently in my natural form." Maxx explains. He looks up at me. "If it means that much to you, go ahead."

Now that I have permission, it seems kind of weird. I mean, he's sentient. Luckily the elevator stops before I have to make a true decision and the doors whoosh open.

"Time to act like a dog," I whisper to Maxx, daring to reach down and pat him on the head. No flames leap up to eat at my drying flesh, so I'm safe.

"Woof," he says, then licks my hand.

Cute. I follow him out of the elevator and through the lobby to the great outdoors. It's just a few blocks from the building to the Big Chicken. Maxx couldn't have chosen a better day for a walk, either. It's another gorgeous day in two weeks of gorgeous days. The hell hound is acting like a typical dog, smelling everything and prancing at the end of his leash. It's going to be a *long* eight weeks. Thankfully, it's that funky 'middle time' of the afternoon between lunch and the time most people get off work. There isn't a whole lot of traffic on the road and those few people who are walking take one look at Maxx and give us a wide-berth. So far, so good. Everything's going great. Then a small calico kitten meanders out of the holly bushes lining the sidewalk and struts straight across the hell hound's line of sight.

"What's that?" Maxx yelps aloud, beginning to tug at the leash.

I try to pull him backward, without success. "Shhh. It's just a kitten," I whisper, worried that someone might over hear him.

"It looks like a cat," his voice turns into growls which is bad because I'm seeing the fur on his back start to stand on end.

"You've never seen a kitten before?" I'm astonished.

"I have seen a cat. This smells different." His nostrils flare and the leash pulls taut. "It smells of milk."

"Maxx, don't do this," I plead. "If you walk by, it'll ignore you. I promise." Please, please, please, I beg to myself, remember you're sentient. Remember you're more than just a dog.

The kitten flicks its tail at him. Good grief. The stupid thing's going to get itself eaten.

Maxx responds in true dog fashion. He yanks me forward at what feels like light-speed.

"Maxx, stop!" I shriek. "Slow down!"

He listens about as well as any other dog does when faced with a cat: not at all. I feel my arm separate from my shoulder at the same time the stitches on my sweatshirt pop. Muscles tear loose and if I could feel pain, I'm pretty sure I'd be on the ground, screaming out my agony. I manage to slow myself down enough to watch the hell hound dash down the sidewalk, the sleeve of my shirt, arm and all, flapping in the wake he creates.

This sucks. I've got to get my arm back before cars start slowing down. Luckily it's my left arm so as long as I stay on the left side of the street, I should be fine. For the first time, I bless the fact that I now have slow moving blood. There are a few drips, but no more than a standard nose-bleed might cause. I continue my walk toward the Big Chicken. I can't see Maxx anywhere, but that doesn't mean he's not around. If he's left this reality, would my arm go with him? I sure hope so because a stray arm on Cobb Parkway would definitely cause a stir among the locals. The air around me bends and Maxx trots out of the bushes. My arm dangles from his mouth, sleeve still attached. He spits it out at my feet.

"Yuck! That does *not* taste like chicken!"

Twenty-Two:

Everything Does *Not* Taste Like Chicken.

"It's not supposed to taste like chicken!" I snap, reaching down and picking up my arm before the increasing traffic notices.

Maxx's ears perk up. "I thought everything tastes like chicken except chicken, which tastes like snake."

I forget for a moment that we're standing on a major intersection and I look like a complete idiot, talking to my dog. "People taste like pork," I reply.

He cocks his head. "How do you know?"

"It's a joke," I say. And then, because well, I just can't help myself, I continue. "But pigs *do* taste like apples."

Maxx narrows his eyes. I didn't know dogs could do that, but he manages it. "I do not believe you."

And here I am, telling him the truth. "It's true. If the pigs eat apples before they're killed, then their meat tastes apple-y."

"Is that why you eat pig brains instead of human ones?"

I pick up the leash that still hangs from his choke chain. "I'm not an animal. I would never eat human brains."

"Actually, you *are* an animal. Every human being is." He tugs at the leash. "Can we continue my walk?"

"Ummm...I kind of need to deal with my arm," I tell him. "I tell you what. Take my arm back to the apartment and grab me another sweatshirt out of the closet. Then we can keep walking. You can do that, can't you?"

"Yes."

I give Maxx my arm. He takes it and trots back into the bushes and the air does a weird bendy thing. After he leaves it occurs to me I could have gone with him. Oh, well. Instead, I stand as close to the bushes as I can. The traffic is growing heavier and I don't need anyone to notice my missing arm.

Thankfully, it doesn't take him long to reappear. I stare in open-mouthed horror as he emerges from the hollies, a cotton candy pink sweatshirt draped over his back.

"You didn't..." I gasp.

He did. It's my 'Hello Kitty' sweatshirt. The one I wear only in my apartment. The one I'd never, ever, *ever* wear in public. And now I don't have a choice. Darn it. I take it, duck down behind one of the bushes lining the sidewalk, and wriggle the torn sweatshirt off. I drop it to the ground and wrestle a knot into the end of the left sleeve of the Hello Kitty hoodie before manipulating it over my head. Geeze, couldn't Maxx have grabbed a zippered sweatshirt instead?

"I picked it because it has a cat. You like cats." Maxx peers around the bush, tail wagging ferociously.

He's pleased with himself and I just don't have the heart to tell him how I really feel. I'm not a huge cat fan, and the only reason I own the sweatshirt at all is because my mom gave it to me last year. I stand up.

"Thanks, it's great." My shoulder throbs just enough to let me know I'm still only mostly undead. I nab Maxx's leash, somewhat surprised he hasn't found a way to rid himself of it yet.

"Damn!!" A guy's voice shrieks at me from a passing car. "You so ugly, Hello Kitty's sayin' good-bye!"

The stupid sweatshirt is so bright it can probably be seen from space.

Maxx growls deep in his throat. "That was cruel. Release me at once." He tugs at the leash. Knowing he could, I appreciate him not taking the other arm off.

"No," I say. "I'm responsible for you. You can't go after them."

"I am a hell hound," he says, the growls still vibrating through his words. "I can go where I want and do what I wish."

Okay, the last thing Atlanta needs is a pissed off, bull sized dog roaming the streets and terrorizing the public.

I squat down and face the Rott sized dog. "No, Maxx. You can't go killing humans just because they're mean." I hug him around the neck and bury my face in his ruff. He's warm. It's comforting. I take a deep breath in and discover he smells of butter cream and vanilla.

"Are you sure you wish to continue the walk?" He rumbles the question.

I nod and speak into his fur. "We haven't even made it all the way to the statue yet."

"At least you are no longer decomposing," he says.

"That's true, as far as I know." I stand up. "Okay, let's keep walking. I do have church tonight."

"Ah yes, I had forgotten. The 'interesting' church you wish me to attend with you."

There are more people on the sidewalk now, but they're still walking in a large half-circle around Maxx and me. I'm not sure if it's because of me or because of him. I'm also not sure it matters.

"Are you okay?"

I turn away from Maxx to face the girl who asked the question. She's young, well, younger than me, anyway. Middle school age, maybe. She doesn't wait for my answer. Instead she holds her hand out for Maxx to sniff. Not sure if he's up on 'doggy protocol', I say 'I don't know if he's friendly to strangers. He's not mine."

"You had your face buried in his fur," she points out. "That's a pretty good sign."

"Well, yeah, but I'm familiar," I say.

Maxx takes matters into his own hands…errr…paws. He licks the hand in front of him. A smile spreads across the girl's face. "Oh, he's a cutie-pie! Are you baby-sitting him?"

I want to say 'No, I'm bull sitting', because it'd be hilarious, but I take what I believe is the higher road and just nod.

"And you're sure you're okay? I heard that guy yell at you. What a jerk."

It's nice to meet someone not jaded by reality yet. "Yeah, I'm fine."

"Okay, then. Well, take care." She leans down and pats Maxx on the head. His tail thumps against the ground as she walks away.

"I like her," Maxx says. "Can we follow her?"

I can see that I have a lot to teach him about manners. And stalking. "No, let's just get to the Big Chicken." This walk has never taken so long before. I dig into my pocket, pull my phone out and glance at it. 3:30 p.m. Not nearly late enough to head to church and walking laps around the Big Chicken isn't my idea of a good time. "Maxx, have you ever eaten chicken before?"

The massive hound shakes his head. "Nacelles

fed me before I arrived. You have no need to give me anything."

"It's not about need," I say. "Call it a treat instead."

"Yummmmm…chicken!" Now he pulls at the leash and somehow, I keep up as he gains speed. We begin to flicker in and out of reality.

I hope no one notices, because that'd be bad.

Twenty-Three:

What Do You Want on *Your* Tombstone?

It's like my whole body's blinking really, really fast. All I can do is hang onto the leash and pray since Maxx, in his excitement, shows no signs of slowing down. We're moving fast enough that it feels like mere minutes before he stops.

I assume it's still lunch time for most of the world. I don't even know what KFC serves for lunch...maybe chicken biscuits? It feels like forever since I've eaten anything except brains, even though it's only been days.

"Maxx, you'll need to stay outside." I make a huge show of draping his leash over a nearby bush. I doubt anyone'll mess with him, but I kneel down. "Don't bite anyone," I whisper. "I can't afford a lawsuit."

"Human flesh is bland," he answers. "I would not consume it."

I swallow. I'm pretty sure my arm is not the only human flesh he's tasted. Part of me is super curious and part of me just doesn't want to know details like that.

"All right, well, I'll go get you something and be back in a minute. Just...stay here, okay?" I don't wait for his assent, but pull open the doors to the restaurant and get in line.

There are a lot more choices than I remember. I

opt for a lunch combo. While I hate to waste everything but the chicken, I'm not giving Maxx any soda. He can try the French fries, though. I don't think they'll hurt him. It's potatoes, after all.

"How'd you lose your arm?" A tiny boy asks, tugging on my empty sleeve. I look down. He's about four, maybe six. I'm no great judge of age, especially in little kids.

"Hush, Marcus, that's not nice." I assume the woman at his side is his mother, but it could be his sister. She looks around my age, at any rate.

"I lost it in a vicious dog walking accident," I say.

The little boy's eyes get huge. "Honest engine?"

I smile and the woman laughs. "No dear, she's kidding. She doesn't want to talk about it. I'm sorry," she says to me, "he's just so curious about everything."

"It's all right." The question does make me wonder, though, if someone can fix my arm. I don't want people to see me as the local one-armed freak.

"Order # 34."

I walk up to the counter, and take the bag from the cashier. It's a short walk from there to the soda fountain to get some water. The little boy waves at me as I put the lid on the cup and leave.

Maxx looks up from licking his paw when I squat down and open the bag. "It smells odd."

"That's because it's cooked and seasoned." I take the sandwich out, dismantle it, and hold the chicken patty out to him. I expect him to act like a typical dog and devour it, but he doesn't. Instead, he bites a piece off and chews it before swallowing.

"I like it," Maxx states. "Is chicken available everywhere?"

I nod. "Some people are strict vegetarians, but others just like a variety in their diet, so yeah. Pretty much everywhere serves chicken in one form or another."

"I approve of Atlanta," he announces.

I laugh. "Are you ready to explore more?"

Maxx mouths the rest of the chicken from my palm, chews and swallows. "Yes. Where should we go next?"

I think about it. "Can you transport us somewhere you've never been?"

He shakes his head. "I must have a point of reference first."

Well, that makes things a little problematic. With only one arm, I can't drive and only service pets are allowed on the MARTA system. "We can walk to the Marietta National Cemetery, if you like. It's not too far from here."

He ponders for a moment before replying. "I enjoy looking at headstones."

My knees pop when I get up. "It's less than two miles away. It shouldn't take us very long to get there."

Maxx sneezes and follows me down the street.

The cemetery is a broad expanse of shortly mown grass, with headstones standing in neat rows around four feet apart. Some of the graves have little American flags in small vases set at the base. I'm drawn to the other ones, though; the ones closer to the tree-line, somewhat overgrown and neglected. I glance around before I bend and unclip the leash from Maxx's collar. It's definitely not allowed, but I doubt he'll pee on a headstone or anything. He's more civilized than that. He immediately snuffles his way over to the oldest tombstones and I follow.

"Isisss, look at this!" Maxx barks. I've never heard him do that before.

I turn from where I'm investigating the grave of a

young girl. The dates read '7 June, 1891 – 24 December, 1896.' My heart breaks for anyone who loses their child that young, let alone on Christmas Eve. What a nightmare.

"I remember him," Maxx tells me.

"Uhhh...remember who?" I look, but no-one is close-by.

"The headstone, look at the headstone!"

It's a weathered, chipped headstone, the carving on it so faint I can barely read it. "William DeHec. Born 1802. Died 1845." There is nothing special about it. I mean nothing other than the fact that my disguised hell hound remembers him.

"You've been wandering around here for one hundred and sixty-eight years?" I ask.

Maxx shakes his head. "I had to track his soul. He was good at avoiding detection. But I was better."

If I was an escaped soul, I wouldn't want Maxx and his posse of 'pest exterminators' following me around. But I *am* curious about the whole thing. "What's it like?"

"Hunting for souls?" He sits down with a plop.

"Yeah. I mean, you've been all over the world, right?"

"It is not as simple as that," Maxx says. "I did not 'travel the world' in the normal sense. I was hunting."

I frown. "And that's different, how?"

"It is difficult to explain. When I hunt, I do not exist in either reality."

"What do you mean either reality?" The hell hound certainly has a way of making me feel dumb. "I thought this was the only one."

"There are three realities," Maxx replies with a sigh. "When is the last time you attended church?"

"A couple of days ago. Why, what does church have to do with it?"

ONE FOOT IN THE GRAVE

He sneezes. "There is Heaven, Hell, and here. When I hunt, I do not exist in either one of the realities I am familiar with; here and Hell."

"That's...confusing."

The dog snorts and I'm just grateful snot doesn't accompany the gust of fetid air from his nostrils. "That is reality."

I blink. Okay, onto the next question. "What was it like, working for demons?"

"Most humans would think Nacelles is a demon." Maxx says. "It is not as though there is a great distinction."

"Other than the fact that Nacelles isn't from Hell," I point out, burrowing my hand in Maxx's fur.

"There is a saying I have heard...to-may-to, to-mah-to? Yes, that is it."

"What do you do if the souls don't want to go back? I mean, they aren't exactly corporeal, so how do you transport them?"

"It is one of my innate abilities." Maxx yawns and I get to see the rows of sharp Rotty teeth up close and personal like. And smell his nasty chicken breath. Gross. I turn my face away, coughing. And see the cute little calico kitten that cost me my arm perched on top of a nearby headstone.

It stares at me with big green-gold eyes.

"No," I say. "Oh no, I am so *not* taking you home."

Maxx cracks open an eye. He seems disinterested in the kitten itself, unlike before. "You could use a pet."

"No. I could *not* use a pet. My apartment doesn't allow pets. Why are you encouraging this?"

"I have learned that humans are less lonely when they have pets to care for. You could enjoy that."

"I don't have time for a pet." I try again, but Maxx is having none of it. Neither is the kitten, which jumps off its perch and saunters over to me.

"What else are you going to do with your time? You cannot hunt for the vampire who turned you forever. That is a sad excuse for a life."

Buddha Maxx. That's what his name should've been. "Stoopid hell hound and your stoopid insight," I grumble, not meaning it. Luckily, Maxx doesn't hear me. Or, if he does, he ignores it.

The kitten wriggles its way into my lap, curls into a ball and begins to purr. It hasn't dug its claws into my leg and *is* super cute. I remove my hand from Maxx's fur and begin to pet the kitten. It purrs harder, arching its tiny back up to meet my palm.

Darn it, it looks like I've acquired a pet. I want to hate that Maxx was right, but I don't have the heart. Petting the tiny thing does make me feel a little less alone. I'll figure out the apartment restrictions later.

Twenty-Four:

Holy Hell Hound, Batman!

Maxx and I, along with my newly acquired pet, decide to go to the church after the cemetery visit. My heart speeds up a bit at the idea of a hell hound at church, but it doesn't seem to bother the dog any.

"I already told you, crossing the threshold of the building will not hurt me."

I nod. "I know, but still...don't you think it's weird, *you* going to church?"

He tilts his head upward to look at me. "Not particularly, especially since you have told me what sort of a church it is. I look forward to meeting Father Moss and speaking with him at length."

I wonder if Father Moss will feel the same way. The beauty of being close to the church is that it doesn't take me long to find out.

I step into the darkened foyer, sun-spots dancing in front of my eyes. I blink to clear my vision.

"You came back." I hear Father Moss' voice with a sense of relief. I'd rather deal with him than with Lydia.

"Uhhh...yeah. Is that okay?"

"Of course," the gargoyle says, stepping into the light. "Are you ready to talk about what happened?"

"Ummm...well, I kind of brought a visitor."

"Then now is not the time." He focuses on my empty sleeve. "It looks like you have other things to worry yourself about. But you cannot avoid it forever, Isis. This is Noelle's home, too."

"I understand. I'll talk to her," I promise.

"Good. Now, who did you bring?"

I glance behind me and see that Maxx is back to a normal size. Well, normal size for him, which means huge for everyone else.

"I smell gargoyle, witch, vampire and human," Maxx states. His tail sweeps from side to side, like a lion's.

"I am the gargoyle, as you can plainly see," Father Moss steps forward, his wings completely unfurled. "I never thought I'd live to see a hell hound in my church. What brings you here? This place houses no souls to hunt."

I open my mouth to reply, but Maxx shoulders me aside. "I come as a guest, nothing more. Isisss was quite adamant about my visitation." He looks sideways at me. "She seems to be under the impression that I will enjoy your sermons."

"I'm surprised she'd say that considering we don't have sermons here."

"I never told you there'd be sermons, Maxx," I admonish. I like the old gargoyle and don't want him to think I'm telling stories.

Father Moss folds his wings down with a loud scraping sound. "My calling is somewhat different than you might have been led to believe," he says to Maxx.

"We were never taught about priests and their callings," the hell hound replies. "Our sole duty was to our demon and to our hunt."

"Let me show you around the premises," Father Moss says. "Isis, what on earth has happened to your arm?"

I'm glad he noticed, though I'm rather

embarrassed about the whole thing. "Maxx tore it out of its socket. But it wasn't his fault. He saw that kitten." I point to the kitten, which looks up at the priest and purrs.

"I can see it has since adopted you," the priest says. I hear the smile in his voice.

"It's adopted one of us, that's for sure," I reply.

"It's cute," Father Moss says. "Come, both of you, the cemetery out back is quite unique. I think you, hell hound, will find it especially fascinating."

That's intriguing. I follow the two of them to the back of the church and out an arched doorway.

It's very different from the cemetery we'd just left; overgrown and ancient. I watch Maxx squeeze himself through the archway and look around.

"Ummm...doesn't Maxx need to be in disguise?" I ask Father Moss.

"Ah, that's his name. You neglected to introduce us," he admonishes me. "My church has protections, Isis. Your guest is safe."

Maxx nods as though in perfect understanding.

I'm stupider. "What does consecration have to do with anything?"

"It is not the consecration," Maxx explains. "It is protected by magic."

Oh. That's cool. "So who's buried back here?"

"Take a look around," Father Moss says.

I wander further into the cemetery, the nameless kitten at my heels. The first headstone reads "Wanda Yates; 1985 – 2006. Born of a human; died a half-wendigo."

What the heck is a wendigo?

"It's sort of like a werewolf, but scarier," Father Moss answers the unasked question.

"This is a half graveyard?" I look around. There are tombstones squished together, set apart, standing upright and flat on their backs. It's haphazard at best. "I didn't know so many existed!"

Maxx sniffs around a downed headstone before lying next to it, his immense head on the stone itself.

"Is that—was that—someone you dragged back?' Considering his behavior at the other cemetery, it's possible. "Do we even *have* souls?" I direct the last question to Father Moss.

"I believe every creature born of God has a soul." The gargoyle glances at Maxx. "No offense meant."

The hound sneezes. "How do you know I am not born of God? Was not the Christian Devil himself one of God's angels?"

The gargoyle nods. "You bring up an interesting point, Maxx, and one I would love to discuss with you at length, if you're so inclined."

I'm bored, so I wander away, their conversation turning into a bee-like background buzz. The other tombstones bear similar epitaphs to the first one. It's amazing how many half creatures there are. Some of the dates go all the way back to the early 1700's and are only visible because I squint at the headstones. I have no idea how they survive the humid summers sort of intact, but they do. Maybe it has something to do with the magical 'barrier' Father Moss says surrounds the church. I spot something curious and bend down to take a closer look.

"Hey, Maxx, did you know this person was in Salem, Mass during the witch trials?

The massive hound turns his head to look at me and I realize I interrupted him. "Sorry, but her tombstone reads 'witch'. Do you think she came here to escape persecution?" I'm fascinated by the idea.

"What is the name on the stone?" Father Moss asks. "I may have known the woman."

"How old are you?" I blurt.

The gargoyle scratches his head with the tip of one claw. Tiny pebbles rain down. "I can't give you an exact figure. I don't know. I've been here, at this church, since around 1720. Or thereabouts."

"That's impossible," I say. "Buildings don't stand that long. Not without restoration."

"They do with preventative and protective measures," Father Moss says. "Has it never occurred to you that no-one but half breeds ever come here uninvited?"

Actually...it hadn't.

"But that doesn't matter," he continues. "What's the name on that tombstone?"

"Anne Wood."

The priest nods his head. "Ah, yes. I remember her. I believe she was one of Lydia's friends. She was a sweet child who wanted nothing more than to study herbs. She used to spend hours out here, just watching her plants grow."

Maxx yawns hugely.

"Are we boring you?" Father Moss asks.

"Hell hounds are supposed to nap frequently," Maxx explains. "It helps us keep our energy charged for our hunts."

"I see," the gargoyle says. "Then I apologize for keeping you up. By all means, nap."

The hell hound closes his eyes.

"So how do you find these people, anyway? The halves, I mean."

"Lydia," Father Moss replies. "She scrys for them."

A deep, terrifying rumble fills the cemetery garden. The ground quivers and headstones begin to topple. I expect lightening to raze across the sky, but when I look up everything is clear.

"What is that?" Father Moss' wings unfurl and he

looks ready to take to the skies. "Are we under attack?"

I glance over at Maxx. His eyes are completely shut and the sounds shaking the foundations of the earth itself are coming from his nose. Good night, the hell hound is snoring.

Twenty-Five:

We're Nothin' More Than Stone Soup.

I start to snicker, but Father Moss isn't as polite. He begins to laugh and if I didn't know better I'd swear we're caught in a rockslide.

The rumbling ceases. Maxx opens his eyes. "What?"

My snickers turn into full blown laughter.

The hell hound quirks his eyebrows.

"You were snoring," I say. "Look around."

Maxx's huge head turns first to the left, then to the right as he looks at the damage he's caused. "I do apologize," he says. "It has been a long time since I slept in my natural form in your world."

"No harm done." The gargoyle reassures him. "A few knocked over headstones won't make a difference. Not in this cemetery. If you're sufficiently rested, would you like to see the rest of the church?"

Maxx nods.

"Isis, would you care to join us? The others will be here shortly, and I'd like Maxx to feel at home before they arrive."

I shrug. "Sure, why not?" I thought I'd seen the entire church, but the cemetery/garden was new. And having Father Moss as a tour guide can't hurt.

Maxx clambers to his feet. "Where will we begin?"

"The church isn't large," Father Moss says,

waddling toward the archway.

"Can you fly?" I follow the gargoyle into the church, and I feel Maxx's hot breath coat the back of my head. It's disgusting, but I do my best not to shudder. After all, it's not his fault he has to breathe.

"Yes, of course," the stone creature says. "But I do only when the occasion demands it." He doesn't elaborate what might constitute an 'occasion', but I'll admit, at least to myself, that I'm curious.

"But your wings look so delicate..."

He laughs. "They're still made of stone, Isis. They're made out of stone, just like the rest of me."

"Gargoyles keep evil away from places of worship," Maxx rumbles.

I stop walking and turn to face him. The kitten winds itself in and out between my feet. "Then why didn't he do anything when you walked in?"

The huge dog huffs out a sigh. "Why do you insist on not understanding this, Isisss? Hell is a place, not a state of being."

Father Moss surprises me when he nods his agreement.

"Oh, I don't know," I respond, "maybe because it's contrary to everything my mom ever tried to teach me."

"If there's one thing I've learned over the centuries, it's that parents are not infallible. Maxx, would you care to see the computer room?"

The dog lifts one paw off the ground as though he's going to offer to 'shake' my hand. "There is no point, since I do not have the dexterity to manipulate the keyboard."

Father Moss smiles. "We'll skip that, then. I would show you my quarters, but neither of you could reach it, I fear." He gestures upward. I follow the line of his sight and see the ceiling.

"You live on the roof?" You know, there are days when everything that comes out of my mouth is just pure idiocy. Today feels like one of those days and the look Maxx throws me just cements the feeling.

"I live in a small room located to the right of the bell," the gargoyle says. "It necessitates flight."

"Where's the rope?" I ask. "Don't bells usually have ropes attached?"

"It rotted away long ago," Father Moss replies. "I used it a few times before that happened, but there's something about flight..." His voice trails off.

"Have you ever flown?" I ask Maxx. Hey, it's possible. After all, he can change shapes.

"Excuse me? Have you ever seen a winged canine?" The hell hound's tongue lolls out. I get the distinct impression that, if he could laugh, he'd be on the floor, convulsing.

I have to reply in my own defense. What's that saying? 'In for a penny, in for a pound'? "But you can disguise yourself as other beings, right?"

"I have never had a need to transform into anything else," Maxx says. "There are enough canines to choose from."

"Isis!"

"Hey, Daniel," I greet the half-vamp. "Did Ink tell you what happened?" I don't want him thinking I abandoned him at the club.

"Yeah, she filled me in. Are you going to go back?"

I nod. "Yeah, actually...I am. It's not so bad."

"I'm glad you enjoyed yourself," he says. "I wasn't sure you would."

"Neither was I," I admit readily. "But I made a new friend, so..."

Daniel glances in Maxx's direction, but before he can say anything, Father Moss speaks. "Kids, take your seats. The others should be filtering in shortly. Maxx, if you would come with me. I'd rather introduce you after everyone has arrived."

The hell hound obediently follows Father Moss into his office.

"You made friends with a *hell hound*?"

"Did you know Nacelles has a herd of them under the club?" I counter.

Daniel frowns. "You met Nacelles Caldemer? Boy, when I tell you to mingle, you really mingle, huh?"

I shrug, now kind of self-conscious about the whole thing. "It just kind of happened."

Other halves start to filter into the sanctuary and I take a seat, knowing full well the Hello Kitty sweatshirt and lack of an arm will garner me a ton of questions. Time to get this party started.

Twenty-Six:

Crow and Humble Pie.

"Group, we have a visitor. Please, seat yourselves."

Okay, that's new. I don't ever remember Father Moss being so formal. Maybe he's worried the others will take one look at the still absent Maxx and go screaming out the front door. I know I would if I didn't know any better.

I totally underestimate them.

"Maxx, please join us." Father Moss says.

The bull sized dog steps out of the shadows, his ears pressed to the back of his ginormous head. He's nervous. And if he wasn't the size of a small car, it'd be cute.

A chorus of "Oooooo..." and "That's a hell-hound!" echo around the sanctuary as everyone, including Noelle, stares at him.

"Is he safe?" Albin asks. His paws are still paws. I wonder if that's a permanent condition. If so, that sucks.

"You'll have to ask him," Father Moss replies. "His name is Maxx and he came with Isis. He'll only be here a few weeks, so be polite, everyone."

Albin is the only one brave enough to actually approach Maxx. "Can I touch you?"

The big dog shakes his head. "I am sorry, but in this form I would burn you beyond recognition. Wait a moment."

The air bends and in Maxx's place is a beautiful husky with his same golden eyes. "Now you may."

The half-were smiles. I get the impression it's not something he does a lot of. He stretches his hand out and Maxx strides forward until he's underneath.

"Where'd you come from?" Albin asks. His tone is almost reverent. "Are there more of you?" I don't know if he expects a reply or not, but the entire church seems to hold its breath for Maxx's answer.

"I am from Hell." Maxx's voice is dry. "As all hell hounds are. And yes, I do have a pack."

That starts the whispering. I get the feeling not every half there believes in either Heaven or Hell. I don't really blame them.

Albin's paw sinks deeper into Maxx's fur. "But what makes you, you?"

The hound cocks his head sideways. "You are very curious."

"My dad's a vet," Albin says. "I guess you could say I was born curious."

I ooze out of my seat, and shrink backwards, away from the crowd. I know, once they've gotten their fill of Maxx, their attention will turn to me and my empty sleeve.

"What's with the empty?"

Dear Mother of...I close my eyes, say a small prayer for patience, then open them again. I just don't have it in me to be polite. "What do you want, Noelle?" It's like my brain's completely forgotten I promised Father Moss I'd talk to her.

She leans toward me. "Look, Father Moss said I need to help you, and so did Daniel. So here I am, ready to help. Now, what's with the empty sleeve?"

I tell her the same thing I told the little boy at KFC. "It was an unfortunate dog walking incident."

Her eyes immediately fixate on Maxx.

"Seriously? And so you brought him *here*?"

"It was an accident. He's not vicious at all." She raises one eyebrow. "No, I swear. I mean, just *look* at him."

Noelle swivels to stare at Maxx, who looks as far from vicious as a dog could possibly get; flat on his back, accepting belly rubs. The half-fae laughs. "I see your point," she concedes.

"So what kind of help do you think you can give me?"

"I have ties to the community my *boyfriend* doesn't. I used to be a dancer. I still dance, on occasion. That takes me places. Places your runaway vampire might be."

"Hold up. Daniel's your boyfriend? He never said anything to me about it."

"Not everyone advertises their relationships," she says, but the look in her eyes tells me it's pretty much one-sided. "Focus, Isis. As I said, I'm a dancer. I can ask questions; see if anyone's seen anything."

"You mean you'll help me as long as I stay away from Daniel."

She stares at me. "That's the deal, yeah."

I shake my head. "I won't agree to that. If you can't accept my friendship with Daniel, that's your problem, not mine."

Her eyes begin to glow, but I refuse to back up. "This is ridiculous," I say instead. "Noelle, get over yourself. You can jinx me all you want, but seriously. I'm not staying away from Daniel. He's pretty much the only friend I've got *in* this place. He likes me and I like him. Deal with it."

The half-fae's eyes dim back to normal. She looks thoughtful, and not at all inclined to turn my fingers into snakes again. "I don't like you, you know."

I shrug. "That's okay; I don't like you, either."

Noelle bites her lip before continuing. "I actually think you and I might be friends someday." She laughs. I can only imagine it's at my dumbfounded expression. "Not today, and not tomorrow. But someday. The truth is, there aren't many halves I like."

I want to say something sarcastic, but she's making an effort and so should I. The problem is, I have no idea what to say.

"Why do you live here?" I finally ask. "You look pretty normal; you could get away with living outside."

"Really? Have you *seen* my eyes?"

It's weird, having Noelle confide in me. "Just tell everyone you've got contacts. No-one's going to care."

"You really don't get it. How old do you think I am?"

"I don't know, eighteen?" She certainly doesn't look much older than me, and *definitely* doesn't act it.

"Not hardly. Add around one hundred years to that guess."

I blink. "A hundred and eighteen? Really?"

"Fae age very, *very* slowly. So do witches. That lovely fact leaves me pretty much stuck looking like a teenager for the next hundred years or so. That's not exactly conducive to living a normal life."

Wow. At least I can move around in the real world. No wonder Noelle's such a…pill. She's right. We might not be friends now, but we're not exactly enemies anymore, either.

"Noelle, can I steal Isis away from you for a moment?" Father Moss startles me. I'm so involved with my conversation with Noelle, I don't even hear him coming.

The half-fae shrugs. "Sure, I'm not her keeper."

ONE FOOT IN THE GRAVE

"Everyone is wondering what happened to your arm," the gargoyle continues, "and how you came to be acquainted with a hell-hound."

I take a deep breath. Regardless of how much the church feels more like home than home does, I don't know if I'm ready to tell every half there my story. But it looks like I don't have much choice. Maybe I'll actually get some friends if I start to confide in people. If nothing else, it'd make my mom worry a little less about me. Luckily, it doesn't take long to tell the story, not with Father Moss and Lydia ensuring there are no interruptions. By the time I finish, saying, "and so I brought Maxx here," I'm emotionally worn out. Lydia seems to sense that, because she motions me to follow her. I do.

"You look flustered," the witch says. "Why don't you take ten minutes in the cemetery? The air will do you good, and I'll make sure you're not bothered by any of the halves."

I literally trip over a tombstone. When I look down, I notice it's one I've seen before. "What happened to the half-wendigo that's buried here?"

"She was killed by a half. Not all of you are safe to be around other people." Lydia states. "There are rooms below us which house the more dangerous ones." She glares at me. "Do not go down there without express permission and a powerful escort."

That sounds like a challenge.

Twenty-Seven:

What Lies Beneath.

"I mean it, Isis. Do *not* go into the rooms below the church," Lydia states again.

I bite my lip. Maybe Maxx can go down there with me. He's a hell hound. What could be safer, right?

"I shouldn't have said anything," Lydia sighs. It's like she can read my mind. "On second thought, why don't you come back inside with me? Father Moss has an announcement."

I was kind of looking forward to sitting outside, among the actual dead, but I nod and follow her back inside.

"Now," Father Moss says right as I walk back through the arches, "if everyone will finally sit down, we're having another movie night soon. Does anyone want to watch anything in particular, or should I make the decision again?"

There are a ton of suggestions. Most of which, in my not so humble opinion, suck. 'You Got Mail', 'The Time Traveller's Wife', 'The Notebook', and 'Journey to the Center of the Earth' (the original one, not the hilarious remake).

Albin raises his hand.

"Yes, Albin?" Father Moss asks.

"What about movies that are more, I don't know, in keeping with our current lives? You know, like

'Dracula' or 'Silver Bullet?'"

"Well, the point of movie night is to keep things lighthearted and fun," the gargoyle says. "But if the general consensus agrees, I'll bow to what everyone else wants." He grins, showing a row of truly impressive stone teeth. "Of course, there aren't any horror movies about gargoyles, so I know *I'll* be sleeping well that night."

Everyone laughs, as I know he meant them to, and start chattering among themselves. I feel kind of left out, even after my 'confession', until Maxx and the still nameless kitten amble over to me.

"Isis, are you unwell?" Maxx pushes himself against me.

I bury my hands in his still husky sized body.

"Lydia told me other halves exist," I tell Maxx.

He blinks those huge golden eyes at me. "Yes, they are in the church."

I shake my head. "Those aren't the halves I'm talking about. I mean the ones under the church. The ones Lydia says are dangerous."

The big dog sneezes. "You wish to see them." It's not a question.

"I'm curious. Wouldn't you be?"

"There have never been half- hell hounds, Isisss. Unlike the human species, we are isolated and very careful where we place our teeth."

I'm almost positive he just insulted me; but I have no idea how. "I want to go downstairs, Maxx. I want to see what Father Moss is hiding."

"I do not think this is a wise course of action," Maxx replies. "There is a reason they have been locked away. If a *witch*, a woman who survived the Trials of Salem, is telling you not to go, why are you refusing to listen?"

"Because the more dangerous creatures might

know where Andrew is. Because I'm curious, and all this is new to me and I'm just plain, flat out *curious*. Why is that such a bad thing?"

"Curiosity killed the kitten," Maxx sneezes again.

"Cat," I automatically correct. "Curiosity killed the cat. And how do you know that saying? I didn't think you'd ever seen a cat before Callie."

"Who is Callie?"

I smile. "I've decided to name the kitten after my grandmother. She was a burlesque dancer."

He tilts his head to one side. "And so you decided to name a kitten after her."

"She loved Calico kittens." I hear myself start to defend the choice. Gah. "You never did answer my question."

"I have seen cats. I have not seen kittens. I have never cried over spilled milk, but I understand the concept of doing so."

Okay, point taken. I've never cried over spilled milk, either. Well, maybe when I was a toddler, but certainly not in recent memory. "So will you go with me?"

He tilts his head at me. "Have you spoken to anyone else about this?"

"Of course not. Both Lydia and Father Moss would tell me I can't go. But I want to, Maxx. I want to see what's down there."

"You will go with or without me," Maxx states.

I nod. It's true. I will. "So will you come with me?"

"I cannot, in good conscience, allow you to go down there by yourself. But you need to understand that Father Moss and Lydia will be quite upset with you." He sneezes again.

"Maxx, you do that a lot. Are you allergic to me, or something?"

He opens his mouth and his tongue lolls out. "I

am allergic to your less than intelligent ideas, Isis. But I like you, and I do not desire to watch you get injured by your choices."

What a polite way of saying I'm a total idiot and have the worst ideas ever. Of course, that isn't going to stop me from doing exactly what I want. "I want to go downstairs."

The dog sighs and lumbers to his feet. "Do you wish me to change my size first?"

It's an awkward shrug, but I manage. "I don't know. Do you think it's a good idea?"

"This is your venture, not mine."

So I'm the one who gets to make all the decisions? Gee, thanks Maxx. I think aloud, "I have no idea where the entrance to downstairs is."

He cocks his head at me. "That is a problem."

Yeah, it is. Father Moss' hearing is excellent; I'm pretty sure he'll hear me looking around. "Will you distract Father Moss while I see if I can find stairs or something?"

"You are using me as a blind." The hell hound states.

"No, that's not what I said," I reply. At least, I don't think that's what I said. Sometimes Maxx confuses me. "I just want you to talk to him."

"That is what a blind *is*, Isisss. I thought you graduated from your high school."

"I did," I protest. "But 'blind' usually means not being able to see, not a distraction."

"You are missing the point, which is that you wish for me to enable your deception."

Well, yeah. That's kind of the point of the whole conversation. "How else am I supposed to snoop?"

"I would recommend investigating the small door on the side of the church," Maxx says. "It appears to be quite old and might contain what you are searching for."

I had no idea the church had secret doors, but then again, I've never walked all the way around it, either. It's pretty cool.

"How do *you* know about the door? You said you've never been here before."

His answer shocks me. "Callie told me."

She did *what*?

"She's a cat." Trust me to state the utter obvious. I'm good at that.

"She is a kitten. And I am a hell hound. We understand each other when I wish it." He quirks an eyebrow at me. "That is not all the time, however. She is young and has a young animal's mind and interests."

Like adopting a perfect stranger in a cemetery. "You'll still come with me, right?"

He nods and gets to his feet. "I gave you my word."

I'm abnormally relieved. If Maxx is there and something goes wrong-the halves break loose and come after me, for instance-I won't be alone. I may get blamed, but I won't get eaten. I hope. "Okay, let's go."

We amble around the left side of the church first, the side farthest away from the cemetery. It's not particularly well-tended, either. Plants and roots grow upward from the ground in a massive tangle that kind of makes sense. It's vibrant, green, mossy, and so very, very *alive*. I wonder if that's exactly what Father Moss intended; a place where us undead could wander around and feel what we'll never be again. The weight of that settles itself in my chest, but it's not as heavy as it used to be. It's more like a fact than a burden.

"See, there it is," Maxx says.

I follow his gaze and yup. There it is. A small door with the biggest padlock and chain I've ever seen holding it shut. "How the heck am I supposed to get in there?"

"You have the vampire's strength," Maxx states. "Use it."

"I've only got the one hand," I retort.

"Then pull on it with one hand," the hell-hound practically sneezes his reply

Oh. Duh. Well, aren't I a bag of smart? I step forward and take the chain in my hand, feeling a lot like The Incredible Hulk. I yank, expecting it to fly apart like tin foil.

The metal rings groan and squeal, but nothing else happens. The chain stays firmly together. How disappointing. I drop it and reach for the padlock. It looks way old and rusted through. I'm sure I'm in for a fight, so to speak, but the thing lives up to its looks and just disintegrates in my hand. A fine black powder rains down to coat my shoes and the chains sag open. Well, that was easy.

Twenty-Eight:

Something Pissed Off This Way Comes.

I put my hand on the latch to the door, twist and push. It opens reluctantly, with a puff of dust *wooshing* out and all over us. I sneeze three times and it's not because I'm allergic to Maxx.

"Great googly ooglies," I swear. Okay, so as far as swear words go, they're pretty silly, but anything else just sounds wrong to my Southern Baptist, hippie upbringing.

"What is a 'googly ooglie'?" Maxx asks. "And why is it great?"

"It's just an expression," I say.

Maxx's fur is now coated a light brown. He shakes and the dust flies. "I do not understand. What is it an expression of?"

How am I supposed to explain made up words to a hell hound that has a better grasp of the English language than I do?

"It's just a better word than an actual swear word." I brush the dust off. "You know what swear words are, right?"

The hell hound nods. "I do, yes. But I have never seen the purpose of using them. It cheapens the entire conversation."

"We weren't having a conversation," I say. "And I wasn't really swearing. Just kind of."

He quirks an eyebrow at me. I sigh.

"Fine. I was swearing because I didn't expect the dust cloud."

"Humans are odd," is his only observation. He sneezes and creates his own dust cloud. "Is this when I should say 'great googly ooglies'?"

I roll my eyes. "Never mind. Let's go inside...actually, you lead. Y'know, just in case something decides it's hungry."

Maxx sneezes again, but this time I know what it means: he thinks what I just said is stupid. I prefer the term 'prudent', myself. Either way, I'm the one following him through the door and down the rabbit hole.

The interior isn't dark and gloomy, though in all honesty I think it should be. Instead, it's brightly lit and hospital clean. All the dust seems to have accumulated on the door itself. There certainly isn't any on the floor or the walls. A vague sense of disappointment fills me. I expected moldering walls and lichen; maybe a drippy sound in the background. Instead, a whining kind of hiss reverberates eerily from the stones below my feet. All the hair on my body stands at attention, as though ready to abandon ship at a second's notice.

"What the heck was *that*?" I don't even realize I said the words out loud until Maxx replies.

"A were of some sort, though I have never heard that particular sound from one."

The next hiss nearly stops my heart. It rolls up from the bowels of the church and sounds entirely too much like a tormented soul from the depths of Hell for my liking. Maxx doesn't even flinch; just keeps on walking. Maybe he's used to it, considering where he's from and all, but it completely freaks me out.

"Maxx, I don't think this is such a hot idea." I

know I'm a coward for saying it, but those sounds are terrifying. I don't think I want to meet the monster they belong to.

The big dog stops and turns his head to look at me. "We can leave if you like, but your curiosity will never be satisfied if we do."

"I know." I *know*, but the thing below us is scary. "It's locked up, right?"

Maxx's answer does nothing to reassure me. "If it was roaming free, it would already be up here, tearing you apart. Do you wish to continue or not?"

Sure, let's go see the insane half. That sounds like a thrill a minute. I nod yes, because I'm stupid like that. And because it was my idea and I do have a sense of pride, misplaced as it is.

The hallway winds itself downward, much like a spiral staircase, but without any stairs or railings of any kind. I rapidly lose all sense of direction, or how deeply underground we are. I just know I'm entirely dependent upon Maxx-so it's a really good thing I trust him. Somewhere underneath our feet, a door splinters; accompanied by scrabbling, as though claws are fighting to gain purchase.

"Uhhh, Maxx?"

His ears swivel back. "I hear it."

"Is that the were? Did it get loose?" Oh my Gawd, Father Moss is going to kill me. He seriously is. I'm so screwed.

"Stay behind me." The hair on Maxx's back bristles and he's suddenly, completely, full sized.

I shrink backward as the scrabbling claw sounds get louder. This is going to be bad. I know I shouldn't shut my eyes, but I do…and say a quick, silent prayer to whatever God exists that I won't get eaten. And that Maxx won't die.

The half-creature comes into view and I shrink

backwards in anticipation of the coming fight between Maxx and it. The hell hound is already growling, low and rumbling; a steady sound I can feel deep in my chest.

Maxx launches himself at the thing and I only get a glimpse of a vague man-shape before the two are tangled together so completely it's hard to tell them apart. It's over almost before it begins. After the initial jump towards the creature, Maxx backs off. I mean, he backs *way* off. The thing doesn't pursue him at all, which gives me all the time in the world to study it. And I kind of want to do exactly that. I mean, it's cool. Other than the fact that it's not even breathing heavily after its tussle with Maxx. That's kind of definitely horrifying.

"It's a...were- lizard?" I'd laugh if I wasn't terrified of it. The thing is beautiful, but it's also around six feet tall and standing on human-like legs. It's covered in deep silver scales that look like they've been spray painted a light gold. The light gold deepens into a more solid color around its eyes. And its eyes are gorgeous in a flat reptilian way. I'm not close enough to see its pupils, but the irises are lava red flecked with the same gold as its scales. It's amazing. I take a step toward it before I even realize what I'm doing.

"That thing is *not* a were, Isisss. It is a half-dragon," Maxx growls. "Stay away from it."

I blink. "You're kidding me. It looks like a lizard."

"It is a half-Komodo dragon. They are giant lizards from Indonesia." He moves closer to me, until I can feel the heat emanating from him. "Are you sure you wish to pursue this further? We can turn around. It does not appear to be hungry at the moment."

I've never heard of Komodo dragons before, so I'm not sure what the big deal is. "Can't we walk around it?" After all, it's hunched against the wall, just squatting there, staring at us.

Maxx sits. "I am not sure it would allow us to move past it."

The Komodo thing's tongue flicks out. It's thin and forked, like a snake. I catch a brief glimpse of shark-like teeth before its mouth snaps shut. Maybe there's a very good reason why Maxx is acting so cautious. I should take a page out of his book and stop acting as stupid as I feel.

"We can go back, Maxx. I'm okay with that, honest." I step backward, and the lizard man hisses at me. I freeze. So. *Not* going back, then. "If it's not hungry, why won't it let me leave?"

It blinks. Sideways. I mean, its eyelids open and shut from left to right. Rapidly. That's a blink, right?

"Can you understand me?" I ask. Hey, if it's half dragon, that means half of it's human, too. And if it's human, it can reason. Theoretically.

It opens its mouth. "Ehhhhh…ehhhhh." It doesn't sound like anything close to human. I'm not sure why I expected something else; I can see the shape of its mouth, after all. It's not designed for human speech.

The creature levers itself to its feet, using its front claws? Pads? Hands? For support. Maxx begins to steam. His fearsome jaws open wide and those fun strings of lavaesque saliva make their sizzling way to the ground. This is going to get real ugly real fast. I press myself back against the wall. The last place I want to be is between the giant hell hound and the massive lizard.

Twenty-Nine:

Fight! Fight! Fight!

The lizard opens its mouth wide and I see the rows of serrated teeth, each as long as the first joint of my pinky. Then it flings itself at Maxx, who is standing sideways, protecting me. The half-Komodo's claws grip him around the middle and rip him away. His body slams into the other wall. Bits of granite rain down from the ceiling to coat us in its dust, but I'm the only one who notices. I sneeze. Maxx finds his footing just as the half-dragon turns its attention towards me. He springs at the lizard, teeth bared. The creature meets him in mid-air, mouth still gaping open. It snaps shut, getting nothing but a mouthful of air. And then Maxx shows me exactly what being a hell hound really means. His eyes begin to glow; his normally black fur burns, orange flames racing across each other before turning to black and repeating the process. My mouth drops open in amazement as my friend sheds his form all together and turns into pure magma. The stones above our heads groan in protest at the heat.

"Uhhh...Maxx?" I don't even know if he can hear me, let alone answer. He's too busy burning the Komodo, who is screaming...ummm...hissing its outrage, but seems otherwise unaffected. Maybe it takes longer to burn a lizard than it does a human. I'm no expert. Its claws try to dig into the hell hound, but it can't get a hold on him. Maxx crackles as the flames leap upward from his back and lick at the ceiling. It's so noisy I can't hear myself think. I hunch down and away, resisting the urge to 'stop, drop and roll'.

"Lydia *told* you to never come down here!"

At the sound of Father Moss's distinctive voice, everyone stops in mid-fight. The half-Komodo backs away from Maxx, one stumbling step at a time, its skin charred and blackened. Maxx doesn't regain his shape, but he sits and tilts what looks like his head up at the gargoyle, which is hovering above us like a very pissed off, and avenging, angel. Minus the flaming sword.

"Ra'kul," he says, then starts hissing and clicking. The half bares its teeth and Father Moss flies directly into its face. It throws its arms above its head, backing away from the stone wings until it vanishes back down the hallway and, presumably, into the bowels of Hell it came from.

Then it's our turn.

"You disobeyed Lydia, Isis, and could have been seriously injured in the process." Father Moss lands at my feet. "Not only that, but Ra'kul was hurt and it's difficult enough to treat wounds when the one bearing them is..." he trails off.

"Crazy? Insane? Wacked out of his head?" I say.

"That's unkind, Isis," the gargoyle replies. "Ra'kul was bitten many years ago, but instead of dying, she turned. She's the only one in existence, and her mind snapped shortly after it happened."

Oh. The lizard thing is a girl. Oops. "She *was* trying to kill me."

"Why do you think I had her locked up? Down here, where *no-one* was supposed to go?" He clatters his wings at me. "Why do you new ones never *listen*?"

I'm not sure which question I'm supposed to answer first, so I just do what I do best; try to justify my actions. "Lydia told me I couldn't come down here without a powerful escort. And I didn't. I had Maxx."

How exactly a gargoyle can glare, I'm not really sure, but Father Moss does it. "*You* are ultimately responsible for Maxx's actions, which caused Ra'kul's burns. The entirety of this mess is on your head, Isis, and it is up to you to repair it."

Well, how in the world am I supposed to do *that*?

"To that end," Father Moss continues, "if you wish to continue to come here, you will help Lydia tend to Ra'kul's injuries."

I open my mouth to protest, but he growls at me. I didn't know he could do that, either. Boy, my education is just increasing by leaps and bounds. My mouth snaps shut.

"It's called personal responsibility, Isis, and you need to take some. You are *not* allowed to run rampant, doing whatever you wish, and if you continue to do so, the next cell you see will be your own."

Wow. That's harsh. I want my eyes to well up with tears. I want some way to show Father Moss that I'm sorry, that I know I wasn't thinking. But, of course, I can't. So I nod instead. "That sounds fair," I say in a small voice. "Should I go find Lydia now?"

The gargoyle shakes his head. "No. Go home, Isis. Just...take Maxx and go home."

My heart drops. His anger hurts, but his obvious disappointment hurts worse. Noelle is going to *love* the fact that I've screwed up. Again. Going home sounds like an excellent idea. I glance over at Maxx, who is now the size and shape of a Saint Bernard. "Can we go home, Maxx? As fast as possible?" God knows I don't want to face anyone in the sanctuary. I suck.

He nods. "Close your eyes."

I don't even argue, just obey. My whole body vibrates once, violently, and when I open my eyes we're standing just inside my apartment.

"I need to fix my arm," I say. I don't want to talk about what just happened. "And I need to change."

Maxx sneezes.

"Don't sneeze at me!" I snap. "I know it was a stupid idea, okay? And now Father Moss is-is mad at me and everyone at the church will know what I did. Okay? You're right; I never should have done it. Are you happy now?"

"There is no reason I should be happy because you are yelling at me," Maxx's voice is calm, which just makes me want to yell at him more.

But I refrain. Because this mess isn't his fault. It's mine, and I know it is. I take a deep breath and release it slowly. "So...about my arm."

He nods. "I do not know how to heal you. We will have to visit Nacelles again."

"Can we just do it tomorrow? I really don't want to go anywhere else today." Truthfully, I just can't take it if the lich says I can't be fixed. I just want to sleep. The only blessing in today thus far is that my mom is nowhere to be seen. I'll introduce her to Maxx later.

"Very well," Maxx replies. "I will return to Father Moss, if you have no objections. He is quite knowledgeable and I am not familiar enough with your world to navigate it effectively."

It's stupid, but I feel like he's abandoning me. "No, go," I say, instead of telling him what I really want to do is curl up with him by my side. "You'll come back tomorrow, right?"

He nods. "I shall be here first thing in the morning."

"Thanks, Maxx." I wait until he transports himself out, and then flop down on the couch. All this emotional crap that's been happening lately sucks. All I want to do is sleep it off, much like a hangover. My eyes drift shut and then the dreaming begins.

It starts out the same as before; Andrew and I walking on the pier in Savannah, him inviting me to walk in the sand, my agreeing. But then it kinda goes wonky, and I'm sitting at The Blood Bank, watching Ink dance with Lorii the banshee. They're both graceful and beautiful and all I can think about is how I want to crack open their heads like watermelons to get at their brains.

I sit bolt upright, my heart slamming against my ribcage. Crap. Not another dream. I glance at the clock. What felt like a few minutes was, in reality, a few hours, but now I'm too scared to go back to sleep. I shed the nasty Hello Kitty sweatshirt in favor of a bright pink, long sleeve silk button down shirt and trade out my jeans for a clean pair. Just the act of changing my clothes helps push the dream to the back of my mind where it belongs. After all, I'm not a monster. I'm only someone who has to eat raw brains. Forever. I sigh. It sounds totally ridiculous, even in my own head. At this point, I realize I'm totally awake. I might as well do something, but I have no idea what. I can't drive a stick with only one arm, so that means driving anywhere is out, and, unless I want to get stared at, so is riding the MARTA transit system. I grab the phone and call Lydia. Might as well find out what exactly my punishment from Father Moss entails.

She answers just as I'm about to hang up. "Yes, how can I help you?"

"Uhhh, Lydia, it's me. Isis," I say lamely. "I, ummm...can we talk about the Komodo dragon thing?"

"She isn't a thing, Isis." Her voice goes flat. "The half's name is Ra'kul. Use it."

"I don't know if Father Moss told you, but I'm supposed to help you with her..." I trail off, feeling awkward beyond belief.

She sighs. I don't know if that's good or bad until she speaks. "I was about to go down to Ra'kul to see the extent of her injuries. How long will it take you to get here?"

"Ummm...small problem...I have no way there without Maxx." And without my arm, but I have no idea what Maxx did with it after our ill-fated walk.

"He's in the cemetery...do you want me to ask him to come get you?"

I shake my head, then realize she can't see me. That's me, brilliant as usual. "No, I don't want to bother him while he's talking to Father Moss."

"Father Moss is in his office," Lydia corrects me. "I'll send Maxx." She hangs up before I can say anything else.

Huh. I wonder why Maxx is wandering around the cemetery. Then again, it's not really any of my business. Maybe he found more headstones. Who knows.

I don't feel anything weird; no air bendy-ness or anything. But Maxx comes trotting out of my bedroom.

"Seriously, Maxx? My *bedroom*? Couldn't you have warped in somewhere more appropriate, like the living room?" I greet him with my hands...hand...on my hip.

He blinks at me, looking every inch like a totally innocent Doberman. "I do not see the issue. Would you rather I used your mother's bedroom? She is in there, by the way, fast asleep. Is she ill?"

"No, it's probably stress and more jet lag. Let's just go."

He doesn't say anything, doesn't even tell me to close my eyes. So I watch the air shiver around us and it's like I'm seeing the earth breathe. A wave of nausea overwhelms me and I slam my eyes shut.

"What are you doing?" Lydia's question makes me realize we've arrived in the church.

I open my eyes. Correction. We're not in the church. We're exactly where I don't want to be; standing in front of the door of doom. "Are you sure we have to go down there?" Now that I'm faced with it, I'm really wondering why I called Lydia. I mean, I know I need to do this to appease Father Moss...but I also know I really don't want to.

Lydia counters my question with one of her own. "Do you want to come back to church?" She holds up a hand when I open my mouth. "Don't be so quick to answer, Isis. You have shown everyone here that you have no real desire to fit in, to embrace a new family. None of us can help you find Andrew. We all have our own problems. So why come back here?"

My initial reaction is to say I'm not sure. I mean, on the one hand, it's been really cool to be able to bring a Tupperware full of brains and not have a single person blink twice at the idea. But answering the question with 'yes' means I'm accepting that I can't revert; that I can't possibly be human again, and I'm not sure I'm ready to do that. I'm not sure I'm ready to live a half-life.

"If I may add something?" Maxx asks. "This is not a question she needs to answer immediately. Let her do her penance; the answer will come to her as she works with Ra'kul."

Part of me wants to protest that I'm *right* here. They don't need to talk around me. But maybe it's better if I don't say anything at all. I suspect Maxx may be right. I need to make sure I think more and react less. In short, it's time to grow up.

The latch turns easily under Lydia's hand. She glances back at me. "Are you ready?"

Gee, why does she ask all the tough questions? I shake my head even as I walk forward. "Not particularly, but it doesn't really matter, does it? It's the right thing to do."

She nods and smiles at me. Step one on the road to redemption, check.

Thirty:

...Could be Worse.

The hissing starts as soon as Lydia shuts the door.

"Are you sure this is safe?" I ask nervously. I'd feel a lot better about the whole thing if Maxx was here, but he opted to go back to the cemetery. He said he found an interesting tomb to investigate, but I'm not sure I believe him.

"No, I'm quite sure this *isn't* safe," Lydia says. "But Ra'kul is in pain, and I can help her."

I reach out and put my hand on her arm. "Lydia, do you think I'm a horrible person?"

She doesn't answer right away, which makes me feel like crap. *And* like a horrible person.

"I think you're trying to find your way," she says delicately. "But honestly, Isis, it's time to decide what direction you want your life to take. Everyone in that church would like you if you gave them half a chance." She pauses briefly before continuing, "Well, maybe not Noelle, but everyone else."

I laugh. She's definitely got her daughter pegged.

"Right now most of the church sees you as a troublemaker; first the fight with Noelle, then what happened to Ra'kul. Quite frankly, you're a walking disaster."

That's pretty brutal. But it's also pretty true. "I didn't start the fight with Noelle," I protest.

Lydia starts walking again and I follow, about a heartbeat behind her. "Yeah, you did," she throws over her shoulder. "But you could have ended it, and you didn't. You chose to fight."

"Is that what you would've done? Walked away?" I feel like I'm walking in one of those round seashells, heading toward the center with no real sense of where exactly I am.

The witch shrugs. "I'm a peacemaker by nature."

Which really doesn't answer the question, but before I can say anything else, I hear what I assume is Ra'kul, clicking her way up the hall towards us. Wonderful. I swallow. "Is she going to attack us?"

Lydia shakes her head. "Doubtful. Maxx hurt her very badly. I can hear it in her walk."

I tilt my head but honestly, all I can hear is the same frightening scraping sound I heard the last time I was down here. It's not at all reassuring.

"So what are we supposed to do?" I can't imagine the half sitting still while we slather her in lotions and potions, but what do I know? I'm just the resident brain eater.

"Take a few steps back," Lydia cautioned. "Give me a chance to talk to her first. She might see you as a threat."

Yeah. I definitely don't want *that* to happen. It's not that I don't trust Lydia to be able to handle whatever Ra'kul does; it's just that...I don't trust Lydia to be able to handle whatever Ra'kul does. Lydia might be a witch, but she's still pretty human looking to me, where the half-Komodo only sort of looks human. If this was a brewing fight, I'd be putting money on the dragon.

"Ra'kul," Lydia's voice is low and hypnotic. "You remember me, right? I've come down here before, with Father Moss."

The hissing slows, as do the clicking sounds on the granite floor.

"That's right," the witch continues. "There's no need to attack. We're not here to hurt you; we're here to help." She steps forward. "Will you let us help you?"

"Uhhhhhsssss?..."

The nearly human sound scares me more than almost anything else. I actually stop breathing for a minute, waiting for her to say more, but it doesn't happen.

Lydia seems to understand her just fine, though. "The half-zombie is here as well."

The hissing becomes a ferocious and sustained growl. I didn't even know lizards could make that sound. I guess I'm not high on her list of acceptable halves. Not that I blame her. After all, what Maxx did to her is totally my fault.

"Uhhh...I'm here to help, Ra'kul." I don't know if what I'm saying makes a difference, but she doesn't growl again, which makes me happy. "I'm really sorry you got burned." Surprisingly enough, I find that I mean it. I *am* sorry. The half-Komodo's life has *got* to suck on the best of days, and I certainly haven't helped matters any.

Lydia must see something in my face, because she gestures me forward to walk by her side. "We're going to come down to you, Ra'kul. Is that all right?"

Ra'kul starts hissing again. Good night, it's got to be seriously messed up to not be able to communicate. I can't even imagine.

"So how're we going to heal her, anyway?"

"We can't heal her," Lydia says. "The best I can do is cast a spell to calm her, take an inventory of her burns, and apply a salve."

So...we *are* going to coat her in lotions and

potions. "Then what am I doing here, other than fulfilling Father Moss' edict?"

"You will coat her in the salve, as necessary."

Oh. Gee. Thanks. My sarcasm rises to the surface, ready to blurt something wildly inappropriate. I pause and think better of it as I remember the extent of Ra'kul's burns. She's got to be a world of pain. "All right," I say humbly.

It doesn't take us very long to reach Ra'kul. The half-Komodo is crouched against a wall, staring at us out of those fabulous gold eyes. Lydia stops around five feet away and I come to a halt behind her. I'm not taking any chances on the half-monster's forgiving nature, especially once I see the bits of black skin flaking off her in chunks.

"This is Isis," Lydia introduces me. "She's the one responsible for your wounds."

Seriously? Did she just tell a monster capable of killing me that I was the one who got her massively injured? What on earth... "It was an accident," I start to babble. "I just wanted to see you...to know you really existed..." That I'm not alone in being a freak, but that's not really true. There are a whole group of people upstairs who are just as freaky as I am, if not more so.

Ra'kul tilts her head, as though listening.

"I really didn't mean to scare you..." I finally trail off. "And I really *do* want to help."

The half-Komodo nods slowly. Now that she's not busily attacking, I can see that she's more...human...than I originally thought.

"Here," Lydia hands me a jar with some absolutely yucky looking greenish purple gunk in it. "Coat every part of her that's black in this."

I squat down, putting the jar between my knees so I can open it. When I do, I'm pleasantly surprised.

ONE FOOT IN THE GRAVE

It doesn't smell to High Heaven, which is exactly what I was expecting. Instead, it smells like eucalyptus and lavender. Not great, but certainly not disgusting. I stick my hand into the jar and draw it out covered in goop. Yay?

Ra'kul's tongue flicks in and out. I glance over at Lydia, unsure what to do next. "Should I approach her?"

The witch shakes her head. "No. Let her approach you."

I swallow, but stand my ground. Sure enough, the half-Komodo slowly climbs to her feet and steps toward me, one hand outstretched as though to touch mine. And suddenly, like a light bulb has gone off in my head, I see her, and myself, and all the other halves, as what they truly are. Not half-monsters at all, but half-human.

Who says I can't learn?

Thirty-One:

Zombie, Heal Thyself.

"I'm woken up the next morning by my mom's voice, calling to me from the living room. "Isis Blue Monroe, why is there a *dog* on our couch?"

If my heart beat normally, it'd be racing. "I'm coming, Mom!" I scramble out of bed, into the same clothes I wore yesterday, and hustle out my door. Maxx must be normal sized, or my mom'd be screaming bloody murder. That's something to be grateful for. And for the fact that he's obviously not talking, because I'm pretty sure that'd send her over the edge, too.

"You *know* we're not allowed to have pets," she greets me.

"Yes, ma'am, but he's not exactly a pet."

Maxx lowers one eyelid in a supremely lazy wink.

"Isis, what is he doing *here*?"

I glance at Maxx.

"He can't answer for you," she snaps.

And that's when it happens.

"Actually," Maxx clears his throat. "I can answer for myself."

My mom screams and collapses into a heap.

"Mom!" It takes me two steps to reach her, and I'm still seconds behind Maxx, who is licking her in the face. How very…dog-like.

My mom comes to sputtering. "What—get off me!" She pushes Maxx away. "Isis, what the *hell* is going on?"

It's the first time in forever since I've heard my mom swear.

Maxx's ears lay flat against his head. "I am sorry for startling you," he begins, but my mom's hearing none of it.

"I don't know what you're doing here, but you need to *get out* of my apartment."

"Mom, he's a friend, it's okay."

She sits up and glares at me from the floor. "It's a talking dog, Isis. That's nothing close to okay!"

I laugh and she glares harder. "It's *not* funny, young lady."

"Actually, Mom, it pretty much is. This *is* my reality. I'm Maxx sitting."

"There's no way we can have a dog here, especially not a Saint Bernard. People will notice and the landlord'll be notified."

I kneel down at her feet, and try to take her face in my hands. When she sees my empty sleeve, she starts to cry. "Oh, Isis, what now?"

"It's just my arm, Mom. It's totally fixable, I promise. As for Maxx, he's not exactly a dog."

She reaches up and does what I want to; she wipes the tears off her own cheeks. "Then what is he?"

"I am a hell-hound," Maxx announces. "Would it help you accept my existence if I changed shape?"

My mom smiles weakly. "I don't know if anything you did would help me accept all the changes I've been forced to deal with lately."

"I did not expect you to find me on the couch," Maxx says. "I expected Isis to be awake before you. She said you were suffering from jet lag." He cocks his head to one side. "Do you need to sleep more?"

She shakes her head. "I'm fine, thanks."

"Ummm...Maxx, where'd you put my arm?"

"It is on your dresser," the hell hound replies. "I was not sure where you wanted it."

"I'll be right back, then we can go," I say. I leave him in the living room, grab my arm off my dresser and hightail it back.

"Excuse me, but where, exactly, are you going?" My mom hasn't bothered getting up from her place on the floor.

"I'm going back to the club, Mom. I've got to get my arm put back on." I have no idea what I'll do if Nacelles can't fix it, but I'll cross that bridge if it happens.

"Are you ready?" Maxx's going to move us from this reality straight to Nacelles. I'm not sure I'm thrilled with the idea, but neither do I want to be stopped by the cops because I'm carrying an unattached arm. Decisions, decisions.

"Yes, no, I don't—" before I can finish my sentence, my body begins to vibrate at a low frequency. It starts at my toes and moves its way up into my chest and finally my head. I shut my eyes to try and dislodge the weird sensation, and that's when the air bends.

Just like that we're standing in front of Tucker the revenant, guarding The Blood Bank lair.

It frowns. "I know you. You're 'not food.'"

It's super flattering to be remembered. "Isis. My name is Isis."

"Tucker," Maxx says.

The six foot tall creature glances down to meet Maxx's gold eyes. "Maxx," it replies. "You are small."

"I am smaller, yes. We have come to see Nacelles." I'm not sure why Maxx didn't zap us straight to the lich, but I assume he knows what he's doing.

"He is not available." The revenant says. Those massive metal beams seated on the floor the last time I was down here are across the door. The club is definitely closed.

"Look, Tucker," I say, stepping forward. The creature's nostrils flare. I remember what he eats and what I'm holding in my one remaining, attached, arm. I step backward. "I need to get in and see Nacelles. Will you help me, or not?"

He tilts his head sideways while he considers me. "Did you bring food?"

I hide my arm, both arms, behind my back. "Uhhh...no, I didn't, sorry. But I'll bring you something next time I come, I promise." I swallow hard. I don't want to ask the next question, but I do anyway. "What kind of meat do you like?" As long as he doesn't say 'human', I'm good. I can handle this.

"Steak is good." Tucker says.

Whew. I can do raw cow. "Okay, I'll bring you a nice steak next time if you'll let us in now. Sound fair?"

"Kobe beef is better," the revenant's tone is hopeful.

Okay, even I know Kobe beef is so out of the realm of my pocketbook it's laughable. "I can't afford that, but I might be able to swing a nice rib eye from the Farmer's Market."

"That's acceptable." The moldering corpse turns, unbars the door and steps aside so we can walk through.

All the lights are on and chairs are stacked on top of tables. There are a lot more of them than I saw before, but then again, the lighting pretty much sucked.

Maxx trots across the floor, his toenails digging into the cinnamon colored carpet. I follow him over to the hidden door.

"Put your hand against the wall," the hell hound instructs.

I remember Ink doing the same thing. I echo what she did, and the door slides open.

"Follow me," Maxx says. "I do not know if Nacelles has released the ghouls."

I remember the ghoul from my first visit to the club, and I cling to Maxx. There's no way I'm risking my life. The corridor is lit, but not well. I can't help but wonder where Maxx is taking us, because as far as I can tell, there's no end in sight.

A tall, thin man dressed in a very familiar suit appears out of the darkness. "Maxx, you've returned." A line of drool snakes down the corner of his mouth and drips off his chin. "And you brought a snack."

"Back off, she is not a snack." Maxx's lips curl up.

The man's eyes flash red. I back up further. I do not want to be between Maxx and anything he's pissed at. Not after the half-Komodo incident, anyway. I know better. He doesn't look pleased at the ghoul standing between us and where he wants us to be.

"Nacelles Caldmer allows us the run of his domain after club hours," the ghoul states. "Any flesh here is ours to consume by right."

The fur on Maxx's back stands to full attention and smoke begins to rise. It's odd to see on a Saint Bernard. "Do not try me, undead. You know I will win."

The certainty in his voice is chilling. I hope the ghoul backs down because I really don't want to see him go all demonic again.

A guttural growl emerges from the ghoul's throat but he takes a step backward, then another, all the while not taking his eyes off Maxx.

"Inform your master we are here," Maxx says. The smoke from his fur continues to rise toward the ceiling, as thick as mist.

"You and I are not finished," the ghoul's voice echoes even as he continues to back down the hall until he's out of sight.

Maxx huffs. "What a stupid creature. It thinks it is superior because it has a human form."

"It wanted to eat me," I state.

He glances at me. "Well, yes. That *is* what ghouls do."

"Does anything here not eat people?"

"I do not." Maxx says.

It's the perfect time to ask. "What do you eat, then?"

"I eat whatever I wish."

"What about souls?"

"My hell hounds do not eat souls," Nacelles steps out of the shadows in front of us.

I squeak.

The lich raises one eyebrow. "Isis, I didn't expect to see you here again." He gazes at the arm in my hand. "Ahhh...I see what the problem is."

I step forward. "Can you fix it?"

"You haven't tried healing yourself yet?" The lich asks.

I blink in astonishment. "I can do that?"

"I don't know what you can or cannot do," Nacelles replies. "Your essence and Ink's mixed. That could produce some interesting side effects. Tell me, have you noticed any strange abilities?"

"Ink can't mesmerize me. And I can keep up with

Maxx when he runs in and out of reality." I remember the fight with Noelle. "Oh, and I threw a half-fae into a wall by accident, but I think that was because of Andrew, not Ink."

"Did you now? Those are significant effects, but not all of them are vampire based. You are quite interesting." The lich's voice is thoughtful. "Come in to my chambers and we can experiment." He turns his attention to Maxx. "Are you hungry?"

"I am," the hell hound replies.

"What would you like to eat?" Nacelles asks.

Maxx's tail begins to thump and the long strings of drool dripping from his mouth sizzle as they meet the floor at his paws. "I want chicken!"

"Ummm...I introduced him to KFC," I say. "I hope that's okay."

The near skeleton shrugs bony shoulders. "It's his palate. If he wants to eat chicken, he can."

Maxx grins at me before vanishing.

Nacelles gestures in a 'come here' way. "Come. Let's see what other abilities you might have."

Thirty-Two:

Ouch, That Kinda Hurts!

Nacelles' chamber isn't what I think a monster lair should look like. I'm not even sure what I'm supposed to expect, but certainly not the warmth and light I find. The same purple couch he summoned before stands against the far wall and scattered cushions litter the carpeted floor. It looks more like the inside of a genie's bottle than anything else.

"Now, how did this injury happen?" Nacelles takes my arm from me and peers at the torn shoulder.

"It was an accident." I'm loath to name the hell hound, though I'm not sure why. Nacelles likes him, and I'm pretty sure Maxx wasn't lying when he said he chose to stay with the lich.

He looks at me. "Maxx doesn't always remember his own strength."

So much for keeping the cause of my accident a secret. "It really was an accident," I repeat. "He saw a kitten."

"I never did get around to introducing him to kittens," Nacelles muses. "Take off your shirt."

"Ummm...*excuse* me?"

"I have no designs on your zombiefied body, Isis," the lich says. "I need to see the wound itself and your long sleeved blouse, while beautiful, won't allow me to do that."

"Turn around," I demand. "This is embarrassing enough."

"Here, wear this." Nacelles reaches into thin air and pulls out a sleeveless, zipper up top. It matches the couch. What an awesome color. I'll look like an eggplant, but I guess it's better than the alternative. I catch the top and wait until the lich turns his back. It doesn't take me long to undo the buttons on the shirt I'm currently wearing, shed it, and put the new one on.

"Okay, I'm ready."

Nacelles turns around. "The color suits you."

Right now, I don't much care. I just want my arm back on. "So how do you plan on fixing me, anyway?"

"I don't," Nacelles says. "I can't heal you, Isis."

The bluntness of it hurts.

"Then what am I even *doing* here?"

"Good question," the lich replies. He strolls over to me and peers at my empty socket. It's weird.

"I thought we could experiment on you, but I wouldn't know where to begin. You're an unusual case-study. Are you sure you don't just want to use crazy glue or screws?"

"I'm positive," I say. "I've glued myself and screwed...ummm...enough, thanks."

"The only thing I can think of is to self-heal," Nacelles says. "You said you've never tried it before. Do you feel comfortable enough to try it now?"

I shrug. "Sure, why not?" I grimace. "It can't hurt, right? What do I do?"

"Vampires don't need to do anything," the lich muses. "But you are only half-vampire in spirit. Try putting the arm up to your empty socket. Maybe the muscles will knit together of their own accord."

I take my arm back and do what he says. I can't help but picture tendrils of ligaments, reaching out like vines to grab the arm and pull it close.

"Is it working?" I drop my arm and it falls with a thump to the ground. Nope.

Nacelles is nice enough to retrieve it and hand it back to me. "Hmmm...let's try this instead. Close your eyes and visualize the arm adhering to your shoulder, looking exactly like it used to be."

It sounds simple enough. I give it a shot. And the world turns purple. My insides are doing their level best to crawl out through my belly button. I can barely breathe. I curl into a ball, hugging my knees to my chest and moaning low in my throat. I'm pretty sure Nacelles is trying to talk to me, but I can't hear anything beyond the roaring in my ears. It feels like hours before I can unkink and open my eyes. A black fuzzy blur greets me. A *huge* black fuzzy blur, which means Maxx is back to his normal size.

"Isisss," The familiar voice makes me smile. Well, grimace. I want it to be a smile, but I can't quite manage it.

"Did—" I growl the first word so I clear my throat and try again. "Did it work?"

"You have an arm," Nacelles says.

"But did it work? Is it attached?" I'm still shaky; definitely not strong enough to stand upright, so I just focus on, well, focusing.

"It is as it was," Maxx replies. "Though I disapprove of what you had to do."

I laugh at the hell hound's indignation. "Yeah, I do, too." His face comes more into focus. "Did you enjoy your chicken?"

His tail starts to wag, which is answer enough, but he speaks anyway. "Yes, it was good. I think it is now my favorite food."

I'm not sure I want to know how much chicken a dog the size of a full grown brahma bull has to eat.

Instead I rotate my left shoulder. It feels...tender...but not sore. I hope I never have to go through something like that healing again. I smile and flex my wrist.

"Does this mean I can heal all the time?" Not that I want to, because, seriously, owww. But if my leg decides it needs to be unattached or something, it'll be a handy skill to have. Once I sound proof the apartment, that is. I'm pretty sure the old ladies would call the police in a New York minute if they heard me screaming and moaning. Plus there's my mom. She might have something to say about it, too.

"It should," the lich says. "But I wouldn't try it unless it was crucial. Screws and glue should work just fine for the little things."

I agree. The less I have to deal with, the better. Life's getting complicated enough without adding 'voluntary pain' to the list. "So why didn't I feel anything when Maxx pulled my arm off?"

Nacelles shrugs. "I have no idea. I hate to tell you, Isis, but you're a giant 'who knows'. You'd probably have to travel to Louisiana and speak to some of the voodoo queens to get all the answers you're looking for."

Yeah. That's not going to happen. I'm not that committed to knowing, honestly.

I take a cab home. I'm just plain worn out. My body's sure it's been running on fumes for miles and all the brains in the world aren't helping me stay full. I need a break. Honestly, I'd rather be at the church's cemetery. There's something soothing about being surrounded by dead people who don't want anything from me, but I'm not sure Father Moss knows I helped Ra'kul yet. I'm not ready to face his possible wrath. Honestly, I feel totally overwhelmed. So of course there's just one person I feel even remotely like talking to.

"Isis, can I come in?"

Before I can answer, the doorknob to my bedroom turns and just like that my mom's here.

"Oh, Isis, really? Purple? You look like an eggplant," are the first words out of her mouth once she actually sees me.

I guess that's what I get for letting a lich dress me.

"What's wrong?" She kicks off her shoes and joins me on the bed, legs curled under her.

"Nothing. Everything. I don't know. I can't find Andrew and it all just sucks."

"Mama Llama likes no drama," she winks at me, and then laughs.

Good grief, she must've just come from her reading stint at the library.

"Mom, seriously? You've been reading the kids those Llama books again, haven't you?"

"Yes, they're adorable. Now hush, and tell me whose rear I need to kick."

And that pretty much sums up the relationship with my mom. All practicality and business under that 'Look at me, I'm going to name my kid 'Isis' because it's the name of a goddess, and oh! Let's all make daisy chains and look for Little Bunny Foo-Foo!' exterior. I love her, though. After all, she crazy glued my mouth. You can't get much more supportive than that.

"It's everything," I sigh. "The date with Daniel was a disaster, kind of, even though I met a really nice vampire and a lich who's not so bad, really. And I still have no idea where Andrew is, but I met Maxx, and he helped me see a really messed up half Komodo dragon under the church who wanted to eat me, but that turned out okay, too, because I'm still alive." Yeah. I just open my mouth and it all comes gushing out, like a flood I can't control.

She holds up one hand to stop me. "Wait. Just...wait. I'm not even sure where to start asking all the questions I have."

I snicker first, then sigh one of those sighs that comes up from the depths of my soul. "That's okay. I'd have no idea where to start answering them. I don't even know if I *can*. Honestly, Mom, everything has been so messed up lately. I mean, I thought Andrew would be able to cure me, but what if he can't? Everyone keeps telling me there's no way. What if I'm stuck like this forever?"

"From what you've told me, you're not the only one, Isis. Besides, what's really different about your life now, other than eating brains?"

Huh. That's the one question I haven't really considered. *Is* my life so different from what it used to be? I actually have more friends...well...acquaintances, really, but they *could* be friends if I tried. Even Noelle might someday fall into that category.

"Nothing, I guess," I admit. "But it's *weird*, Mom."

It's her turn to laugh. "Weirder than being raised in a commune, or learning how to grow your own food and sew your own clothing? Honey, you were *made* for weird. Out of all the people in this world, you can handle this."

I nod, actually starting to believe it at least a little bit.

"So now that we've established that much, tell me everything else. I'm here for you, Isis."

"Albin's pretty cool," I say. "He's the half werewolf whose dad is a vet; he gets along really well with Maxx. And there's Lydia, the Salem witch. You met her already, remember? She's the mentor of us all."

"That doesn't sound like so bad a life." She shifts so she's no longer sitting on her feet. They must be falling asleep.

"I've messed up," I say. "I went and saw the half-Komodo and she got injured. It was totally my fault."

"Do no harm, Isis."

"That's a Wiccan belief." And even then, she kind of mangled it. She raises one thin eyebrow at me. My mom may be hippie in spirit and dress, but she grooms herself immaculately. "That doesn't make it untrue."

I'm not going to argue it. There's really no point. Besides, she's right. Luckily, I *did* try to make it right. I just hope Father Moss sees that.

Mom glances at her watch, shaking her bangles away from the face so she can read it. "I hate to cut and run, baby, but I have an appointment with some farmers. They're conducting a seminar on upside down growing, and I don't want to be late."

I'm sure there's a huge market for growing food upside down, but I don't know where. Or why. I stifle my laughter and pull her close for a hug. "Thanks, Mom. I guess I just needed a dose of common sense."

"That's what I'm here for." She slips her sandals back on and waves at me.

The door shuts behind her with a click and I realize I actually *do* feel better. A lot better. My mom is awesome. Now I'm ready for a day of watching Netflix and munching on brains. Eh. It might not be the life I envisioned, but at least I'm not a half-Komodo dragon who lives in the basement of a church, right?

Thirty-Three:

Help! I Need Somebody.

My landline rings early the next morning, and I mean early. I think even the birds are still asleep. I know I am as I scramble for the stupid thing, miss the end table and wind up on the floor, the phone lying next to me. Ugh. I grab it and bring it up to my ear.

"Hrug?" It's definitely not English and the voice on the other end sounds confused.

"Isis, is that you? It's Andrew."

I swipe my hand across my face in a vain attempt to clear away the nighttime cobwebs, not sure I heard correctly. "Excuse me?"

"It's Andrew." His voice is both rushed *and* hushed. "I really need to talk to you, Isis."

"You're out of your mind. There's no way I'm talking to you." I hang up.

The phone immediately begins to ring again. I snatch it up out of the cradle. "Seriously? Quit calling! You're going to wake up my mom."

"Then don't hang up on—"

I click the receiver down and unplug the cord attaching it to the wall. Unfortunately, my cell starts buzzing. I snatch it up and press the green 'talk' button. "Andrew," I growl, "I mean it. Stop. Calling. Me."

"Isis, you don't understand. They're hunting me."

That gets my attention. "Who're hunting you?"

"I don't *know*," he whispers. "But I think they want to kill me. Isis, please...didn't you get my letter?"

He sounds absolutely panicked, and my sluggishly beating heart melts just a tiny bit. "I did," I admit. "But you're still a jerk." My words don't have as much heat behind them as I might wish.

"I just loved you," he whispers.

"I'm half a zombie," I whisper back, mindful of my mom, sleeping soundly in the bed across the hall. "I had a *life*, Andrew. And you totally screwed that up."

"Look, I really need to talk to you. In person. Will you meet me?"

I tap my index finger on the bedspread. "Not alone," I finally say.

"Come to the church."

"The *church*? What're *you* doing at the church?"

"Hiding. Please, Isis."

I haul myself up off the floor and run my free hand through my hair. "I'll be there within the hour, Andrew." I click the phone off. I have no idea why I'm willing to help Andrew, but I am. It doesn't take me long to stagger to the bathroom, splash cold water on my face and cram myself into a pair of old jeans and a t-shirt. I roll my healed shoulder forward to make sure it won't fall off. Nope, I'm good to go. I grab my apartment keys and hurry out the front door, stuffing my cell into my front pocket. The faster I reach the church, the better I'll feel. I press the button for the elevator, grateful beyond belief that I'm alone. Thankfully, the elevator arrives on time, the door swooshes open and I step inside.

And stagger as my feet sink into damp soil. Where the heck did the dirt come from? In the split second it takes for the thought to form, the blue black of an early morning hits me full in the face. I blink my bone dry eyes, wishing once again for some blasted tears. My vision finally clears and I know where I am. Callie mews at me from her perch atop a stone angel's head. Yeah. I'm in the church cemetery. I just have no idea how I got here.

"Isisss, I did not know you could move through reality."

I'm surprised, but happy, to see Maxx. "I thought you were staying with Nacelles."

"I enjoy it here," the hell hound says. "And this is a solution which works for all of us, as I cannot stay at your apartment. Besides, Father Moss has chicken."

Of course he does. "Maxx, how did I get here?"

The big dog sneezes and my hair blows back in the wind he creates. "I already told you, Isis. You moved through reality."

"What do you mean?"

"What were you thinking about before you arrived?" He asks.

"That the faster I got to church, the..." my voice trails off. "Are you telling me I can teleport at will?" I have brief images of just appearing wherever I want, whenever I want. It would make sitting in traffic on Spaghetti Junction a thing of the past. How cool is that?

"Not exactly," Maxx says. "But the idea is similar. For instance, if you tried to teleport now, I doubt you would succeed. I believe it is based on the strength of your need, rather than the strength of your desire."

I frown. "I didn't know vampires could do that."

"In ancient times vampires were thought to be able to transform into bats," the hell-hound replies. "In reality, they simply relocated from one place to another. Since in those times, vampires chose to inhabit the same areas as bats, the assumption was a logical one."

Interesting. "So Ink gave me this ability?"

"Very likely," Maxx says. "She *is* quite old."

"But I can teleport?"

"Only when the need is great, it appears."

Well, darn, so much for no traffic travelling. "I'm here to – to speak to someone, Maxx."

"Ah, yes. Your errant boyfriend. The kitten you left here found him." Father Moss lands with a significant thump on the ground next to the hell hound.

"Hello, Isis." I hear Andrew from behind the stone angel Callie is perched on. "I'm glad you came."

Thirty-Four:

Rut-Roh.

Hearing him is like pouring salt on an open wound. I lose my ever-lovin' mind and try to claw my way past Maxx, but the stupid hell hound refuses to budge and pushing on him is like trying to move a mountain. "Maxx, move your carcass!"

"I cannot do that," Maxx replies. "That would not be a wise course of action for either of us."

"I'm not going to kill him," I growl. I attempt to get around Maxx, but he stands his ground. Who decided hell hounds need to be the size of ginormous cows, anyway?

"Your actions tell me otherwise." The hell hound refuses to move.

The vampire peers around the angel's head. "You said you'd talk to me."

"Look, I don't even know why you're *here*. Say what you have to say. Oh, and Andrew? Keep it short."

"I needed somewhere to go," my ex admits. "I'm not old enough for anyone to take me seriously and too old to be someone's protégé."

I know I shouldn't feel sorry for him, I know I shouldn't, but I do. I guess I'm not all that hard-hearted, after all. And he looks like crap. Those gorgeous black ringlets I love so much are dull and lifeless and his teeth are no longer white, but starting to yellow. "What's wrong with you?"

"I'm being hunted, like I said. I haven't been able to eat properly."

I blink. "You mean you have to drink blood to look good?"

"And from what I've heard, you have to eat raw brains," he snaps. "What's your point, Isis?"

"You *changed* me." I finally say it out loud, and the unspoken accusation that's been lodged in my chest just dissolves like magic.

"You're right. I changed you. But the monsters changed me, too; they changed *both* of us."

My anger at him kind of goes away at that point. I mean, how can I stay mad at a guy who's just as messed up as I am? We are what we are. I guess it shows on my face because he comes out from behind the angel and sits, cross-legged, in front of Maxx. The hell hound sinks to the ground and closes his eyes. I guess as far as he's concerned, the danger's over.

"Oh, Andrew," I say. "Now *we're* technically the monsters."

Andrew nods. "I know. This hasn't been easy for me, Isis. And now it's even less easy. What'm I going to do? If I can't eat, I'll die. I'm not like you. I *will* starve to death. Eventually."

I bite my lip. "I know someone who might be able to help you."

"You do? Awesome!" He grins at me and I remember how he used to look when I first met him. Maybe his drinking blood to regain some of those good looks isn't such a horrible idea, after all.

"Have you ever been to a club called The Blood Bank?"

"Sure," he says. "Plenty of times, why?"

"Let me check something out first. I'll get back to

you in a couple of days, okay?" Speaking of days, I glance up at the sky. "Andrew, look."

"Yeah?" He follows my line of sight. "Oh, don't worry; I can feel it right before the sun rises. I've got a few minutes still."

"The sky is turning blue," I point out.

Maxx sneezes and Father Moss snickers, proving that he's been listening to our entire conversation.

"The sky is always blue," Maxx points out. Trust him to point out the obvious.

"That's not what I meant," I say. "I just...I don't want him to burst into flames."

Andrew smiles at me and my heart remembers, *again*, how cute he is. "I'm touched. But you're right; it's time to go. Can I still stay here? Or would you rather I leave?" He pushes himself off the ground and waits for my answer.

I remember he's got nowhere to go. He may be a full-blood, but he's like the rest of us. Worse than the rest of us, actually. We have homes. He doesn't. "Stay here," I say. "There's no reason for you to leave."

"Thanks, Isis. That's nice of you."

That's me, your friendly neighborhood zombie. I wait until he retreats back into the crypt before I turn to Maxx. "Is he going to be okay?" I ask. I don't know why I'm worried about him, but I kind of am. Maybe it's because, after meeting Ink, Tucker, and Nacelles, he's not all that frightening.

"Andrew can stay in the crypt for now, but he'll need to find his own road," Father Moss says. I'm surprised. He seems more compassionate than that. I guess my shock shows, because he continues. "You misunderstand me, Isis. Andrew doesn't belong here. He's not a half. He can have a family of vampires if he wants."

"And what if he doesn't want them?"

"Isis, this is none of your business," Maxx stretches before rising to his feet. "Nacelles can introduce Andrew to Ink. She is his family." He grins at me, a huge doggy smile. "As a matter of fact, I should introduce myself properly before he turns in. If you will excuse me…"

I don't know if I've ever met a creature with better manners than Maxx. I smile at him and he just…vanishes… presumably into the crypt. I almost wish I could be a fly on the wall for that conversation. It's bound to be an interesting one.

"Now that that's done, I have a couple of questions for you." Father Moss squats closer to the ground. "First of all, how did your meeting with Ra'kul go?"

"Oh. Ummm…so Lydia told you about that already?"

He nods. "She told me her perspective, but I'm interested in hearing yours, as well."

"I feel sorry for her," I say. "She's so…so…*human* underneath it all."

"I'm glad you're able to see that, Isis. I wasn't sure whether you'd be able to fit into our family until this point."

"So this means I can come back to church, right?"

"If that's what you want to do, yes."

I smile. "Thanks, Father Moss. I'm sorry I've been such a pain in the…rear."

He tilts his head to one side. "You do know you'll have to make peace with Andrew, don't you?"

"I kind of already have," I state. "I mean, I've pretty much forgiven him. After all, I'm almost positive he didn't want to bite me any more than I want to eat raw brains forever."

"That's very mature of you," the gargoyle says.

"Yeah, well, it happens." I'm really not all that great with compliments. In my opinion, there's no real way to accept them gracefully. 'Thanks,' sounds dismissive and anything else sounds kind of conceited. "You said you had another question," I prompt Father Moss to move on instead.

"How exactly did you get here? I know you didn't have enough time to come via the usual methods."

Oh. That. "I'm not sure," I say. "Maxx told me it's called translocation or moving through reality or something. Andrew called, said he wanted to meet me. I guess I was more worried about him than I thought. I got dressed, got into the elevator, and when I went to get out, I wound up in the cemetery."

"That's an interesting skill," the gargoyle snaps his wings open and shut. "And not one every vampire has, but Ink is quite old and maybe that explains it."

"That's what Maxx said. Do you think it's something I can use whenever I want to?" I seat myself on the ground next to him.

"Maybe once you're more practiced at it. You'd have to ask Ink about that." Father Moss admits. "I'm no expert when it comes to vampires."

I hide a yawn behind my palm. Today just started way too early for my comfort, and it's all Andrew's fault. Speaking of lemons…there's something I want to do, and there's only one person I trust to have my back. "Where's Noelle?"

"She's inside with Albin," Father Moss replies. "Yesterday was hard on him."

Poor Albin. "Is he okay?"

The old gargoyle nods. "His Great Dane has been stressed since Albin was turned. Last night was particularly bad, and Rufus snapped at him. Albin decided to spend the night here to give the poor creature some space."

I shudder. What a nightmare. My stomach starts to rumble. I don't have any brains with me, either. I sigh. When it rains, it pours. I get to my feet. "I've got to go," I say. "Breakfast calls."

"There are raw pork brains in the church refrigerator," Father Moss says. "I stocked them after your first visit."

"Ummmm...thanks," I'm surprised at his thoughtfulness, though I'm not sure why. "I guess I'll go get some, then. And, ummm...yeah," I trail off.

Father Moss laughs. "Go. Eat. I wouldn't want to keep you from your brains."

That's something I never, in my wildest dreams, imagined someone would ever say to me. This unlife is so weird, but I think I'm starting to get used to it.

Thirty-Five:

Hi, Ho, Hi, Ho. It's off to the Lich We Go!

I scrape the last of the brains out of the plastic container with a spoon. Noelle's sitting across from me, her arms folded across her chest. I run my tongue over my teeth. I'm not used to eating in front of people and she's making me nervous. Albin is nowhere in sight.

"You're not the only one who screwed up by going under the church, you know."

I blink. "I'm not?"

"I'm pretty sure Albin's the only half who *hasn't* gone through that little side door. Father Moss uses that darn half Komodo as a lesson in obedience. I think he makes sure that particular cell door is built out of paper mache." She flashes me a quick smile. "You *are* the only one who took a hell hound, though. That was pretty smart. The rest of us just ran for our lives." She pauses for a minute before continuing. "Supposedly, there was an even more dangerous half under there in the 1800's – it even killed another half. A wendigo. It was really messy. Father Moss buried her in the cemetery."

I nod. That explains the headstone. "Did you all have to help Lydia heal Ra'kul afterward?"

She shakes her head. "Nah, you're the only one who's managed to injure her, to my knowledge."

"Well, that was more Maxx than me, but okay."

"You look rough," Noelle says. "You okay?"

"I've been dreaming about eating brains."

She just stares at me. "How's that a nightmare?"

I sigh. "They're human brains."

Her nose wrinkles up. "Ewww. Gross."

Yeah. You could say that. "It scares me," I say honestly.

"Talk to that creature you told us about...the one you met at the club."

I blink. The solution's so simple; I have no idea why I haven't thought of it sooner. Nacelles or his legion of undead club-goers might know something about brains. In fact, if they don't know, it probably doesn't exist.

I scoot my chair back from the old wooden table and stand up. "I'll go see him later."

"I'll go with you," Noelle makes an unexpected offer. "I've never met a lich before. Sounds like it might be interesting."

I decide to be blunt. "Why? You don't even like me." I take my bowl and spoon to the kitchen sink and turn on the faucet. Hot water pours out and I turn on the cold to balance out the steam I see rising from the sink.

"Someone needs to make sure you don't kill yourself," she answers. "And Father Moss would never forgive me if something happened down there."

"Yeah, okay. You can come with me." Trust has to start somewhere, right? I frown. "Does Nacelles sleep during the day?" Were liches even related to vampires? I have no idea.

Noelle shrugs.

I add dishwashing detergent to the now lukewarm water, turn off both taps and grab a sponge. Yeah, I'm more domestic now than I was when this whole mess started. It's a good skill to have, just in case I ever wind up with a boyfriend. I almost giggle at the idea. My heart hasn't healed from Andrew yet, and I'm not quite sure it ever will.

"What're you doing up so early?"

The half-fae shifts from foot to foot. I don't expect her to answer but she surprises me. "I have some abilities I can't explain well," she says. "They make sleeping through the night kind of problematic."

Huh. That's not an answer I thought I'd get. "You mean like the illusions?"

She mumbles something under her breath and I strain to hear her reply. "What'd you say?"

"Wait, I'll show you." Biting her lip, Noelle closes her eyes. I'm not sure what to expect, so I just watch her. Before long, she starts to hover. Like feet off the floor, around two feet up, the hem of the long dress she's wearing held in one clenched fist.

I blink. "You...fly?"

She shakes her head. "No. I hover. Father Moss is teaching me how to control it, but I still tend to float at night. I've bumped against the ceiling more than once."

Yikes. "What do you do all day?"

"Go to auditions when I can, teach dance when I can't." She smiles. "It's not so bad. I love kids and at Christmas time I take a few of the little girls to see the behind-the-scenes stuff when The Nutcracker comes to The Fox. They love it."

I wouldn't have pegged Noelle to be so...what's the word? Altruistic? It's kind of cool. I wish I had a passion like that. The only thing that's been keeping me going is the hunt for Andrew, and becoming human again. The whole revenge idea's pretty much fallen apart after our last conversation, though. I wonder if that makes me a sucker.

"So, let's go see this lich of yours," she says.

"Day's not getting any younger."

No, as a matter of fact, it's not. The sun is beating against the kitchen window like it's determined to pierce the stained glass and come inside. I've become such a night owl that a trip to The Blood Bank might be just what I need to wake up completely, odd as that sounds. I eye Noelle. The dress she's wearing is a blinding lime green. Maybe it will keep the ghouls confused long enough to reach Nacelles.

Father Moss is nice enough to call us a cab from the church. I guess he's got one on retainer for emergencies because I overhear him say 'I've got a pick-up', nod a reply and then hang up. And just like that we have a ride to The Blood Bank which doesn't cost us a dime. I don't remember the address, but the taxi driver gets us there, no problem.

"Didja need a pick-up, too?" The cabbie asks as we get out.

I pause with one foot still in the taxi. "Ummm...I have no idea." I look at Noelle. "Do we?"

She nods. "I'd think so, yeah. A couple of hours should do it."

"A'ight. Be outside at..." he glances down at his wrist. "Twelve. I'll be here."

"Thanks," I say, closing the back door. The huge bouncer, whatshisname, isn't on duty and the neon lights aren't lit, either. It looks pretty dismal in the light of day.

"This is where the lich lives?" Noelle asks.

"Not exactly." I pull at the club door, which doesn't open. What a shock. "He lives under the club."

"So how do you expect us to get inside? Got a key?"

I bite my lip. Hadn't really thought of that, darn it.

I'm so fixated on getting to Nacelles, I forgot to figure out how to actually get inside the locked building. "Ummm..."

Noelle rolls her eyes. "Seriously, Isis?" She reaches up into her hair and pulls out a bobby pin. Putting the ends in her mouth, she spits out what I assume are those weird plastic ends.

"Are you really going to pick the lock with a hair pin?" If the police come by, we're so screwed.

It takes her like a minute and a half to jimmy open the door. I slip inside, praying the ghouls aren't out. I don't hear anything weird, so I gesture to Noelle. She follows me and pulls the door closed. It doesn't take us long to reach the staircase.

"Do you know what a revenant is?" I ask her. I don't want to scare her, but she deserves to be warned. Tucker is, well...Tucker.

She shakes her head. "Is it like a ghost or something?"

"No." There's no easy way to say it. "He's a reanimated corpse that eats meat."

Her face is blank, so I elaborate. "Flesh, Noelle. He eats people."

The half-fae gasps. "And that's where you're taking us?"

"Tucker just mans the door to Nacelles. And he can control himself." I try to reassure her, but I'm not sure if it's the truth. The last time I was down here was with Maxx. Maybe the hell hound was the only thing keeping Tucker from chowing down. It's a sobering thought, but I try not to let the growing dread show on my face. It's pretty much too late to back down. I need answers.

Thirty-Six:

Experimentation is the Name of the Game.

"Tucker, we need to see Nacelles." I face the revenant head-on. "Is he here?"

"You promised me steak." His voice is flat.

Crap. I had. "You're right," I say, "but I don't eat steak anymore and I forgot to buy some."

"You promised me steak." His eyes are fixed on Noelle. If he thinks I'm giving the half-fae to him instead he's mistaken.

"She is not food." I use his own terminology against him.

"*You* are 'not food'. She is alive."

"I'm Isis," I say, not so patiently. "She's my friend, and she's not on the menu." I shrug when Noelle glances at me. It's easier to call her a friend than to explain 'frenemie' to a corpse.

"I require food."

Boy, he really does have a one track mind.

"It's super important," I plea. "How about taking two steaks next time?" Bargaining like this makes me feel like Wimpy of the old Popeye cartoons. 'I'll gladly pay you Tuesday for…' Sheesh! I assume Tucker's thinking about it because he doesn't say anything. After a long and agonizing minute, he pulls the door to Nacelles' hallway open and gestures us inside.

I release the air I don't have to breathe anymore. Now all that's left is the ghouls. And I really hope they're not roaming the halls in search of their next meal.

A phalanx of glowing golden eyes greets us as soon as we step through the door. Noelle turns around immediately, but it's too late. Tucker's already bolted us in.

"They're the hell hounds," I whisper. It's weird, seeing row upon row of eyes without bodies. Before I can wonder if Maxx has that ability, too, a pair of eyes steps forward and blurs into a hound as massive as my friend.

"This is not your domain," it growls. "What are you doing here, half? You were not summoned."

"I need to see Nacelles Caldmer." I'm determined to keep my voice firm. If dogs can smell fear, does that mean the bigger the dog, the more fear it can smell? I sure hope not.

"You are not expected." Its voice is a lot deeper than Maxx's.

Yeah. We pretty much established that already. "This is kind of impromptu. Unplanned," I add, in case it doesn't understand me. I needn't worry.

It bares its teeth at me and I'm pretty sure it's not smiling. "I am not unaware of what the word means." It's a lot more formal than Maxx, and that's saying something. "I'm sorry," I apologize. "But it's important."

"I will take your request back to him," the giant beast says. "What is the nature of your visit?"

"Brains," Noelle says. "She needs to talk to the lich about brains."

The hound's nostrils flare. "*You* have no business here, half-fae. Our master does not deal with the living."

I'm shocked when Noelle stands her ground. I guess she's making an effort, too. "I'm here for Isis," she says.

The beast cocks its head to one side, as though it's listening to something neither Noelle nor I can hear. Then the rows of eyes begin to fade. "Follow me. I will take you to him."

"Did you just communicate telepathically with Nacelles? How cool is that!!"

The hell hound in question sneezes. Thanks to Maxx, I know exactly what *that* means.

"We're not going to run into any ghouls, are we?" I ask.

"Our master does not allow them to roam during the pack's time," it replies. "We do not get along well."

I recall Maxx's showdown with the red eyed man in the gray suit and believe it. Neither of them looked happy to see the other one in the hallway. Nacelles' control over the hell hounds and the ghouls is amazing.

"Are you sure this is safe?" Noelle asks.

No. As a matter of fact I'm not, but I nod. "Of course it is."

"If you are quite ready," the hell hound says, "our master will not wait forever."

"All right, we ready, Noelle?"

The half-fae nods.

"Hi ho, hi ho, it's off to Nacelles we go…" I start to sing under my breath but see the hell hound's ears swivel back. Oh yeah, they have super hearing.

I kind of expect the hallway to go on forever, but it doesn't. It just ends and I frown. "Wasn't this longer the last time I was down here?"

"This underground is outside time. The rules do not apply," it replies. "Our master is through that door." It tilts its head to the left, and I glance over. Sure enough, there's a door there, where I'm sure there wasn't just a minute before.

Our 'guide', for lack of a better term, dissolves like the Cheshire cat, but without leaving behind any grin. Or anything else, for that matter.

"Come in, Isis, and bring your friend." I can hear the lich's voice through the door. "I am most curious what brings you here, uninvited."

Well, that bodes well for this meeting. I pull the door open and Noelle and I step inside.

The lich is sitting at what looks like the biggest desk ever created, his skeleton frame at home behind it. He leans forward. "My hound informed me you believe your visit is of vital importance."

Boy, he just cuts straight to the chase, doesn't he? "I eat brains," I blurt. Idiot, thy name is Isis.

The lich leans back. "Yes, you do. That is the standard zombie fare, so I cannot imagine why you consider that important."

"It's the brains," Noelle steps into the conversation, about as successfully as I started it.

"Yes," Nacelles says. "We've established that."

"I've been dreaming of eating human brains," I elaborate. "That can't be normal."

The lich leans back in his chair. "Have you been tempted to eat them yet?"

I gag. Is he serious? "Why would you even *ask* me that?"

"It's not an unreasonable question. You're a zombie, Isis. It *is* what they eat. So why haven't you tried them?"

"Because it's cannibalism and it's disgusting!"

"You're an interesting puzzle," the lich says. "But I think we might be able to come up with an answer, if you trust me."

He hasn't led me wrong thus far, so I nod. "What do you want me to do?"

The skin around his mouth stretches taut, almost as though he's smiling. It's creepy, to say the least. "Why, eat brains, of course."

"Ummm..." I frown. "I'm already doing that."

"You misunderstand me. I want you to try monkey and human brains for a change."

I push myself up and out of the chair. "There's no way."

"You're crazy," Noelle chimes in. I'm actually glad she's here and on my side.

"Look," Nacelles says. "You came to me for help. You haven't tried anything other than pork, am I right?"

I nod.

"All zombies are mindless undead, Isis. You're the only exception. Aren't you the least bit curious why?"

"I'd actually never thought about it," I admit, feeling beyond stupid. Because, of course, now that he's said something, I'm super curious why. Don't get me wrong, I don't *want* to be a full zombie, but it'd be nice to know why I'm not. Not to mention, it'd be awesome to know how *not* to turn into one.

"I suspect it's the brains you're eating." He leans forward. "I think the zombie part of you is craving human brains, and that's why you're dreaming of them. That's pretty important information to have, all things considered. Imagine if you eat raw human by mistake, and that causes you to turn...the consequences could be disastrous."

Visions of 'The Walking Dead' scroll through my head, with me as lead zombie. Yuck. Yeah, that'd be bad.

"If you – if I turn into a complete zombie, can you bring me back?" It's terrifying to think I might get stuck, wanting only to eat other people's brains.

The lich half shrugs. "I might."

"Is that the best you can give me?" I ask. "Maybe you can fix me if I become a raving lunatic?"

Nacelles nods. "It's not without risks, but I think the end result would be worth it."

I turn to Noelle, who's just been sitting without saying anything. "What do you think?" Might as well ask for her opinion; she's the only other human here. Sort of. She's already shaking her head.

"I wouldn't do it, but it's not up to me."

I take a deep breath and release it. "Okay, when do we start?"

"Immediately," Nacelles says. "Your cage is through the far door."

"You're not putting me in a cage," I say.

Nacelles shrugs. "Then I can't help you."

Check and mate.

"Fine. Then what? You slip brains through the bars at me, palm flat so I don't bite you by accident?" Okay, I know I'm being more than a little bit sarcastic. But my voice is shaking and so are my hands.

"Don't be ridiculous," Nacelles replies.

"I'm the one who'll be eating brains," I say. "I don't think I'm being ridiculous at all."

"What about me?" Noelle asks. "Do I have to stay down here with her?"

"Of course not," the lich says. "You're free to leave whenever you wish."

"How long do you think this process is going to take?" I walk around the massive desk where he still sits. His chair swivels to keep me in his line of sight.

"I have no idea," Nacelles says. "This whole thing is a gamble. But why don't we start off slow? Go back to your apartment, gather what things you need for a possible overnight stay, and I'll do what prep work I can here."

"When should I come back?"

"This evening will be soon enough," he replies.

I nod. "Okay, and...ummmm...thank you," I say, though I'm not sure what I'm thanking him for. I mean, he's going to feed me brains. That's so not awesome.

"Will Tucker let us out?" Noelle asks. She's obviously better at remembering names than I am.

"The door's already unbarred. The ghouls are in for the night and the hounds won't stop you." Nacelles bends over his desk, studying something I can't see. I guess that's our cue.

"Well, see you later, then."

He doesn't respond.

I shrug at Noelle. "Let's go."

She follows me out and it's not long before we're back in the taxi, riding to my apartment building in complete silence.

Thirty-Seven:

I Kind of Wanted to Eat That...

I pack my bag. It's not like I have that much to take, but I'm still procrastinating as long as I can. I don't much relish the idea of sleeping in a cage, whatever the reason. Maybe the dreams'll go away by themselves. I sigh. Yeah, I don't really believe it, either.

"You have to go," Noelle reminds me. She's sitting on my couch, watching me stuff clothes into an old backpack.

"I know, I know." I pull the drawstring tight. "I'm just sorry I didn't get to see Maxx first." The hell hound hasn't shown up for his daily 'walkies'. I wonder what's up with that.

"You don't think you'll see him at The Blood Bank?"

"I have no idea. I hope so. But maybe he's busy herding souls or something." Or eating his weight in Chicken McNuggets. That's always a possibility, too.

"You're delaying."

"I *know*!" I first snap, then apologize. "I'm sorry. It's just..."

"Do you want me to come with you again?"

I'm surprised she offers. "No. Not a chance. What if I turn...y'know...evil?"

"You'll be in a cage," the half-fae says. "I won't be in any danger."

"It's not just that," I respond. "It's embarrassing. I mean, it could be. I just…I appreciate it, Noelle, I do, but no."

"All right, I'll be at the church when you guys finish." She walks to the door, opens it and turns back to me for a minute. "Good luck, Isis."

"Thanks." I take a deep breath and grab my backpack. "Wait up. I'll walk down with you."

We walk to the elevator together.

"Can you transport yourself wherever you want?" Noelle asks once the elevator doors swoosh shut behind us.

"No. Maxx says it has something to do with how much I want to be somewhere. And before you ask, I can't transport myself to Nacelles. I don't particularly want to be there, remember?"

She throws her hands up in the air, laughing.

The elevator grinds itself to a halt and the door opens. We both step into the foyer. "Thanks for going with me," I say. "I guess I'll see you tomorrow."

"I hope so." She winks at me before walking through the foyer and out the double doors of the apartment building.

The same taxi that had taken us from the church to the club and back again is waiting at the curb, as requested. I have no idea what kind of special arrangement the service has with Father Moss, or how he's paying the fares, but it must be awesome. I stride over to the bright yellow cab and get in.

"I need to go back to the club," I say.

"Sure thing," the cabbie replies. He puts the car into gear and eases into the light Atlanta traffic.

I close my eyes for a moment. I can't believe I'm doing this.

"You can trust him, you know." The cab driver says.

I open my eyes. "Trust who?"

"Nacelles Caldmer. You can trust him." The cabbie smiles into the rearview mirror.

"How do you know who I'm going to see?" I inch toward the door, wondering how much it'll hurt if I throw myself from a moving car.

He laughs. "You halves aren't as insulated from the real world as you think you are. We're familiar with the lich and his doings."

My eyes narrow as a sneaking suspicion grows. "You're not human, are you?"

The cab driver flexes his shoulders and, just for an instant, I swear I see the shadow of wings unfold.

"You're an...and you drive a cab?" I'm astonished at the idea of it.

"I work for The Angel Cab Company," the cabbie says. "Printed right there on the side of the taxi, but I can see you didn't bother to notice."

He's right, but then again, there are so many quirky cab names in the city, why would 'Angel Cab Company' be any different than the others? "Did God send you here to watch over us?"

He laughs again. "God gives us as much free will as He gives you."

My eyebrows rise. That's an interesting concept. I wonder what Father Moss would make of it. "Since you guys...angels...exist, do demons? Do you, like, battle it out?"

"You've been watching too much television," he replies. "But as far as demons go, you're asking me that? You've got a hell hound for a friend, don't you?" He turns on his signal and merges over to the curb. "We're here."

"Ummm...okay, thanks." I'm still a bit floored by the fact that a freakin' *angel* just drove me to my destination. Talk about service!

"Tell Nacelles to call the cab company when you're done. One of us will come pick you up."

"How many of you are there?"

"Cabbies? We number in the multitudes," he replies with a smile.

Not exactly what I meant, but I suspect he knows that. I pause with one hand on the door latch. "Does that mean angels aren't in Heaven anymore?"

"Some of us live here, some of us live there. As I said, it's all about free will. There will always be angels in both places, just like there will always be demons to balance us out both here and in Hell."

And just like that, my mind is blown. I think I'm done with this conversation. I definitely don't want any information on how many demons are roaming the streets of Atlanta. I'd never sleep again. I open the door. The sidewalk in front of the club is hoppin'. The bouncer is trying to turn the milling crowd into something resembling a straight line. I close the cab door and walk to the front of the nebulous demarcation.

"Hey, that's not fair, cutting in line!" "Why does she get in first??"

The protests rise, but I ignore them. Explaining I'm not going to the club when I'm walking in the front doors would just be an exercise in futility. The bouncer lets me in. Good memory, I guess.

The noise hits me square in the face. Good thing I love swing music. All the tables are full and it's standing room only close to the stage. It doesn't take me long, even in my distracted state, to notice why. The woman onstage is breathtaking, and it's not just her voice, which sounds like a chorus of angels. It's the freakin' *wings of fire* that flow off her back and trail sparks as she paces from one side of the stage to the other. I want to watch her, but I have the sneaking suspicion Nacelles would *not* understand my fascination. I navigate the undulating sea of people, skirting the edges of the crowd, heading straight for the secret door and Nacelles' staircase. No-one pays any attention to me and I reach the door at the bottom in record time. It stands open, almost like an invitation. Tucker is nowhere in sight. Instead, Maxx is waiting on me. I can't help myself. I smile.

"Hey, Maxx, are you here to escort me to my cell?" I try to joke about it, but I can hear the nervousness in my own voice.

"Nacelles thought it might be easier if I was here," the hell hound replies. He looks at me. "It will be all right, Isisss. His experiment will not harm you."

I wish I could be as sure as he is, but I just nod and follow him down the hall that never ends. Until, y'know, it ends in the cell, which is weird but down here we're playing by Nacelles's rules. The cell takes up the entire width of the hall and it's got a bed that looks more comfy than the one currently in my apartment. That's not what I expected, and not so bad. I'm pretty sure I can deal with it.

"So how does this work?" I turn around to speak to Maxx and find myself facing Nacelles instead. That's relatively disconcerting.

"Once you're settled in, I'll array a sample of raw brains on covered plates just outside the cell," the lich explains. "When I uncover each plate, you'll smell the brains and tell me what, if any, reaction you have."

"I thought I had to eat them..." I trail off when I realize I sound kind of disappointed. Yuck.

Nacelles laughs; it's like he knows what I'm feeling. Who knows, maybe he does. "I considered it for a time, but if you're dreaming of eating humans, I'd rather not risk it."

I look around. "So what am I supposed to do in the meantime? Twiddle my thumbs?" It's snarky; I know it is, but my nerves have gotten the better of me. "Can I go back upstairs and listen to the singer?"

The lich shakes his head. "I'm afraid our experiments can't wait, and Phoenix is only in town for a short while. Besides, it's past time I fed the ghouls, and you would not be able to return. I'll come back once that is done, and we can get started."

"Is she an actual phoenix, or is that just a stage name?"

"Her story is…complicated," Nacelles replies, "and doesn't get us any closer to your brain conundrum. The cell, if you please."

I walk inside and close the door. "Do I get something to eat, too?"

"You didn't eat before you came?" The lich asks.

"Well, no. I kind of thought the point was to come hungry, so I could taste test…" I trail off when I realize how weird that sounds.

"I will ensure you're brought some pork brains," he replies. "Since we already know you can stomach those."

Gee, he sounds so magnanimous, allowing me to eat before subjecting me to his experiments. I almost feel warm and fuzzy.

"I will keep you company," Maxx offers.

Nacelles raises his almost invisible eyebrows as he looks at first Maxx, then me. "It appears my companion has taken a liking to you."

"She introduced me to chicken." Maxx licks his chops.

"I took him to KFC *once*," I sound defensive even to myself.

"I see," Nacelles replies. "Stay if you wish, Maxx. I don't need your services tonight."

The enormous hound lies down in front of the cell door and rests his giant head on his paws.

I don't want to see those skinny, shark toothed ghouls that'll be wandering around down here. The idea is terrifying, since I'm at least somewhat alive and they eat flesh. I have no idea how strong they are and if they can get in the cell, I'm so screwed. But I do trust Maxx and I think that's enough to keep me safe. I sit on the bed, lean back against the wall and close my eyes.

"What are you doing, Isisss?"

I open my eyes. The hallway is empty, except for Maxx. "I'm willing the ghouls not to come in here," I admit. It sounds stupid now that I'm saying it out loud.

He tilts his giant head to look at me. "There are no ghouls here," he states. "However, Nacelles has not released them yet, and even if he had, you would not be able to will them away with the power of your mind. You are flesh and they are hungry."

Great. I can't wait 'til they get here, then.

"I can keep you safe." Maxx understands my apprehension, though I can't imagine anything big enough to scare him.

"Thanks," I say, right as the weird growling moans I've heard before echo down the hall. Oh yay. It's dinner time.

Thirty-Eight:

Feed Me, Seymour!

It's said dogs can smell fear, and I guess that applies to hell-hounds too, because Maxx's nostrils flair as he scents the air. I'm not sure if he smells me or the ghouls. I think it's me, since the idea of the ghouls scares me silly and I'm pretty sure those monsters aren't scared of anything.

"Move to the back of the cage," Maxx instructs.

I'm already sitting against the wall, but I squish further back. I definitely don't want them reaching through the bars and grabbing me. "Can they...are they strong enough to break the bars?"

Maxx coughs. I think it's his version of laughing. "They were human," is his only response.

That's not comforting and it becomes even less so when I can hear the tapping of men's dress shoes on the concrete floor, heading in our direction. It's not long before I see them, marching towards me in neat rows. They almost look human, if not for the bared teeth and the drool snaking down their chins.

Maxx rumbles low in his throat. "This food is not meant for you."

"All the food is ours," one of the ghouls says. I'm pretty sure it's the same one who threatened me before, but I'm not sure. They all look alike.

Maxx lumbers to his feet, hackles rising across his back in rows. It'd look impressive on an extra-large dog. On an eighteen hundred pound hell hound 'impressive' seems like a super shallow word to use. I wonder if he's going to turn into lava, I mean magma, again. "Not this food."

The lead ghoul narrows its eyes. "We answer to the lich, not to you." Its tongue snakes across its lips. "And we're hungry."

"Then go find the meat Nacelles left for you," Maxx growls. Saliva drips from his jowls to the concrete and steams in puddles the size of my palm.

The ghoul bares its teeth and turns to its companions. They huddle together; I can only assume mumbling and plotting.

"Hey, Maxx," I whisper, hoping they don't hear me. His ear flicks back in response. "I wonder if they taste like chicken."

"Mmmmm...chicken..." he rumbles, so low I feel it more with my skull than hear it with my ears.

It's mean, I know it is...but hey, they want to eat me. I think sic'ing Maxx on them is fair, though Nacelles might not agree. Maxx's ears flatten and he rushes the bunched up ghouls. Oops. To their credit, they don't scatter. I know I would. I mean, he's eighteen hundred pounds and freakin' *huge*. Even though I can see the writing on the wall, I don't close my eyes. It's like watching a train wreck; you know it's going to be bad, but you can't look away.

It's way worse than bad. Maxx doesn't change shape, but it's still a massacre. The ghouls don't stand a chance. I almost feel sorry for them. Almost, but not quite, all things considered. I change my mind and squinch my eyes tight when the lead ghoul screams. Turns out I'm not that interested in watching the blood-bath, after all. The sounds are bad enough. Maxx's growls rise above the higher pitched screams of the undead. A continuous wet tearing makes me shudder.

"Thish," Maxx says. I crack open one eye. He drops an arm, an entire freakin' arm, at my feet. What is it with him and arms, anyway? "Does not taste like chicken, either." His tone is accusing and I stifle a totally inappropriate laugh.

"Did you kill them all?"

He shakes his head. "They are ghouls. After a time, they ran."

"Do you think they'll be back?" I refuse to look beyond Maxx. I'm sure I'll see bodies. I can live without that.

"Maxx, come here."

Maxx's ears flatten against his head at the sound of Nacelles' voice. He shrinks down to the size of a baby elephant and almost oozes across the floor to where the lich stands, foot tapping.

"Well?" Nacelles doesn't sound particularly angry at Maxx. He doesn't sound like anything. His voice is just flat. And he's got a bowl of what I hope are brains in one hand. My stomach growls in response.

"She said they would taste like chicken," Maxx mumbles.

I flush. "I didn't exactly say that...and they wanted to attack me!" I protest. I refuse to let Nacelles make me feel bad for what I said. Darn it.

"You're caged," the lich points out. "And the ghouls would not have attacked unprovoked. Maxx, you are becoming quite attached to our zombie, it seems."

Maxx nods. "She entertains me. And I like her church."

"Then I believe it's time for us to part ways. At least for a time," Nacelles says. "You seem to be able to keep Isis alive, and I think remaining her companion would benefit both of you."

I want to cheer, but instead bite the inside of my cheek hard enough to draw my sluggishly running blood to the surface. I swallow the copper tasting stuff with not even a shiver. Maxx is going to live with me. How cool is that?

Maxx sneezes a couple of times. Usually that's a sure sign of 'Isis, you're being stupid!' but in this case I have no idea if that stands for 'Okay, this is awesome!' or 'Crap, I'm stuck with her.'

"Are you mad at him?" I ask Nacelles. "Is that why you're punishing him?"

The lich raises one leathery eyebrow. "I'm not punishing him. He's taken a liking to you, and hell hounds don't make friends without a lot of thought. Besides, this way he can eat chicken as much as he wishes, and the burden of it will be on you, not me."

"How much longer do I need to stay in here?" I rattle the bars.

"We can begin our experiment now, if you wish."

"Do I get to eat first?"

The lich tilts the covered Tupperware through the cage and I take it, popping the lid open and tilting the bowl upward. So I'm hungry.

Nacelles ignores my non-existent manners and waves one hand in a shooing motion. The ghoul bodies, which I still refuse to look directly at, melt into the floor at the same time a table with five covered dishes appears. "There are five different types of raw brains," the lich informs me. "There's deer, goat, monkey, human and dog."

Maxx barks more than once. I think he's a bit concerned, so I try to reassure him. "I'm pretty sure hell-hounds aren't on the menu."

He sneezes again. It's all I'm going to get. I put the now empty bowl on the floor and wipe my hand across my mouth, staring at the covered dishes. "So all I have to do is smell the brains?"

The lich nods. "When I direct you, close your eyes and breathe, as though smelling your favorite steak."

Sounds simple enough, even if the steak I'll be thinking of is a slab of raw meat that oozes blood when pushed. "Why don't you have any cow brains?"

"We don't want to propagate Mad Cow Disease, do we?"

Well, I hadn't thought of that. Huh.

Maxx strolls back to me, full size once more. He sits close to the cell; his back pressed near enough that I can stretch my hands through the bars and touch him. I do exactly that, combing my fingers through his fur over and over. It's almost like rubbing a worry stone. I feel the nervousness slide off me.

Nacelles nods at me and I close my eyes, trying not to think of the fact that I'm inhaling brain stench.

"How do you feel?" The lich asks. He reaches up and pulls a small black notebook out of thin air, complete with a pen. I guess he's planning on taking notes.

If not for the utter ridiculousness of the whole situation I'd almost believe he was the count from The Princess Bride book. Unlike Westley, though, I don't cry. I open my eyes and shrug. "Fine, I guess. How should I feel?"

Instead of answering me, he continues with the interrogation. "What does it smell like?"

My nostrils flare as I breathe deep. "It smells sweet and citrusy." I close my eyes. "Like pineapples coated in oranges."

"Anything else?" He scribbles something in the notebook. Makes sense; he did say he's a researcher. And I'm the current research.

I'm not sure what he's asking, but I take another

breath. And a rush of saliva fills my mouth. I swallow. "It's...good."

He frowns. "Do you want to eat them?"

I open my mouth to deny it, but pause instead. "Yeah, I do." I open my eyes. "Should I?"

"There isn't any wrong answer to this, Isis." He covers the plate again. "It's interesting to note that those were monkey brains, which are closer to human than any other brains on the table. Are you ready to try another one?"

Not really, but what else can I say? This is what I'm here for, right? I nod and he lifts the lid on another dish.

It smells like grass. That's what immediately hits me, but even that's kind of wrong. It's not like lawn clippings, but like how I imagine wild grass tastes. "It tastes...woodsy." I wrinkle my nose. "And to answer what you haven't asked yet...no, I don't want to eat them."

"It's deer," Nacelles answers. "You're doing really well, Isis."

Gee, does that mean I'm going to get a gold star at the end of the test?

"Let's try this one." He lifts one more lid.

"Sure, why not?" This whole testing thing isn't so bad. I close my eyes again and take another breath. The brains smell weird. That's the best description I can come up with. Weird. I inhale again and the smell puts me on the floor as it fills my nostrils. I gasp.

"Isisss, what is wrong?" Maxx's voice sounds far away; like I'm listening to it through a pillow.

I can't breathe. The scent spirals upward; I can almost follow the tendrils I'm sure no-one else can see. Growls start to fill the hallway, and I wonder what Maxx is so upset about. Then I realize it's not the hell hound. It's me. Those guttural, inhuman sounds are coming from *my* throat. It's *my* hands reaching through the bars, fingers curled into near claws as I scrabble for the plate.

"It's the brains," Nacelles states. "They're human." I want to kill the lich for what the squiggly meat curls are making me feel, but I'm too busy drooling onto my own chest. It's humiliating. I moan louder.

Maxx comes to my rescue. "Nacelles, it is making her insane. End it."

The lich nods. "Agreed." He snaps his fingers and the human brains plate disappears from the table.

I sag in relief as soon as the tantalizing smell dissipates. "What..." My throat feels raw. "What's next? Do I need to sniff more brains?"

"I have one more plate I'd like you to try."

I wish I hadn't asked... I sigh. "Okay, bring it on." I close my eyes and brace myself, but when I take a deep breath in, all I smell at first is poo. I crinkle my nose. "Ugh. Nacelles, this is disgusting."

"Try again," the lich insists.

I take another breath. This time I try and focus past the yuckiness. "It's like...fake meat in fake gravy." I open my eyes. "It's dog, isn't it?"

Maxx's growling is confirmation enough.

"I think I have the information I'm looking for," Nacelles says.

"Plan on letting me out of here?"

He quirks an eyebrow at me. "I see no need for you to stay confined, unless you want to stay."

Not really. The bed here may be super comfy, but I'd rather be in my own apartment, on my own crappy bed and with my mom sleeping right down the hall.

I expect him to wave a hand and open the cell

door. Instead, he sticks his hand in his pocket and produces an ordinary key, fits it into the lock and twists. The cell door swings open. I take a deep breath and step into the hall. "What happened to me?"

Maxx pushes his nose into my palm and I notice he's only about the size of a Great Dane.

"If my assessment is right, even the smell of human brains will cause you to revert to your natural state. Your body is actually starting to crave them, at least subconsciously." The lich gestures and a table with two chairs appear. He sits down and motions me to do the same.

"My 'natural' state is not a mindless eating machine!"

"The lady doth protest too much, methinks," Maxx says. I glare at him. Do I need a hell-hound quoting Shakespeare at me? And...did he know Shakespeare? I mean, the actual, living, Shakespeare? I add it to my list of endless questions.

"I'm not a full zombie." I feel like a broken record. Haven't I been saying this for what feels like forever?

"I believe what he is saying is that you will be if you eat, or smell, human brains." Maxx clarifies. His answer doesn't help my state of mind any. But there's one upside.

"I have no intention of ever eating those so I'm good...right?"

"Now that you've smelled them, your body might continue to crave them." The lich shrugs his weird bony shoulders. "I have no idea. You might be fine. You might not. You are, I'm sorry to say, a gigantic 'maybe'. But you're no worse off than the rest of them."

I blink. "No worse off than the rest of whom? I thought I was the only one."

"No worse off than the rest of your family, of course." He elaborates when I stare at him. "The half-turned."

Yeah, they kind of are my family, aren't they?

I don't know what makes me believe life'll return to normal after my jaunt to Nacelles' lair. Wishful thinking, I guess, but after the phone call I get just as I walk into the apartment, I'm sure God is laughing His holy…asp…off at me.

"What now?" I growl into the phone. I don't even care who's on the other end. Maybe if I'm super rude, they'll hang up.

No such luck.

"Isis? I need your help."

I can't hear him well, but I know who it is and as much as I want to, I can't hang up on him.

I sigh instead. "What's wrong now, Andrew?" Aren't vampires supposed to sleep all day? "Why aren't you asleep?"

"It's nighttime, Isis. I really need to talk to you. Can you meet me at the club?"

I rub the palms of my hands across my face. "Why can't you just tell me whatever it is over the phone?"

"The church is surrounded," he whispers. "By a whole bunch of vampires. I think they're waiting for me to leave."

"How do you expect to get to the club unnoticed?"

"Maxx," Andrew says. "He said he could transport me there. I really need to get these vampires off me, Isis."

"So why don't you just ask Father Moss to help you? It's his church. Doesn't he have some protections or something he can use?" I cross my arms over my chest.

"Maxx said I should call you."

"What else did Maxx say?"

"He said the lich likes you and I've got a better chance of telling him my side of the story if I show up with you. Isis, those vampires are going to kill me. Will you help me, or not?"

"Tell me something first," I demand. "Why'd you try to bite me?"

"I don't really have time for this," he says, but I'm not buying it.

"You turned me *undead*, Andrew. *Make* time!"

He mumbles something I can't hear under his breath.

"Excuse me?"

"I already told you in the letter," he snaps. "I was lonely. I *am* lonely. I wanted some company, and...I really like you, Isis."

"Okay, but Andrew? It really does need to be tomorrow night. I'm exhausted and I just came from the club. I have *got* to get some sleep. Father Moss and Maxx won't let anything happen to you."

The sigh I hear through the mouthpiece is laden with disappointment, but he simply says, "All right, Isis. I trust you."

It's three simple words, but I'm flattered by them. "Thanks, Andrew. I'll see you tomorrow night, okay? I have to run an errand, but I'll make sure you get to see Nacelles. I promise." I have no idea if the lich can actually help him, but what kind of a monster would I be if I didn't try?

I can hear his smile through the mouthpiece and I realize I can't let him die again. After all, a twice dead vampire is nothing but completely dead.

"Thanks, Isis."

"Uh-huh."

ONE FOOT IN THE GRAVE

I really don't want to go back to the club. Not again. But Andrew needs my help and I have to be there for him. I just do. It's the right thing to do. But for tonight? Sleep. Lots and lots of sleep.

Thirty-Nine:

A Future so Bright, I Gotta Wear Shades!

"**W**here are you going now?" My mom crosses her arms and glares at me. "You've been bouncing from the church to that club and back to the church. Don't *think* I haven't noticed!"

"I'm not going anywhere yet, Mom. I can't go back to the club until after dark or Andrew…" Crap. I haven't told my mom about finding Andrew. She's so going to flip.

Her eyes narrow to slits. "What does Andrew have to do with anything? Isis, what's going on?"

"It's a long story, Mom. Can I get some breakfast first, please?"

"No, but you can get some lunch; you've slept the day away. Or hadn't you noticed?"

"Last night was rough," I admit.

"Apparently, since you found Andrew." She sits on the couch. "Maxx, you might as well make yourself at home. Isis and I need to have a serious conversation."

The Great Dane shaped hell hound obediently lays down, head resting on his paws. "Very well."

"What's up, Mom?" I take my bowl o' brains out of the 'fridge and carry it back to the couch, where I plop down next to her.

"Isis, you know I love you and I totally respect what you've been dealing with these past few weeks, but I'm getting kind of concerned."

"I'm fine, Mom. I mean, apart from being undead, everything's peachy."

"For now," she says. "But what about later? Have you thought about that, even a little?"

I eat a spoonful of brains before answering. "I've been a *little* busy, Mom."

"And now you have time."

Great. I really don't want to have this conversation; primarily because I have no idea what the future holds. I sigh.

"Do you know how long you're going to live, Isis? How does this undeath work, anyway?"

"Ink implied I could live for centuries," I admit.

"Then we *definitely* need to have this conversation, because I won't live that long."

"Mom, I *don't* want to hear this."

My mom narrows her eyes. "That's tough, baby."

"It is important for you to consider all the possibilities." Maxx raises his head off his paws to stare at me. "Your mother is very wise."

"I see how it is. Two against one; thanks a lot, Maxx. Fine." I fold my arms. "To answer your question, I have no *idea* what comes next. I'm half-dead. I don't think college is an option anymore."

"You could always take night classes," my mom replies. "Or go to school online."

"Or I could take the summer to get used to all this, and figure everything else out later. It's what I was planning on doing anyway, so not much has changed. Not really."

"There are other considerations you must think about, as well." Maxx states. "What will you do as you grow older?"

I shrug, not following his line of thought. "Grow older."

The hell hound shakes his head. "You are undead. Do you not understand what that entails? Isis, you are done aging."

"Huh? But Ink told me I'd live…"

"Yes, for centuries," the dog continues. "And you will. Very likely. But your body will not age. You are, for all intents and purposes, done at – how old did you say you were?—seventeen?"

"I can't *be* seventeen forever," I protest.

"Centuries is not forever," Maxx says calmly.

"Even one hundred and ninety-nine years is close enough," I snap. "How am I supposed to live with that?"

"Much like the vampires do, I would imagine," Maxx sneezes.

My mom nods her head slowly. "You'd have to move every ten years or so to maintain your identity."

"Or live at the church," I think aloud. "Noelle and I could be roomies." Wouldn't *that* be fun?

"I do not believe you and the half-fae would be able to live together long term without damaging each other." Maxx states. "However, your existence there *would* be interesting to any group dynamics that might form."

"I'm not going to live at the church for the next umpteen hundred years, Maxx. I'd go completely mad."

My mom snaps her fingers. "I've got it, Isis! I've got the *perfect* avenue for you to take."

Remembering my mom wanted to be a professional soap maker when I was younger, I'm a bit scared to hear her idea now. "Ohhh-kay, shoot."

"A translator," she says triumphantly.

It's actually a perfect idea. It'd give me the freedom to move around; heck, that'd pretty much be a requirement of the job. And if I'm going to live practically forever, I can learn just about any language out there, which will make me super marketable. "That's an awesome idea, Mom."

"Isis, we should leave." Maxx scrambles to his feet. "It is after dark and we have a prior commitment."

I glance at the clock. Crap. Andrew's most likely waiting on us. "Sorry, Mom, but he's right. We have to go."

"Wait, Isis, what about Andrew?"

"I've kind of made my peace with him," I tell her. "We're – good."

She looks unconvinced. "What reason did he give for biting you?"

"Believe it or not...he wanted company, Mom. *My* company."

"You sound almost enamored."

"No way." I'm dismissive, but I know the idea's already taken root somewhere. If I wasn't at least a little bit still interested, I wouldn't be helping him. I hate it when my mom's right. "Maxx and I really do need to leave."

She sighs and nods. "Maxx, I'm holding you responsible for her. Isis, if you're not home tomorrow, you'll be in big trouble."

"On my soul, I'll keep her safe," the hell hound swears, rising to his feet and shaking himself.

On that lovely note, we *shiver* out and reappear in a...tomb? What has Maxx gotten me into?

Forty:

It's Meat, Flavored with...Meat!

"Whose tomb is this?"

"Does it matter?" Andrew asks, stepping out from behind a huge stone candle holder. "It was overgrown and Father Moss said I could use it."

"We should go to Nacelles as soon as possible," Maxx says.

"Wait," Andrew says, "I think Isis needs to know why—"

I hold my index finger up to my lips and he subsides. Maxx twists the air and just like that, we're standing in my parking garage. Thankfully, it's empty. I turn to Andrew.

"Okay, now tell me everything you weren't telling me before" I say. "And I mean everything, Andrew. Including the stuff you haven't said."

"The vampire who turned me wasn't supposed to," he says. "I was food."

There must've been stupid pills mixed in with my brains. "Huh?"

"I was food, Isis. Good enough to drain, but not good enough to be immortal."

Maxx seems to understand my confusion. "It is customary that food is never turned."

Andrew wilts a bit.

"That's pretty harsh," I say, petting Maxx's soft ears.

He sits at my feet and tilts his head up. "You misunderstand. It is an unspoken rule that has been in place since the creation of the first vampire. It was not a judgment against him."

"But it's not Andrew's fault he got turned!" I argue.

"Isis, I am only the messenger. You need to convince Nacelles Caldmer to speak on Andrew's behalf to the Master Vampire. That is the only way to call off the hunt."

I'm tempted to say 'Why me?' but I'm pretty sure it won't help. I just close my eyes for a minute. "Fine. Maxx, can you take us directly to Nacelles?"

"I can," he replies. "But you stated that you have an errand to run."

I nod. "I do. I'd drive us, but you won't fit. My car isn't exactly big."

"I can shrink down further, if it is necessary." He's not pleased at the idea, though. His ears are down and his normally round with curiosity Great Dane eyes are droopy, a sure sign of his unhappiness.

I pet his head. "Trust me, it is."

He shivers and some sort of spaniel is standing in front of me. I'm not expert enough in dogs to know the exact breed, but he's got long droopy ears and a wonderful coat.

"That'll work," I say.

"Where'd all your weight go?" Andrew asks.

"I cannot contract all my mass," Maxx explains. "This body weighs as much as the Great Dane did."

Yikes. That's one heavy spaniel, but at least he doesn't weigh in at eighteen hundred pounds anymore. He'd break the suspension on my car otherwise. "I need to go to the Farmer's Market before the club, Andrew."

My ex raises his eyebrow at me.

"I owe someone there a couple of rib-eyes. It's kind of out of our way, but I wouldn't feel right not bringing them. Besides, he might not let us in otherwise."

Maxx tilts his head.

"I'll leave the window rolled down," I promise. I don't feel like explaining to Andrew about Tucker. Some things need to be experienced to be believed. And yes, I did just say that. Andrew doesn't say a word when we reach my car. He just climbs into the front seat and buckles his seatbelt. Safety first. Maxx clambers across Andrew's lap and into the back, where he sits upright on the seat and stares first at the seatbelt, then at me.

"Maxx, I'm not buckling you in. You're a *dog.*" Sheesh, has he never ridden in a car before?

"I am a hell hound," he replies. "There is a difference."

"Right now, at this very minute, you're a spaniel," I say. "Besides, I don't have a special harness for you. It wouldn't work."

"Isn't the Farmer's Market in the opposite direction as the club?" Andrew asks.

I get into the front seat and insert the key in the ignition. It turns over without a hitch. If there's one thing I've learned over the years, it's to baby my car. The Marta's great for the short term, but no-one who's lived in Atlanta for a long time wants to use it for, say, grocery shopping and stuff.

"It'll just take a minute. You and Maxx can keep each other company."

"I need to get this done, Isis."

I'm about ready to snap at him, but then catch a glimpse out of the corner of my eye. He looks scared.

"I'll be as fast as I can," I promise, easing the

Bug into traffic. "But things'll go a lot easier if I have rib-eyes. Trust me."

I expect Andrew to say something snarky, but he just leans his head back on the seat and closes his eyes. "Just make sure I'm back before daybreak," he says.

This time I do roll my eyes. After all, he can't see me, and even if he could, what's he going to say? He's the one who came to me for help. Does he seriously think I'm going to let him burst into flames?

It's pretty much a straight shot down 75 South to 285 North, then off the freeway at East Ponce to the market itself. There's not much traffic now, which is perfect, since The Farmer's Market closes at nine.

"What sort of a market is this?" Maxx asks. "I see no farmers."

"It's like a giant grocery store," Andrew doesn't even open his eyes. "Except that instead of normal stuff, they have a huge produce section. It's got all kinds of vegetables from around the world and different kinds of meat."

"I'll only be a sec," I say. I open the door, slamming it shut behind me. I'm not mad or anything, but if I don't use force, sometimes the door sticks.

Maxx barks at me, but I ignore him. I'm just grateful he's not shouting out the car window something like, 'I want chicken!' That'd turn some heads.

I miss buying food at the Farmer's Market. The fruits and vegetables always seem to last longer than from anywhere else. Also, it's food without the middle man; pretty much from farmer to table. In short, it's hippie heaven.

I make the run as fast as possible. I don't eat anything normal anymore, so it's easy to stay away from the entire right side of the warehouse sized...ummm...warehouse. The meat section is a lot harder to resist. After all, it's raw meat. Counter upon counter of juicy, oozing steaks, ground beef, ostrich, turkey legs...Oooo...I pause and grab a turkey leg for Maxx. The man behind the counter just smiles at me — I think it's a default reaction because he does it to the woman right behind me, too. Ah well, I know I'm not pretty anymore. It kind of sucks, but there it is. Next up is the rib-eyes. I wait for my turn. Why're there so many people in the meat department so close to closing, anyway?

"Who's next?"

I raise my hand and step forward, but a woman tries shoving her way past me. "Excuse me," she mutters, not sorry.

"I was here first," I say.

She turns toward me, but something in my glare stops her in her tracks. "I—I'm sorry," she says instead, stepping away from me. "I didn't see you."

We both know it's a lie, but I just shrug and turn back to the counter. "I need two of the largest rib-eyes you've got."

He raises his eyebrow at me. Okay, I know I'm only around 5'0" and, in this stage of the game it's doubtful I'll grow any more, but staring at me isn't going to help.

"Bone in or bone out?"

"Bone in, please."

He weighs out two steaks and I darn near expire at the price. $30.05. Tucker better appreciate these. And I better get to see Nacelles whenever I want from now until eternity. I get the meat, take it to the cashier, pay my bill, and hightail it out to the car, where I find Maxx and Andrew deep in conversation.

"...but he's a magician," Andrew is protesting.

"A magician, not a miracle worker." Maxx's nose

flares. "Isisss, what is that?"

"The steaks are for Tucker, so paws off," I answer even as I dig into the bag and get out the turkey leg. "This one's for you." I hold it out to him, blink once, and while I'm busy blinking, Maxx nabs it. I feel his warm doggy breath as the weight of the leg leaves my palm. Then the car's suspension groans, and Maxx the Great Dane is laying across the backseat, cracking the bone in two. I guess he likes turkey...

"It is not chicken," he says.

"No," I agree. "It's not. And why did you change form again?"

"It is much better than chicken," he replies, "and the spaniel is not my favorite form."

Well, then... "I'm glad you like the turkey," I say. "It's smoked, though, which gives it a whole different flavor than regular turkey."

"I am glad I am staying above ground," Maxx says. "I do not think I would experience such things with Nacelles Caldmer."

I have to agree with him. I mean, the lich seems cool, but I don't think he's one to go out of his way to help Maxx try out new food. Poor hound had never tasted chicken before, and he's how old?

"Now that the touchy-feely stuff is over, can we get on with solving my problem?" Andrew whines.

"Sure." I turn the ignition on, pull out of the parking lot and back onto the freeway. Blood Bank, here we come.

Forty-One:

And Miles to go Before I Sleep.

The club's hoppin' again, but I'm not surprised by that fact. After all, it's night. My mom's right. I'm doing nothing but travelling between the church and here. I'm pretty much running in circles. Maxx stops me as I start to get out of the car.

"I will take us straight to Tucker," he says. "It will be less troublesome." He grins at me.

I hold tight to the bag containing the rib-eyes with one hand and put the other hand on Maxx.

"I can't hold onto him," Andrew protests. "I'll go up in flames."

"Untrue," Maxx replies. "I only burn in my natural state. You will be safe."

"If you say so…" Andrew's tone is skeptical but he puts one trembling hand onto the hell hound. Nothing happens, and I breathe out a sigh of relief. I may not be ready to admit how I'm starting to feel about Andrew, if I ever really stopped feeling it in the first place, but neither do I want to see him light up like a Roman Candle.

The air around us twists as Maxx does his magical hell hound thing, and then I'm standing almost nose to nose with Tucker. My nostrils flare, my eyes widen, and I take a step, or three, backward.

"Uh, hi, Tucker."

The corpse grins at me. "Hello, 'not food'."

"Isis," I say, for what I think is the third time. "My name is Isis."

"I smell meat." He says. Maybe his conversational skills are being hindered by the fact that he's been dead longer than any of us have been alive?

"I brought you rib-eyes," I reply. He just stares at me, so I elaborate. "Bone-in steaks."

He holds out one rotting hand. I give him the whole bag, trying my best not to touch any part of him, because ewwww...He doesn't bother opening the bag, just starts shoving the whole thing into his mouth.

"Ummm...he's going to choke if he continues..." I trail off as I feel both Andrew's and Maxx's stares. "What?"

"He's dead, Isis. We all are, remember?"

Huh. "Speak for yourself," I snap. "I'm half-dead."

"And I am not dead at all," Maxx interjects.

"Fine," Andrew snaps back. "I'm dead, okay? I'm the freak. Happy now?"

"That's not what I meant," I say.

"This is neither the time nor the place," Maxx says. "Tucker, we are going to see Nacelles."

The revenant pays us no attention at all. He's busy picking bits of plastic bag out of his teeth. Between him and Ra'kul, I'm rapidly learning that things really could be worse.

We file past Tucker and into the hallway that never ends, except when Nacelles decides it needs to. The song from Lambchop goes through my mind...'this is the hall that never ends...it goes on and on my friends...some people started walkin' it not knowing what it was...and they'll continue walkin' it forever just because...' Rinse. Repeat. Okay, yeah, I have way too much time to just think.

"Isis, what brings you back? Do you need more brain testing?" Nacelles strolls around a corner I don't even see. I'm starting to hate this hallway. It's like some crazy fun house, but without the fun.

"I — my friend Andrew has a bit of a problem," I say. Andrew isn't my friend, but I'm not sure what else to call him.

"So, naturally, you brought him to me?"

Andrew swallows and steps forward. "Vampires are trying to kill me."

The lich tilts his head to one side. "And why would they do that?"

"I don't know. I wasn't supposed to exist." He glances at Maxx. I wonder if the hell hound was the one who told him.

Nacelles nods. "You are a mistake."

Wow. Did he just call Andrew a mistake? And I thought what Maxx did to him was mean. But Andrew finally mans up. A surge of warmth washes through me.

"I'm not a mistake," he declares. "Just because I'm not supposed to be here, that doesn't mean I don't deserve to be. Why should I have to die just to meet some ancient vampire law I know nothing about?"

"So you're here, asking for what, exactly?" The lich steeples his skeleton fingers together.

"I don't want to die," Andrew says. "I want you to get them to stop hunting me."

"There are certain protocols. What you're asking of me is highly unusual, but not completely unheard of. I do demand payment in return for my services."

The look on Andrew's face pretty much mirrors the look on my face when Nacelles told me the same thing. Though I'm sure Andrew won't get the same answer I did.

"What sort of payment?" I ask. I know, it's none of my business, but I'm curious.

"That is between Andrew and I." He holds up one hand when Andrew opens his mouth. "I can't ask for a certain payment when I have no idea what the price to me will be. I must speak to the one who created you, Andrew. Do you know who he or she is?"

"I have no idea," Andrew admits. "It was dark, and..." he hesitates before continuing. "I'm not even sure if it was male or female."

My eyebrows try to crawl into my hairline all by themselves. "How could you not know that?"

Maxx answers me, his voice soft. "Vampires can be androgynous. It is possible to be face to face with one and not know."

So if I ever made out with a vampire, I could be kissing a girl vamp and not even know it? Well, ain't that all warm and fuzzy and super creepy?

Nacelles' voice draws me back to the conversation at hand. "That's a problem, Andrew. It means I need to meet with the Master himself and see if he will remove the bounty on your head."

"I have a *bounty*?" Andrew's voice rises on the last word. I don't blame him for freaking out.

The lich shrugs. "It's a common practice for an uncommon situation." He turns to me. "Isis, I'd like you to come with us."

Huh? "Why?"

"You are immune to mesmerizing," he says. "I'd like to see just how good you are."

"Against a Master Vampire?" I blurt. "Are you crazy?"

"Not against a Master, Isis. Against *the* Master. He mesmerizes without intent," Nacelles says. "That's why he remains underground and his food supply is brought to him. If he ventured into the night, there'd be a whole city full of mindless zombies. Not your kind of zombie, just people without free will or thought."

I sigh. "Fine. So when do we leave?"

"Immediately," Nacelles says. "The longer we delay, the more likely your friend will die."

All I want to do is rest. I'm still beyond exhausted, but I guess there's no rest for the undead. At least, not tonight.

"I will remain here," Maxx states. "I do not care for most vampires."

That surprises me. I thought hell hounds and vamps would get along great.

"Is it far from here?" Andrew asks.

The lich raises one leathery eyebrow. "Have plans I don't know about?"

"Uh, no. Just curious."

"It's in Woodstock," Nacelles says.

I giggle. You'd think Woodstock would be an area of hippie 'stuck-in-the-60's type people, but it's not. It's pretty normal. At least, until you get into Towne Lake Hills North. They have million dollar homes and stuff. It's crazy.

"How're we going to get there?" I know it's mundane to ask such a silly question, but someone would notice us. Nacelles is like 6'14" and super leathery, Andrew looks dead, and I'm, well, me.

Nacelles smiles at me. "We'll take my car, of course."

I didn't even know he could drive.

Forty-Two:

Vampire, Meet Thy Maker.

I stare at the car, and grin. It's a full blown, honest to God hearse. As in a vehicle to transport the dead. I do like Nacelles' sense of humor.

"Ummm...where are we supposed to sit?" I ask. After all, this thing was not meant for vertical passengers.

"There are seats in the back," Nacelles says. "I had it converted."

Well, that's a relief. I do not like the idea of lying in a coffin built for two, or some other weirdness. Andrew and I sit on the super plush seats, which sink down even as they cradle us. This must be what it's like to have money to burn. I'm almost disappointed when Nacelles doesn't slide in next to us. I don't want his company, but I expect a driver. So maybe being rich doesn't make up for the fact that he's a living dead guy.

It only takes us around half an hour to get to our destination. And what a destination it is, too. We turn toward Towne Lake Hills North and it's like we're in Wonderland for adults. There are huge mansions; ginormous manicured yards and cars I've only ever seen in magazines. They line the driveways; Lamborghinis, Ferraris, even the kind of car James Dean crashed and died in. I mean, I'm talking crazy rich.

I'm not sure why, but I'm sure the house we're going to wind up at will be like the Haunted Mansion at Disneyland. It's not. It's a modest (considering what I've seen, anyway), castle. That's right, the Master Vampire, or whoever built it, decided a castle was the way to go...in the middle of Corporate Georgia. That takes some guts. And some very solid cash flow.

Nacelles parks the car on the cobblestone drive and turns in his seat. "Andrew and Isis, let me do the talking. Mikeal isn't particularly tolerant of outsiders."

Ummm...why'm I here, again? I nod. I'm not super excited by the idea of discovering whether a Master vamp can kill me...I'm already pretty sure he can.

"What're you going to say to him?" Andrew asks.

The lich sighs. "I plan on asking him to make an exception to his rule. I plan on asking him to spare your life."

"Do you think it'll work? I mean, will he do it?" I open the car door and get out, because it doesn't look like valets are going to come and escort us to the throne room, or wherever. I don't know. This whole thing just keeps getting weirder and weirder by the minute.

We trail Nacelles up to the huge wooden doors, where there's an honest-to-gosh bell pull instead of a doorbell. I'm not sure how it's not moldy and nasty, considering it's made of purple velvet, but it's not. Looks brand new. I yank on it, and hear...nothing. Huh?

"I don't think this works," I say.

"It works," Nacelles replies.

"Then why don't I hear anything?"

"Mikeal soundproofed his home."

The whole house? Errr...castle? "Why would

someone even do that?"

"To contain the screams during parties," the lich says, as if it's not the creepiest thing in the whole, entire world.

Andrew blanches. I mean, whiter than white. Whiter than me. Pasty, even.

Oh my gosh. "And we're going in here? On purpose?" This sounds like a super lousy idea, the more I think about it.

Nacelles raises an eyebrow. "Do you have a better option?"

Darn.

Andrew takes a deep breath. It's weird, watching his chest rise and fall with unnecessary air. But I guess I can do the same. It's all a matter of perspective. "Okay. Let's do this."

At that exact minute, the door swings open. Not of its own accord, or I might've run screaming down the driveway, Andrew be...darned.

"You must be here to see my dad." There's a kid standing there. A super cute red-head, around twelve years old, who looks like God took a salt-shaker and sprinkled him with freckles.

"We're here to see Mikeal," Nacelles replies. "May we come in?"

The kid opens the door wider. "Yeah, come on in. He's in the pool out back."

Of course he is. Because that's what rich vampires who have kids do after dark...go swimming. Now that I can see the kid better, I see he's dressed in swimming shorts and his hair is spiky and wet looking.

"How'd the vamp get a kid?" I ask. Unfortunately, I forget about what great hearing vampires have and it's the kid who answers my question.

"Didn't they teach you sex-ed in school?"

Ewww...But, since I'm me, I don't just stop; I segue right into another 'none of your darn business' question. "What about your mom?"

"Isis, enough!" Nacelles reprimands me. "You're being rude."

"Nah," the boy replies. "Everyone new here asks. It's no big deal. My mom's human. Kind of."

"So she's still alive?" Why can't I just shut up?

He laughs. "Of course! She's in the pool with Dad." He gestures in front of him. "See?"

Yup. I see. Two French doors with stained glass are wide open, I guess to let in the night air? Right in front of us, just outside, is a massive infinity pool with only two people in it.

"Hey, Dad, some people are here to see you!" The kid sort of introduces us, then cannonballs into the pool, tucking his legs up to his chin right before hitting the water and sending a tidal wave of water racing towards us.

Nacelles raises one hand. The water just slams into the air in front of us and falls to the ground.

The man, I assume it's the Master Vampire himself, laughs. "You need to be more devious, Stephen. Successful attacks are always planned in advance. You cannot depend on blind luck."

Those pearls of wisdom fall on deaf ears as the kid butterflies his way across the blue expanse.

"Nacelles Caldmer, what brings you to my home?" Mikeal levers himself out of the water, and wraps a towel around his waist.

"I have a favor to ask," the lich replies.

"What sort of 'favor' does a lich need from my husband?" A woman's voice asks.

I peer at the pool and see the head and shoulders of a, I don't know what...she looks human. Sort of. Except that her hair is kind of greenish blue and her face shimmers in the moonlight. And not in the 'Look how healthy and wonderful her face is' kind of way. I'm pretty sure she's covered in little scales.

"This boy," Nacelles propels a nervous looking Andrew forward. "Has a bounty. I would like it removed."

"And her? Why did you bring a zombie/vampire hybrid into my household?"

"If you don't mind, Mikeal, I would rather you discover that for yourself. What you'll learn is worth it."

The Master Vampire inclines his head. "We only put bounties on the mis-turned." He glances at his son, who's eavesdropping. "I think we should continue this inside. Kalliope, watch Stephen?"

The fishy looking woman nods and we follow the Master vampire back inside.

"He cannot drown," Mikeal says. "But Kalliope needs to learn the finer points of acting human." He smiles, as though the idea of having to act human is so commonplace. I don't know. Maybe, for him, it is.

"What is she?" Yeah, I do ask it. Yeah, it's rude. But then again, it's me.

Mikeal glances at me. "My wife is one of the last sirens."

I rack my brain. I know I've heard of them before...Oh! Wow. "Doesn't she sing men to their death?" Yeah. I'm all class. Just ask anyone.

Nacelles glares at me, Andrew bites his lip, but our host starts to laugh. "She is quite entertaining," he says. "Is that why you are keeping her?"

The lich's shoulders stiffen. "She's not my pet," he declares. "Isis is her own person."

Mikeal raises an eyebrow. "But not without your help."

"No," Nacelles agrees. "Not without my help."

"And yet here you are, asking for help for another stray." His glance includes Andrew, but not in a kind way. More like someone would look at a homeless dog who wandered into the house by accident, cold and hungry.

"I'm not—" Andrew starts, but the Master Vampire cuts him off with a flick of his wrist.

"You are a mistake," he says. "Whether you will remain so or not is the only question."

The kind guy, swimming around the pool with his family, is gone. That guy, I would've pegged at around 35 — 40 years old. This guy is ancient and power oozes off him in waves. I don't like it.

Mikeal seats himself in a leather-backed chair and waves to us to take identical seats. "If I remove the bounty, there will be payment involved."

The lich nods. "I understand."

The vampire shakes his head. "Not from you, Nacelles. It is not your bounty I would be removing."

"Wh—what kind of a payment are you talking about?" Andrew's voice shakes. I don't blame him one bit. I'm scared, too, and the Master Vampire's not even talking to me.

Mikeal leans back in his chair. "Service," he says. "I could use another...procurer of food."

Andrew blanches. So do I. At least, white washes over my vision for an instant and I feel cold and clammy.

"So you want me to find you people?"

"Our human sources are already willing," Mikeal says. "You would be transportation." When Andrew looks confused, he continues. "You would be a driver. That is all. Just go pick them up and bring them back here. It is not that difficult."

"For how long?" Nacelles interjects. "What are the terms of the agreement?"

"Oh, I do not know, how about a year and a day. That is pretty standard 'fairy tale' stuff, is it not?" Why is he looking at me when he asks that? Am I supposed to be some kind of expert?

"You are not mesmerized," the vampire observes. "Nacelles, do you realize what you have brought me?"

"She's here of her own free will," Nacelles leans forward and rests what's left of his forearms on his jean clad thighs.

"It has been a long time since I have had the pleasure of speaking to someone not under my thrall," Mikeal states. "A very long time, indeed."

"Dad," Stephen pokes his head into the room. "Mom wants to know if you're coming back out."

The Master Vampire stands up. "I think our business is done. Stephen, tell your mother there will be extra places at the dinner table."

I open my mouth to protest. Whatever it is they're all eating, I doubt my food's on the menu.

"Stephen, tell the cook we need a bowl of raw monkey brains marinated in white wine for our zombie. Are there any other special dietary considerations I do not know about?" No-one says anything. "Good." He smiles at my amazement. "I have lived for a thousand years, Isis. You are not the first zombie I have had for dinner."

For dinner, or to dinner? And...do I really want to know?

"So how come your wife isn't a vampire?" I blurt, in a massive attempt to stop my own random thoughts. So instead of staying in my head, my thoughts come flying out of my mouth at light speed. Sheesh.

Mikeal stares at me for a long, silent moment before answering. "Kalliope and I married years before I turned."

"Wow. You must love her a great deal." Mouth, insert foot. I mean, how dumb was that?

A tiny smile tilts his mouth upward. "I am quite fond of her, yes. Over a thousand years will do that."

Okay, I think I'll just shut up now. If nothing else, that'll make Nacelles happy.

"Why do you keep talking?" Andrew grabs my arm as I walk by. "What'll happen if you piss him off with all your endless questions?"

I yank my arm away. Now that I know I can heal, I'm less concerned about losing a limb. "I babble when I'm nervous. And he's not angry. He was smiling."

"Nacelles wasn't amused," Andrew continues, trailing along behind the vampire and the lich. I keep up with him.

"Is Nacelles ever amused...by anything?" I ask.

He shrugs. "You know him better than I do."

And isn't that a scary thought?

Forty-Three:

Yet Another Thing to Do.

It's a short walk to the dining room. The castle is all modern inside, or I suspect we'd be eating at trestle tables and using our fingers instead of forks. The table's set already but there's no one in sight. I guess lots of money buys super-efficient slaves...I mean, servants...or whatever.

"Have a seat," Mikeal seats himself at the head of the table, where there is nothing in front of him except a tall goblet and a wine bottle. I'm 99% sure it doesn't have wine in it. We all follow suit, scraping chairs back and sitting. Andrew's got a similar goblet, filled, I assume, with blood. A large bowl of itty, bitty meat curls are in front of me and there's...nothing where Nacelles seats himself. I guess he's not eating.

"You didn't have to wait dinner on me."

I stare at the woman coming into the room. If a harp could speak, it would have her voice. It's like a waterfall of melted butter. I blink. What's wrong with me? Even at my most creative, I've never been a poet.

"This is my wife, Kalliope," Mikeal smiles, as if he knows exactly what I'm thinking.

So that's what a siren can do. I'm pretty sure I don't like it.

"What's for dinner?" Stephen asks. He bounces

in his chair and grins at his mom, as if he already knows the answer.

"Sushi," Kalliope replies. "As you well know."

I'm riveted by her voice. It's annoying, because what I really want to do is stare at her face. I was right about what I saw in the pool. Her face is covered entirely in tiny fish scales, which refract the light from the chandelier hanging above our heads like a diamond ring worn on a woman's left hand. Gah. There goes the poetry again.

Mikeal leans forward, resting his elbows on the eggshell colored tablecloth. "Andrew, tell me, why should *you* be the exception to the rule?"

Andrew takes a deep breath. "It's not my fault. There's no reason on earth why you should murder me. I'm not hurting anyone."

Mikeal nods. "That is true. But the bounty has always existed. Again, I ask you. What makes you so special?"

"Not a darn thing," Andrew says. "But doing something just because it's always been done isn't the right decision. Take slavery, for example."

"I owned slaves," Mikeal states. "I did set them free when I could, though."

"Because you knew it was wrong." Andrew sounds confident.

"Because my wife demanded it," Mikeal corrects. "But she is not speaking on your behalf tonight."

"I will owe you a favor," Nacelles says. "You know my power and know my favors don't come cheap."

The older vampire leans back in his chair and steeples his fingers together.

Kalliope walks around the table to where I'm sitting and takes the seat next to me. Great; I'll likely be reciting poetry in my head all night.

"You are an interesting creature," she says.

I laugh, because I'm kind of thinking the same thing about her. I want to ask her where she's from, but can't figure out how to without sounding rude. Or reciting a string of poetry a mile long. Either way, I think I've had enough of "foot –in-mouth" disease for tonight. My stomach growls and I close my eyes for an instant and breathe deep. It smells good.

"We do not stand on formality here," the siren says. She pours a dab of A1 onto her plate, next to two pork chops.

Huh. "I would've thought you'd eat fish."

"I am not a mermaid," Kalliope states. "I do not consume fish."

I glance over at her son, who has a sushi roll in each hand. "But your son does…"

She nods. "Yes. Stephen loves fish." Her cute little nose wrinkles and the scales on her face sparkle like champagne bubbles in a tall glass. Kalliope looks at my plate. "Do you eat what your parents do?"

Now that's just not a fair question. "I did…before Andrew turned me."

Mikeal's head swivels in our direction. "*Andrew* turned you?" He's shocked. "Nacelles, that changes everything."

"Does that mean you're unwilling to remove the bounty?" The lich asks.

The vampire takes a sip from his goblet. "I will lift his bounty immediately." He points at me. "But only if you agree to come back."

"What? Why do I need to come back?" I ask.

"You intrigue me," Mikeal says. "Do you have any idea how long it has been since someone fascinated me?"

I'm not sure whether I like that or not. It feels like I'm a small penguin staring down the gullet of a large polar bear. "So if I say 'no', then Andrew will die?"

He nods.

"Well, that's not fair," I blurt out.

The vampire that's not Andrew laughs. "You are quite young. Even you must learn that life is not fair."

"Please, Isis," Andrew pleads. "Just say yes."

I bite my lip, weighing my newly admitted feelings for my ex to the idea of being at the Master Vampire's beck and call. "I'll do it."

Andrew smiles. "Thanks, Isis. It's not that I'm not grateful for the reprieve, but why are you willing to remove the bounty at all?"

"You are the zombie's father," Mikeal says.

I drop my spoon and brains spatter across the floor. "What?"

Andrew waggles his eyebrows at me. "Isis, I am your father…"

Considering I'm seriously debating the possibilities of dating Andrew again, I'm supremely unamused. "What the…heck…are you talking about? How can Andrew be my father?"

"He created you," Kalliope says, her voice low velvet.

"And it's not cool to kill parents," Mikeal's kid chimes in, around a mouthful of sushi.

This conversation is so weird I feel like I should've taken a swig of NyQuil before I came, just so I could understand it. "So does that mean Andrew's—father," I stumble over the word, "is still alive? I mean, undead? Errr…a vampire?"

"He was laid to rest for his transgressions." The Master Vampire's tone doesn't invite further questions.

I bite my lip. Yikes. I guess this whole 'turned by accident' thing is pretty serious.

Kalliope lays a hand over my spoonless one. "Do

not concern yourself," she says. "It is a rare thing Andrew has done in turning you into what you are. My husband will ensure his safety."

The rest of dinner is uneventful. Kalliope fills it with small talk, which keeps everyone enthralled and me reciting silent poetry. Finally, Nacelles pushes away from the table. "It's almost daylight, Andrew. If we leave now, we'll have just enough time to make it back to the cemetery."

"You live in a cemetery?" Mikeal asks. "Please tell me you do not sleep in a coffin. Stereotypes are so overdone."

I laugh.

"He's staying at Father Moss' sanctuary," Nacelles says. "Until other quarters become available, of course."

"Of course," Mikeal agrees. "He will have to assimilate."

That sounds super Borg-ish. "Is resistance futile?" Sometimes I can't help myself.

Both vampires tilt their heads to one side, thinking. Well...I guess neither of them are Star Trek fans.

The lich stifles a smile. I guess he is.

"Thanks for the brains," I say. "I mean, they were good."

Kalliope stops me as I'm getting up. "Isis, if you ever want to talk, you can call me." She smiles. "I know what it is like to navigate a world that is no longer yours."

"Thanks." I don't know what else to say so I just stand by my chair and shift my feet.

Andrew takes another gulp from his goblet before getting to his feet. I'm relieved to notice that his color is looking better and his hair is back to its lustrous self.

"I'm not sure what to say," he starts, but Mikeal stops him with one raised hand.

"Ink will help you adjust to your circumstances. Do not turn anyone. Am I clear?"

Andrew swallows. "I wouldn't dream of it. Sir."

"You will," the Master Vampire corrects. "We all do. Just do not do it, or you will be laid to rest beside your father."

And that pretty much takes care of everything. We say our goodbyes and pile back into Nacelles' hearse. Traffic is almost non-existent. I close my eyes and cat-nap for the entire ride back to Marietta. I don't even realize where I am until the lich shakes my shoulder to wake me up.

"Isis, we're here. Wake up."

"Here where?" I mumble.

"We're at your apartment building. Go inside, Isis. Get sleep." His voice is gentle and about lulls me back into dreamland.

A light mist begins to coat my skin. My eyes snap open. It's raining. Inside the hearse. Wow. That's just not right. Now I'm awake.

"Alright, fine, I'm up. Stop the rain already."

"It's mist," the lich corrects, but the dew eases up.

"Where's Andrew?" I rub my eyes.

"At the church, where I left him. You slept through it."

I clamber out of the back seat and lean back through the open window. "Thanks for the ride, Nacelles."

"You're welcome, Isis. Goodnight."

'Night' seems kind of a misnomer considering streaks of light are beginning to coat the sky, but okay. "G'night."

I watch the hearse pull away from the curb, then

walk inside the building. Bed's never sounded so good. I hope my mom's asleep. I really don't want to have another conversation. Not until I talk to Andrew about some stuff.

Forty-Four:

A Life by Any Other Name...

I'm so tired I feel like I can sleep for days. And I pretty much do. I crawl into bed and leave it long enough to eat, then crawl right back in again. My mom's come in a couple of times to check on me, but other than that, she's pretty much left me alone. For which I'm intensely grateful.

The phone rings. I answer it. "Wha?"

"It's Friday, Isis." It's Father Moss on the phone. I wonder how he can hold the receiver.

"Ummm...Okay." Maybe my brain is misfiring due to fatigue, but I have no idea what's so special about Fridays, other than being the start of the weekend.

"It's movie night," the gargoyle elaborates. "You *are* planning on coming, aren't you?"

"Sure, all right," I mumble, only half paying attention. I drop the phone back onto its receiver and close my eyes again.

This time it's the persistent knocking at my apartment door that does the trick and forces me out of bed. I glance at the window on my way to the door. It's dark. Crap, I slept the entire day away.

I peer through the spyhole in the door and my breath catches. It's Andrew. What's he doing here?

He knocks again. "Come on, Isis, open up. I know you're there."

This is not who I want to be dealing with dressed in pajamas. "I—uhhh-I can't open the door, Andrew. What're you doing here?"

"Father Moss sent us," my erstwhile boyfriend says.

I crack the door open. "Who is 'us'?"

"Him and I," Ink flows out of the darkness of the hallway.

I smile. I like the vampire...and if she's there, I can focus on her and not on my feelings for Andrew. I can deal with that. "Okay, come in and give me a few. I've got to get dressed." One of these days, I'll ask Ink if the whole thing about vampires having to be invited in is real or not. But not tonight. I leave them in the living room and shut the bedroom door behind me. It doesn't take long to get dressed and rejoin them.

"So what's the movie?" I shut the apartment door behind me and lock it.

"Newbie's choice," Ink replies.

"Have you been to one of these things before?" We follow Andrew to the elevator and it opens immediately.

"Yes, even though I'm not one of you, Father Moss allows it." She smiles at me, her fangs long and sharp.

I nod and even manage to conjure up a smile when Andrew glances my way. He looks phenomenal. Eating regularly definitely agrees with him.

The cab waiting for us is, of course, an Angel cab. What a shocker. We all slide into the backseat, Ink sitting in the middle to keep Andrew and I separated.

"I'm Ezriel," the cabbie says. "Sit back, relax and enjoy the ride. It shouldn't take me long to get you to the church. Traffic's usually pretty light at this time of night."

I take him at his word. I'm still bone tired, and don't have a clue why. Maybe it's just the exhaustion of dealing with everything. After all, since Andrew turned me I haven't had much of a chance to just be. I let out a breath, close my eyes, and feel my shoulders relax.

The taxi slows and I open my eyes. Wow. That was fast. Maybe the cab has some angel power or something I don't know about. It's not likely, but I giggle at the thought and Ezriel glances at me in the rearview mirror. He winks. "We're here. Enjoy!"

We pile out of the taxi and file into the church. Everyone's crammed into the sanctuary. Even Maxx, who's taken up a semi-permanent housing in one of the cemetery's tombs, is there. I try not to think about it. I still want him to live with me, but I get why he opted for the church instead. There's no way I could keep him a secret from the apartment manager. Honestly, I spend so much time here, I still see him a lot.

Someone's lowered a huge white screen where the altar would be at a normal church, and there's an array of DVDs spread out across the steps. Ink nudges me forward. "Go, choose."

I smile. There's only one movie I'm interested in...I just hope it's one of the options in front of me.

Noelle grins at me when I hand her the DVD. "I knew there was a reason I kind of liked you." She puts it in the player and pushes 'play'. The opening scene is innocuous; a car driving up a dirt road, with a farmhouse in the background, all in black and white. Then the name of the movie appears and groans erupt from the pews.

"*That's* the movie you pick?"

Popcorn flies over my head. I laugh. Someone needs more practice throwing stuff.

"Really?"

"George Romero! That's an awesome choice, Isis!" Much to my amazement, that last comment comes from Andrew, of all people. I smile and take a seat close to him. I'm not sure how he'll take it, but it's time to say something. I nudge him gently in the ribcage. He turns to face me.

"I miss you," I murmur, knowing full well there are at least a handful of people who'll be able to hear me over the opening credits.

His gorgeous blue eyes widen. "You do? I mean...you don't hate me?"

I shake my head, finally realizing it's completely true. I don't hate him. Far from it, in fact.

He takes my hand in his and something finally 'clicks'. Everything's starting to make sense. I look around. I've got a bunch of supernatural half-breeds as friends. I've also got a lot on my plate; Ra'kul, visiting the Master Vampire so my not so ex-boyfriend doesn't die, keeping the peace with Noelle, and everything else. But I've also got a mom who accepts me unconditionally and 'Night of the Living Dead' playing on a big screen in a church sanctuary. It's not anything close to normal, but that's okay. If there's one thing I'm learning to accept, it's that my undead life may be super weird and kind of quirky, but it's a lot more interesting than the life I had when I was completely human. I'm not seeing a problem with that.

***